S0-BJM-865

FROGMOUTH

A Yellowthread Street Mystery

William Marshall

MYSTERIOUS
PRESS

THE MYSTERIOUS PRESS

New York • London • Tokyo

MYSTERIOUS PRESS EDITION

Copyright © 1987 by William Marshall

Cover design by George Corsillo

Mysterious Press books are published in association with
Warner Books, Inc.
666 Fifth Avenue
New York, N.Y. 10103

A Warner Communications Company

Printed in the United States of America

Originally published in hardcover by The Mysterious Press.
First Mysterious Press Paperback Printing: June, 1988

10 9 8 7 6 5 4 3 2 1

The Hong Bay district of Hong Kong
is fictitious, as are the people who,
for one reason or another, inhabit it.

FROGMOUTH

ANIMUS

In blackest still night, all over Hong Kong, the sleepless lay awake in their beds, their eyes flickering at shadows and wan plays of light on ceilings.

There was a steady rain falling. Without force, without breaking the silence and the stillness, at 4:00 A.M. it turned all the deserted roadways coal dark and ran in courses down the yellow faces of streetlamps and blurred them.

"Daisy." In Yat's Animal and Bird Life Park and Children's Zoo on Kwai Chung Street near the harbor, the rain caught in the leaves of trees, grew heavy with weight and overflowed onto unlit stone walkways and ran away in drainage channels by the cages and wire fences to discharge through a pipe across rocks at low tide out into the sea.

In their beds the sleepless turned and glanced at the outline of those who could sleep beside them. They listened to their breathing.

"Daisy . . ." CROCODYLUS TOMISTOMA: SUMATRAN CROCODILE. *"Daisy."* DO NOT PUT HANDS OR ANY PART OF THE BODY AGAINST THE FENCE. The same warning was painted in Chinese characters on the wooden sign below the English. Below that was the warning in another language: Hindi or Arabic—in the poor light all the symbols were dim.

The awake tossed and touched their thumbs and forefingers to their temples: they could find no sleep.

1

"Daisy . . . !" It moved. In its warm earthy place beneath a half-submerged log in its pool, the crocodile moved.

"Daisy—" Beneath the log the rain made filmy cascades at the mouth of the hole and pushed ebbs and currents. The crocodile, only its snout showing above water, opened one eye.

"Daisy."

All was darkness. The eye saw a movement.

The movement—a blur through the rain, a silhouette—something solid and living and moving, came closer. The crocodile, with no effort or sound, came up a little from its submergence.

There was a beating. The figure was making the sound. It was the sound of a hundred rapid heartbeats.

The figure bent down to see into the hole and the beating turned into a sudden fall of water into the pool.

In all the cages and compounds of Yat's Animal and Bird Life Park there was only a stillness. Everything slept or did not sleep and was silent.

Beneath its umbrella, the bending figure at the edge of the pool called again.

It was cold and wet. The crocodile was snug in its hole. It heard the heartbeats.

"Daisy . . ."

The rain, falling suddenly heavier, hammering on corrugated iron cage roofs and in the pool took away the sound of the beats.

The crocodile began sliding out of its hole. Both its eyes were open. The figure, the shape, was at the very edge of the pool, in the sand. It thudded something hard on the sand: a stick, a rod. The vibrations came in the water. "*Daisy—*"

It was cold and wet. The crocodile, five and a half feet long and young and hungry, began moving a little at a time.

"Daisy—" There was a sense of something that registered far back in a gland or a cell or a memory of the crocodile. The sense tingled in its jaws.

"Daisy . . . Daisy—"

It began to come out. The figure, black, indistinguishable, but living and flesh, changed its shape. There were two shapes. The second was only a thing.

At the water's edge the figure put down its umbrella.

The crocodile caught the sense of rain and flesh and fear.

"Daisy!"

It came. It began to come out.

"Daisy!" It heard a thud again as the stick touched the sand. It came effortlessly, half-submerged. All the other creatures in the place were silent. It touched sand. It saw the figure move back through the rain—like all creatures at night the figure was black. The crocodile's legs bottomed and its snout rose to the sand. It paused, unblinking, the tingling in its jaws turning into an ache. Its guts pained with hunger. The pain, the ache, the spark, accumulating, reached its tail, its rudder. The tail tensed, grew stiff, gathered strength for the rush.

"Daisy . . ."

"Daisy . . ."

"Da-i-sy . . ."

The other shadow by the figure was lifeless: it was a shape, an object—the umbrella—all the heartbeats as the rain fell on its fabric were coming from it. The crocodile—Daisy—for an instant—

In that instant it died with its head crushed by a single blow behind the eyes from an iron bar.

In that instant—

In that instant the iron bar, coming down again and again, smashed its brain to pulp.

In that instant, the figure, pulling hard, dragging it from the pool, turning it over with effort, with a long glittering blade, with a hard, two-handed dragging movement, starting at the soft skin at the center of the sternum, disemboweled it.

There was only the rain. All over the city in the darkness there were the sleepless—the still awake. They tossed with half-dreaming fears, half-remembered words, the sounds of rain and other days and days to come. Those that had them glanced at their sleeping partners at peace and envied or hated them.

> *He thought he saw an Elephant*
> *That practiced on a fife:*
> *He looked again, and found it was*
> *A letter from his wife.*
> *"At length I realize," he said,*
> *"The bitterness of life."*

In all of Yat's Animal and Bird Life Park and Children's Zoo on Kwai Chung Street near the harbor there was only the increasing intensity of the rain. The figure, gathering its umbrella and shaking it, moved as an unhurried shadow toward the wire fence of the pool and the warning sign in three languages.

Hong Kong is an island of some thirty square miles under British administration in the South China Sea facing the Kowloon and New Territories areas of continental China. Kowloon and the New Territories are also British administered, surrounded by the Communist Chinese province of Kwantung. The climate is generally subtropical, with hot, humid summers and heavy rainfall. The population of Hong Kong and the surrounding areas at any one time, including tourists and visitors, is in excess of five and a half million. The New Territories are leased from the Chinese. The lease is due to expire in 1997 at which time Hong Kong is to become a special semi-independent administrative region of the People's Republic with British laws and, somehow, Communist Chinese troops to enforce them.

Hong Bay is on the southern side of the island, and the tourist brochures advise you not to go there after dark.

The sleepless, at 4:20 A.M., counted the hours until dawn. Perhaps, intermittently, they dozed.

In Yat's, all the other animals and birds were silent. All their cages and pens were broken open and in each of them all the occupants were silent.

They were each one of them gutted or stabbed or bashed. They were all dead.

At dawn with the light and the end of the night and the rain, from the crocodile pool, in lines along the walkways up to and inside and all around the children's Tame Animal Section and Pets' Corner they lay bloodless and washed clean and awkwardly extinct.

The figure had gone. With the rain it had left no footprints.

In their beds, in their homes, at the end of all the darkness, from their terrible, brief dormancy, the sleepless, one by one, awoke.

The rain ceased.
It became day.

1

What it all came down to in the end was just you, the fly and The Terror That Had No Name. You hobbled, limped, staggered, reeled, and sometimes ran toward it (the fly got there by air) and, when you finally arrived, The Terror That Had No Name was there to try you.

In the Detectives' Room of the Yellowthread Street Police Station, Hong Bay, Senior Detective Inspector O'Yee was watching the fly.

In the room, the Assistant Feng Shui Man, little round mirrors stitched here and there to his official feng shui coat was watching his lo pan, his geomancer's divining compass. He was squatting down near the far wall with Constable Lim moving his compass first this way and then that, divining evil influences in the room and, generally, checking how the delicate balance of the psychic forces in the universe was doing. It was a nice compass, one of the old style: clay with the symbols for Yin and Yang, and, baked on in the center of all the other lines and circles that represented the eight symbols of nature, the twenty-four hills of the Middle Kingdom, the seventy-two elemental combinations, and finally—beautifully done—the 360 constellations.

O'Yee looked at the fly. It was a nice fly. Hovering around above the Assistant Feng Shui Man's and Lim's heads, it went in happy, lazy circles just below the light and didn't even make a buzzing sound to discommode people. It was a Hong Kong horsefly, *Tabanus maculcornis haematopota Oriental*—nice.

5

It was doomed.

Squatting down, the Assistant Feng Shui Man said just to make sure, "The nine dragons of Kowloon are—" He pointed north. He was speaking Cantonese. He dropped his voice. "—are in that direction?"

Lim said in a whisper, "Yes." He looked at O'Yee sitting at his desk staring straight ahead and nodded.

"Ah." The Assistant Feng Shui Man, adjusting his lo pan, said confidently, "A simple matter." Somewhere someone or something had dislodged the balance of the world or called up a malevolent interest. He made a throaty sound. But it wasn't much of an imbalance or a malevolent interest. Child's play. The Assistant Feng Shui Man said, "Just a matter of rearranging the tiger's tail of heaven where it sometimes droops over the edge of the world." He began taking off one of his little round mirrors to put it in the right place against the wall. He asked Lim, "Did you call me in?"

"Yes, sir." Lim was nine months in the force, his brass and leather belt still shining. Lim said quietly in Cantonese, "I thought it the only thing to do."

The fly was still hovering. It hovered above Lim and the Assistant Feng Shui Man, looking down with interest. It was having an interesting time.

It might as well. So might they all. The fly was doomed. So were they. O'Yee made a groaning noise.

The Assistant Feng Shui Man said, "He isn't Chinese, is he?" Lim said, "No."

"American?" Out of the corner of his eye, the Assistant Feng Shui Man, pretending to check up on one of the holes in the universe where the dragon's breath came out, glanced at O'Yee.

Lim said, "American-Chinese-Irish." Lim said in Cantonese, "Mr. O'Yee is Eurasian."

The Assistant Feng Shui Man said, "Bad luck." He asked, "He doesn't speak Cantonese?"

"Yes."

The Assistant Feng Shui Man said in a whisper, "Oh." He turned his eyes from the dragon breath hole and smiled to O'Yee. The Assistant Feng Shui Man, smiling and nodding, said, "It's the weather. Lightning in the sky always upsets the forces of—" He didn't want to tax him too much. "Always makes the—gets the forces in the world we Chinese believe in a little . . . jumpy." That explained two thousand years of celestial metaphysics—

more than enough for the average Westerner. "Don't you worry now. It's just a little thing Constable Lim and I have to do and it won't take very long and then everything will be all right again." Through the window by O'Yee's desk there was a sudden flash of heat lightning that lit up O'Yee's face and showed every hollow and line on it and turned it haggard. The Assistant Feng Shui Man said, "You just sit there and—" He followed O'Yee's eyes. "And—" He asked Lim, "What's he doing?"

Lim said softly, "He's watching the fly."

"Why?"

Lim said, "He's a detective."

"Oh." The Assistant Feng Shui Man, totally at a loss to understand the Occidental mind said, "—and watch the fly." They were inscrutable, Westerners. And they didn't say much. The Assistant Feng Shui Man said as if he were dismantling a bomb, "I . . . am now . . . going to . . . place a reflective mirror against . . . the wall . . . so the spirits will see only their own reflection and think there's no one human . . . in the room."

Lim said in gratitude, "Thank you very much." He looked over at O'Yee. He was stone-faced, unmoving, watching the fly. There was only the faintest tic working at the side of his mouth. In the air, the fly did an Immelmann turn above the Assistant Feng Shui Man's head and began gliding toward the wall where he worked. Lim said softly in English, "It'll be all right Mr. O'Yee. You'll see. He's only an assistant feng shui man, but my brother-in-law who recommended him said he does wonders with evil spirits."

O'Yee said in Cantonese in a strange voice, "The only thing to do is to tear the entire place down and build it somewhere else."

Lim said, "No, sir. Trust me . . ."

"It is." O'Yee staring at the wall, staring at the fly, staring, said with his face haggard and white, "And then, after it's been torn down, get a big three-inch steel plate and bolt it into the earth above the hole."

The Assistant Feng Shui Man said, "There!" He had his little mirror in place against the wall. The fly flew over to have a look. The Assistant Feng Shui Man said, "There, now all that's—"

O'Yee shouted to the fly, *"Get away from the wall!"* It was going in a beeline for the glittering mirror like a lover, entranced by the picture of the fly in the mirror also going in a beeline like a lover for it. O'Yee, jumping up as lightning flashed in the window, shouted, "Don't go near the—"

The Assistant Feng Shui Man said, "Calm yourself—"

Lim said, "Sir— Mr. O'Yee—"

The fly, in heat, went *bzzzzzz* . . .

O'Yee yelled—

There was a *zap!* and the fly, touching the wall, straightaway, without a twitch—poor goddamned fly—fell down dead.

The Assistant Feng Shui Man said in amazement, "Well, I must say, I—" He looked down at his little round mirror.

Against the wall, the mirror fell over.

The Assistant Feng Shui Man said, "That's strange." He looked at Lim.

In the wall, somewhere, there was a strange creaking.

He looked back at O'Yee and there was lightning in the window.

There was a groan. It hadn't come from O'Yee.

The Assistant Feng Shui Man, touching at one of his mirrors on his coat, said thoughtfully, "That's funny . . ." He looked at O'Yee's face. The Assistant Feng Shui Man asked, "There isn't anything you didn't tell me?"

O'Yee said, "No."

The Assistant Feng Shui Man said, "Because I—"

He heard something in the wall. It wasn't any dragon. It wasn't an evil spirit. It wasn't any tiger's tail swinging. It was . . . It was a sort of moving sound, an unwinding, a— The Assistant Feng Shui Man said, "Um . . . The science of geomancy, wind and water and all the influences in the celestial mechanism, has been effective in China for—" He said, "The— My master has always taught me that the—" He heard a hissing sound, then another groan, then a sort of building-up sound like steam, like something breathing, like something coming closer. The Assistant Feng Shui Man, backing away from the wall and squelching the dead fly with his heel, said nervously, "Um . . . It's been going on since—since dawn, you say." He scratched his head. He would have made notes. If he had had a pad. The Assistant Feng Shui Man, backing toward the door, said, "Did you ever see that movie *The House That Dripped Blood?*"

O'Yee said in a strange, strangled voice as the noise in the wall got louder and louder, "So far there hasn't been any blood." He saw the fly. There was blood. O'Yee said, "Yeah, I saw that movie."

"Now, now, sir." Lim, going forward and touching the Assistant Feng Shui Man on the shoulder, smiling at O'Yee, said, "Now, sir, surely as three intelligent people from differing cultures, with a world of experience and knowledge at our disposal . . ."

From inside the wall, The Terror That Had No Name had had enough. The Terror That Had No Name shrieked, "AAARRAGAH—*Wah!*"

Lim said in English, "Oh, shit!"

The Terror inside the wall shrieked, "RAAAHHGGGG!!" It moved. It shuddered. The whole wall, about to drip blood at any tick of the clock, went WHOOMPH! and moved.

AAAARRAGAH—*Wah!* RAAAHHGGGG! . . . Whoomph!

Doomed. They were all doomed.

Gathering up his broken mirror and his feet as the wall, moving, pulsating, working itself up went Whoomph! Whoomph! Whoomph!, the Assistant Feng Shui Man didn't even stop to say good-bye.

"Are you out of your mind?" In Old Himalaya Street, Detective Inspector Auden, his mouth hanging open, said in a strangled gasp, "Are you crazy? You said it was a slight rise, you didn't say it was a ladder street, you didn't say it was a fucking mountain! You didn't say it was *Sagarmatha Hill!"*

He got a reassuring pat on the shoulder. What he should have gotten was a wheelchair. Detective Inspector Spencer, smiling (it was obviously one of Auden's little jokes), said with a careless toss of his head, "I know you can do it."

King Charles I once tried a little careless toss of his head too. Auden, looking around for an axe and a black mask, said in horror, "That's Sagarmatha Hill! You said P.C. Wang took a little turn—if he pounded up Sagarmatha Hill after the bloody Tibetan Tornado he didn't take a little turn, he probably dropped dead from fucking *altitude sickness!"* He looked down the end of the still wet road to where what had once been a natural hill had been turned by dint of over ninety years of hard work, excavations, town planning and redevelopment into what looked like a mountain. Auden said, "It's a ladder street! It's so fucking steep that they had to put stairs on it so a bloody human being could even get up the first twenty feet to take a breather!" He counted the stone landings. Auden said, "There is a landing every eight steps!" Auden said, "Look, at the top"—at least he thought it was the top—"there's a bloody mist up there it's so high!" Auden said, "Let me get this straight: you want me to chase after someone all the way down Himalaya Street after he's swiped a handful of money from a customer working an autobank and—and if I don't catch him on the flat—you want me to chase after him up those stairs!" It was obviously a joke. Auden said, "Where's P.C. Wang now?"

Spencer said, "Anyone could catch him on the flat. The real challenge is to catch him on the stairs." Spencer said, "He runs barefoot for God's sake!"

"He runs barefoot so that when the paramedics come they won't have to waste time cutting his shoes off before they amputate both his legs!" Auden, his eyes narrowing, asked, "Where's P.C. Wang now?"

"P.C. Wang was weedy."

"P.C. Wang was the Police Weightlifting Champion for three years in a row!" Auden said, "Where is he, Bill?"

Spencer said, "Mmmpzxzzp tripmphhgern."

"What was that?"

Spencer said, "The St. Paul de Chartres gerzuffgarn . . ."

Auden said, "Oh."

". . . hospital, ghizzm ward."

Auden said, "Uh huh."

"Intensive care!" Spencer said, "Look, you can do it, Phil. You're fit. He's just a weedy little Tibetan who steals money from an autobank and runs away like a thief in the night up a little hill and then—"

"Why can't you do it?"

"It's a challenge I can't meet." Spencer said, "I haven't trained my body the way you have. When you go to the gym in your lunch hour, I read." Spencer said, "*Chariots of Fire, Rocky*—all that." Spencer said, "Don't you feel the need to strive, to fight, not to yield?" Obviously, from the look on his face, he didn't. Spencer said desperately, "The New Conservatism needs *heroes*!"

Auden said, "Wang had a coronary, didn't he?"

"A mild one." Spencer said quickly, "But he's all right. From what I could make out when I spoke to him, he's even happy. He said that at his time of life it was a good thing to test himself physically and realize that his best days were over. He said now he's found inner peace."

"How old was he?"

Spencer said, "Twenty-three." Spencer said, "You can do it, Phil. Are you going to let a Tibetan thief in the night lay you low?" Spencer said in his best Churchillian, "Phil, never surrender, never, never, *never!*" Spencer said, "You'll do it, right?"

Auden said, "How long does he take to do the hundred yards down Himalaya Street, grab the money, catch his stride and then get up the hill?"

"He's slow."

"How slow?"

Spencer said, "Twelve and a half seconds."

"*WHAT?*"

"More or less."

"I couldn't get to the bank from the other side of the street in twelve and a half seconds!" Auden said, "He's hit the bank six times in two days. He isn't slow, he's like fucking greased lightning! Even if he gave me twenty yards start I still couldn't—"

"You could."

"I couldn't!"

"You could." Spencer said entreatingly, "Do it for P.C. Wang!"

"P.C. Wang is happy! P.C. Wang has inner peace!"

"P.C. Wang hasn't got any money! P.C. Wang isn't going to get any inner peace until he gets a decent stake from—" Spencer said suddenly, "Phil, if you could have seen him lying there in that public ward looking so pathetic and broken . . ."

Auden said, "Tough."

". . . all his youth and dreams gone in a single cruel twist of fate . . ."

Auden said, "Huh."

". . . with nothing to look forward to but a lifetime of friendless penury and a pension so niggardly and . . ." Spencer said, "Beaten by an unwinnable challenge, defeated by odds so great that only a man of superhuman muscle development and . . ."

Auden said, "Oh, no."

Spencer said, ". . . viselike endurance and—"

Auden said, "You've bet on me, haven't you?"

". . . a will to win . . ."

"You've found a goddamned bookie and you've laid Wang's pension on me, haven't you?" He could hardly hear himself bawl for the violins and hearts and flowers, "*Haven't you!*"

Spencer said, "Poor P.C. Wang was so—"

"*Haven't you!?*"

Spencer said, *"Yes!"* Spencer, admitting it, said, "Yes! I bet on you! They all said it couldn't be done, that the only way to catch the Tibetan Tornado on Sagarmatha Hill was to shoot him and then—"

Auden said, "Whoever they are, they're right."

"—but I told them that out there there was a man to whom no battle was too great, no call too distant, no cause too lost, no burden too great . . ."

Auden said, "I don't even like P.C. Wang—"

"—no fellow human too low, no cur too loathsome that he—"

"Bill, I don't think I can do it."

Spencer said, "You can do it." Spencer said, shrugging, "Anyway, it's only a small pension. Considering that Wang was going to have to try to support his wife and three children and his wife's grandmother on it, he's probably better off without it. The medical bills would have swallowed it all up anyway." He said, nodding, "You're right, you can't do it. P.C. Wang is better off just dying quietly in the hospital with no hope of recovery at all. It's kinder on his family. At least they'll have one little moment of importance at his funeral." Spencer said, "It'll give them a little glow, all the pageantry, to warm them on their cold, friendless, ragged walk back from the cemetery to their doorway or cardboard crate in the street."

Auden looked up at the hill. It was like looking up at the Eiffel Tower. At the top of the hill there was a haze of carbon monoxide where it met Wyang Street. Either that or it was a mist of cloud where it met the sky. There was a flash of lightning. Either that or it was a comet. Auden said, shrugging, "Maybe I could do it . . ."Auden said, "The guy at the gym did say if I hadn't been a cop I could have been a pro footballer or a—" Auden said, "I keep myself fit and clean, you know . . ."

Spencer said, "I know."

Auden said, "I read books too. It's just that you have to choose sometimes between the mind and the body and there are some of us—"

Spencer said, "Lucky for the poor and downtrodden and sick like P.C. Wang—"

Auden said, "This Tibetan character or whatever he is, he probably doesn't keep himself in shape anyway. If he has to grab money off people at autobanks he obviously can't afford to go to a good gym or—" Auden said, "I'll do it."

Spencer said, "I knew you would."

Auden, getting excited, said, "Did you see that movie *Rocky*? Did you see the way he went up those stairs in Philadelphia? Did you see—"

Spencer said, "No, I missed that one."

Auden said, "I'll do it! I'll do it for P.C. Wang and I'll do it for me and I'll do it for all the—"

Spencer said, "I knew you would."

Auden said, "It's a challenge!"

Spencer said, "Right!" He patted him again on the shoulder.

Auden glanced up at the hill. It was nothing. He felt his calf muscles flex. Auden said, "You're a good man, Bill. You have a real concern for the underdogs of this world. You're—" He asked out of interest, "What odds did you get on me, by the way?"

He saw Spencer's face.

Auden said with sudden alarm, "Bill? Bill? Bill, *what odds did you get on me*?"

Auden said, "—*Bill?*"

Fifty miles out to sea there was the remnants of a typhoon moving northeast toward Japan. In the whorls of boiling winds, high up, there were plateaus of pressure and currents spreading out toward Hong Kong. Like the arms of a monstrous beating rotor they were turning the upper atmosphere black and seething. As they diminished away from the center, coming closer toward the land, they became flashes in the sky, reflections of power, explosions of silent lightning in the sky like artillery, bringing, alternately, heat and then rain, light and grayness.

In Hong Kong, the Observatory was not going to post a typhoon warning: the center and the swirling arms would stay out to sea, come no closer and, finally, destroy themselves somewhere above the South China Sea off Taiwan.

In Hong Kong, high up, there were only the sudden sheets of lightning.

In Hong Kong, before that lightning had come, all the sleepers had come through their night.

In Hong Kong, at Yat's, everything—everything that had lived or roosted or perched in all the cages and compounds and enclosures, everything that had walked or crawled or flew or hidden, everything—with the coming of morning . . .

Everything was dead.

* * *

In the Detectives' Room, all the phones rang at once. Picking up the one nearest on his desk, O'Yee said, "Yes?"

"Herk, herk, herk, *herk*!" It was a Heavy Breather.

O'Yee, watching the wall as it settled down to make vague, evil grinding noises, said in a rasp, "What the hell do you want?" O'Yee said, "Oh, God . . ." It wasn't the phone. In the phone, there was only a steady dial tone.

"Herk! . . . herk! . . . herk . . . !"

It was in the room, in the wall, everywhere. O'Yee said, "Oh, shit . . . !" He looked at Lim at one of the other phones. At one of the other phones, Lim had a funny, stone-faced, glazed look. O'Yee said hopelessly, "Anything?"

"Herk! Herk! HERK!"

It was coming closer.

"Sir—" As a man with only nine months' experience, Constable Lim, as it was clearly laid out in all the manuals, looked to his senior officer for guidance. He guided him. Standing there with the phone stuck against his ear like stone, with a wild look in his eyes, O'Yee said clearly and efficiently and encouragingly to the lower ranks, "OH SHIT—!"

At the phone, in command, he ducked.

In Old Himalaya Street the 8:00 A.M. rush hour had begun. The street was filling up, coming to life. Up and down its hundred-yard length, getting ready for the business of the day, there were shops, businesses, stalls, cars, buses, people on their way to work, coming and going from all over Hong Bay, and, behind his car in an alley, the odd medieval Knight readying himself in his courtyard for King Richard's Army and the Crusades against the Tibetans.

Hee girdeth hisse loins.

Hee preparedfth himselfe as forre the bayttle.

Hisse loyalle Squire Spencer hee accompaniefth.

Spencer said softly, admiringly, taking Auden's coat and folding it like a flag, carrying it in his hands to the back seat of the car and there placing it respectfully, neatly down,

> Reioyle England, be gladde and merie,
> Troth, ouercommeth thyne enemyes all,
> The Scot, the Frencheman, the Pope, the Tibetan, and
> Heresie, overcommed by Trothe, haue had a fall:
> Sticke to the Trothe, and euermore thou shall

Through Christe, King Henry, the Boke and the Bowe
All manner of enemies quite ouerthrowe.

He taketh his master's .357 Magnume for too lighten him. He taketh the contentes of his pockets. He taketh: his key ringe, his noxious tobacco weed and hisse tinder and flame maker for to lighte them, hee taketh the scabbard for the .357 Magnume and hee taketh spare ammo. He sayeth, "Verily, My Lord, thy fleetness of foote is legend."

Auden looked at his watch.

Hisse Squire relieveth him also of his timepiece. Spencer said, "Stand up straight." He closeth the car door. Spencer, touching him lightly on the iron muscle in his shoulder, said softly, "You're doing a good thing, Phil." He said so no one else heard the battle cry, "A Wang! A Wang! Scourge of the Tibetans."

He wasn't going to tell him the odds. Sometimes you just got through life the best you could. Sagarmatha Hill . . . Auden closed his eyes in silent prayer.

Spencer said, "Andrew Marvell." He said, quoting the death of King Charles, "He nothing common did or mean, Upon that memorable scene. He—"

He loseth hisse patience. Auden said, "All right, I'm here! I'm ready! For Christ's sake, just get on with it, will you!"

It was 8:02 A.M.

Sir Phillip, Auden Cœur de Lion . . .

He touched at where, for the moment at least, that poor dumb bastard his heart was pumping away unconcerned and happy and . . . softlie . . . *sigheth*.

Out of the walls there dripped a dank, dark liquid. It wasn't blood. It was condensation. It was near enough. In the room, Lim, with O'Yee at the window in the lightning as all the phones went on ringing and ringing, Lim, twisting his hands together in front of his shining brass belt buckle, said in a whisper, "Sir, do you think we should do something?"

O'Yee said in a whisper, "Yes."

"Like what, sir?"

There was, now, from somewhere inside the wall, from somewhere Down There, a faint moaning sound. It was just the Prince of Darkness getting up out of his coffin for the day. There was a rusty hinge creaking sound as he opened his coffin.

Lim said in a tiny voice, "Sir . . . ?"

O'Yee said, "Right!"

He felt better about that.

O'Yee said, "Right!" Behind him, in the window, the lightning flashed in silent sheets of light. There was no thunder. O'Yee said, "Right!"

O'Yee was a Eurasian, the product of a Chinese father, an Irish mother and a San Francisco upbringing. If he had thought about it for a full moon, the Prince of Darkness couldn't have found a better candidate.

He was also a cop, an armed, trained defender of the citizenry, a person of good repute and honest and true demeanor who could be relied on in any emergency to take charge.

He took charge.

O'Yee said, "Right!"

Lim, nodding, also a trained defender, but only trained for nine months and not so good at it yet, said, "Right!"

That settled that.

O'Yee, wondering what the hell he was saying it about, said again just to make sure it was absolutely clear, ". . . *Right!*"

He steeleth himselfe in the face of the sheete lightning for the Hordes. Auden said, "I'm ready. Bring on the Tibetan Tornado."

He giveth a weak grinne.

He seeth Squire Spencer taketh out his Omega stopwatch and sayeth to himself, "Oh, shit."

8:28 A.M.

In Old Himalaya Street the rush hour had started.

In Old Himalaya Street, the autobank machine on the wall of the Russo Harbin Hong Kong Trading Bank went click and opened its little smoked glass window for the day's business.

It was 8:30 A.M. exactly.

In the Detectives' Room, having got them right where it wanted them, the wall, dripping condensation, went, ". . . Creakkk . . ."

2

The crocodile was over five feet long from head to tail. After it had had the top of its head smashed in with what had probably been an iron bar, it had been half dragged over the railing of its compound and disemboweled. By it, there was a dead fallow deer that, before or after, must have tried to run. It had crashed into a mesh netting where there had been sheep, become caught on the wire, and had its throat cut. It hung with its head down on the path with both its eyes open, looking surprised. In the compound behind it, both the sheep were also dead. One of them had a broken leg: the first blow with the bar or whatever weapon had been used had missed the head. There was very little head left. After the blow that crippled it, it had been beaten to death in a frenzy. There was a sign in English and Chinese on the compound that read MR. AND MRS. SHEEP AND FAMILY. The family was a single lamb that had had its throat cut. Along the path that led away from the compound there were two dead rabbits and, crushed and twisted around the base of the trunk, a guinea fowl.

In the bird section, all the cages had been broken open and whatever lived inside there beaten to a pulp where they roosted.

It had happened at night, in the rain: whatever lived in all the cages had been asleep, safe, sheltering, bunched-up together.

There was a Chinese ring-necked pheasant a little way up the wooden path, its wings spread out in an attitude of a stiff, silent glide. It had been gutted. As he turned it over with his hand, Detective Chief Inspector Harry Feiffer drew in his breath. Feiffer

17

said softly, "God in Heaven—" He stood up from the bird and looked across to where Constables Yan and Lee were also with the dead animals. He saw Lee stand up and shake his head.

Yat's Animal and Bird Life Park and Children's Zoo covered a little over three acres, set up in a series of meandering circular paths that took in all the cages and compounds arranged around them and then traveled off onto steps and little picnic areas.

All the animals and birds had had names. *Benny*. On the sign wired to a cage past the pheasant there was a cartoon of a yellow-billed macaw leaning down from a tree reading a newspaper. The newspaper said in Chinese, MACAWS VOTED ZOO'S MOST POPULAR PET. It was dead. One of its clipped wings had been severed at the root and it lay dead and ugly and misshapen at the bottom of its cage in its own dung.

A little farther up the path, the kangaroo enclosure had been hit. Feiffer read the sign. They were not even kangaroos, they were wallabies, less than four feet high. There had been four of them. He had come to see them once with his own son. When he had seen them it was a warm day and they had all been lying around on the grass picking at their fur with their front paws waiting to be let out into the picnic area at lunchtime to see what they could mooch.

Everything, everything was dead. Everything.

In the night, in the rain something awful had come by this way and in the night, in the silence—dark and silent itself—methodically, maybe even in some mad order, it had climbed all the fences or broken into all of the cages or merely caught hold of anything that was free and harmless on the paths or at the base of the trees, and it had slaughtered them.

There had been what looked like a bite mark on the neck of the pheasant.

Feiffer took out a cigarette and lit it.

Ting. It was the name of a tiny spider monkey that hung down from its parrotlike perch and wooden box by a litter bin. There was a cartoon on the perch: if you handed Ting your small piece of litter—your candy bar wrapper or tissue or even something you brought with you for the occasion—he would toss it into the litter bin for you. Hanging from one leg by the silver chain that tethered it to its pole, it looked with its stiffened fingers like a dead child.

Feiffer must have dropped the cigarette without noticing. He put his hands together and rubbed at his palms and the cigarette was gone.

Across the picnic area, Constable Yan yelled out in a strange voice to Constable Lee coming toward him, "How many?" and Lee called back in the same, stilled, ghastly tone, "Sixty-four."

Everything was dead.

Before it had stopped at dawn, the rain had washed anything out that might have helped: a single footprint—anything.

Everything was dead.

There was a large colored sign with a cartoon of what looked like a cross between a Chinese junk and a giant wooden barge full of animals stuck into the ground ahead of him with a black plywood arrow pointing left. The sign read in English and Chinese and one other language that looked like Urdu, NOAH'S ARK THIS WAY!

It was Pets' Corner. It was where the goats and pigs and hares and squirrels and talking parrots and cats and dogs and peacocks were.

It was where Yat waited.

NOAH'S ARK THIS WAY!

He saw Lee and Yan glance at each other and shake their heads.

The silence of all the deaths was tangible.

Feiffer, drawing a breath, began walking slowly toward the worst of it.

In Borley Rectory, Lim looking hard at the wall of the Detectives' Room, said as an inspiration, "It isn't what's in the wall, it's what's behind it! The wall is acting as a sort of eardrum for it and it's—" He looked down at the Public Works Department's renovation blueprint of the place on O'Yee's desk. What was behind the wall was air. Lim said, "Maybe from the cellars!" He was thinking hard. Things like this shouldn't be allowed to beat you. Lim, tapping hard at his teeth with his thumbnail, said, "Maybe it's—" He had run out of maybes. His thumbnail stuck to his teeth, sweat starting on his brow, Lim, all his brass tarnishing as O'Yee watched, said in sudden panic, "Sir! Mr. O'Yee, *what the hell do you think it is?*"

"I've got it!" Lim, starting to jump up and down, said in triumph, "It's the ghost of someone you beat to death in one of the cells downstairs and he's come back to exact his revenge and the terrible howling sounds and the scrapings and the chain-rattling"—so far there hadn't been any chain-rattling, but if he was right that would come later—"and the shrieks and laments

are the psychic sound of the boot being put in and the blood
flowing on the tiled floors and the cries of—" He was getting
carried away. Keep it professional. Lim asked, "How many
people have been beaten to death in this station over the years,
would you say, sir?"

O'Yee said, "None."

"Suicides!"

O'Yee shook his head.

Lim said, "Bad accidents! You know, people falling down and
cracking their heads and their spirits coming back to—" Lim said
in self-criticism, "Right. If they weren't dead, they wouldn't come
back as spirits." It was how detectives worked things out: a step
at a time. Lim, hitting it, said, "It's like *The Exorcist*—it's the
psychokinetic outpourings of a girl in that most spiritually
traumatic of all times, puberty!" He looked happy. Lim said,
"There aren't any girls in puberty around here, are there?" Lim
said gently, "I don't suppose . . . I don't suppose we could both
be imagining it, could we?"

. . . Creak . . . herk . . . AAARRAGAH—*Wah!*
RAAAHHGGG! . . . *Whoomph!*

Lim said sadly, "No."

8:31 A.M.

In Old Himalaya Street, he was ready.

Auden said softly, "I'm ready." He looked across from the lane
to where Spencer was being inconspicuous looking into the
window of an empty shop next to the Russo Harbin Hong Kong
Trading Bank and said softly to any part of his anatomy that might
be listening, "I'm ready."

He wondered what odds Spencer had gotten. They were
probably . . . reasonable . . . Auden said softly, "Bring on the
Tibetan Tornado."

8:32 A.M. He looked at the clock on the wall of the bank. He
wasn't going to have long to wait.

He kept himself fit.

He looked after himself.

"A Wang! A Wang!" He peered out around the end of the lane
and saw Sagarmatha Hill.

Auden said to his body, "*I can do this!* I-can-do-this!"

8:33 A.M.

He sat down with his back against a wall and his head in his
hands to have a little rest before he did it.

* * *

In Pets' Corner, Yat looked at him. Yat was a short, bald Southern Chinese in his fifties who, like all Hong Kong businessmen, no doubt spoke perfect English. He blinked. All around him the police and his keepers were laying out dead animals in rows. Looking hard at Feiffer he shook his head.

Feiffer said in Cantonese, "Do you employ a nightwatchman?"

Nothing made sense, not the English, not the question, not anything. Yat said, "No." He tried hard to understand the question. He did not understand anything. His two keepers were his two teenage sons, neither of them very good at school and, like the other children who came to the park, merely happy to be with animals. The animals in Pets' Corner were dogs and a Manx cat, flightless rhea chicks, doves, lambs, a donkey and two tiny Shetland ponies. They wandered free. In the cages around the ark and the kiosk were barn owls and a pelican, peacocks and more doves and pigeons. They were all dead. They were fur and feathers in mounds on the ground. Yat, still shaking his head to the question, said, "No." At the dead donkey the white-coated government vet, like the policeman, a tall, fair-haired European, was bending down doing something with what looked like a pair of forceps. The donkey was dead: it felt no pain from the glittering instrument. Yat said, "Everything's dead."

The cages where the birds had been, like the others in the main body of the park, had been broken into. The locks on the wired gates or grilles were tiny, cheap Japanese padlocks that had been yanked off with the knife that had gutted the donkey. The barn owl had been in a cage by the refreshments kiosk. The lock there must have been a little stronger or the wooden door frame newer: there were score marks where the knife had been slipped in and wrenched back and forth until it gave.

At the donkey, the vet, standing up, said something in English to one of the uniformed cops, and the cop, looking down with a strange expression on his face, nodded and then looked away.

The cop, walking across, said in a whisper, "He says it's one person." He looked at Yat. On his khaki shirt the cop had the name Lee on a plate in English and Chinese characters. He had a little colored flash on his shoulder showing he spoke English. Yat also spoke English. He could not remember the words. The cop said in Chinese to the man asking him all the questions, "He says it was all done by one person." The uniformed cop had children: you could tell by his face. The cop, jerking his head back toward the main park, said in Cantonese, "He says one person would have been able to drag the crocodile over the fence." He looked down at his hands, but not at Yat. He had been here with his children, Yat could tell. The cop said, "The government vet says, so far, there's no evidence of sexual assault." He looked away.

"Do you have any enemies who might do this?"

Yat said, "What?" Everything was dead, everything. Yat said in Cantonese, "I'm sorry, but I don't—" Yat said helpfully, "Maybe the kiosk was—"

"No. It wasn't touched."

"I keep money in there—"

"It's intact." Feiffer, reaching out, putting his hand on the man's shoulder to get his attention, said, "The kiosk hasn't been touched."

They didn't move. They lay there torn to pieces; they were all just feathers and gray fur and they did not move—they were piles of useless feathers and fur—and they . . . *and they were all dead!* Yat said, "They're all dead! All of them! They're all dead!" He looked and he saw his two sons in their keepers' uniforms and they were not real keepers at all but only his two boys who liked animals and they looked dressed up and they were weeping by the dead donkey looking down at what the vet was doing and he— Yat said, "People come here to be happy! They come here— it's for children! Children—" Yat said, "Was it a person?"

"Yes. It was someone acting alone."

"They're tame! All the animals are tame!" He knew all their names. They all had names. Yat, starting to turn to see all the dead things on the ground, chopping at the air with his hand to find words, said, starting to shake, "They're all tame. They all come up to children and they're all tame . . . They—" He asked suddenly, "Who did this? Have you found him? Ask him why he did this!" He was turning, looking. He looked down at the ground. "Look for footprints, for—for—"

"The rain washed everything away that might have been here."

"Then look for—look for—" He was still chopping the air, bringing his hands together as if he wanted to clap hard at the air and, with the sound, dispel something. He could not get his hands together. "Then—then—" He saw the vet bend down over the donkey and take something out from his bag to take a specimen. Yat said, "Sexual assault—are you crazy? What are you talking about? *Are you crazy?*" The hand-painted sign on the owl's cage read in English and Chinese and Urdu, MR. SCHOLARLY OLD OWL WHO KNOWS SECRETS. Yat, turning, wanting to get away, finding no way out, seeing only all the things on the ground, all the uniforms, all the instruments and plastic bags, his two boys dressed up to go out crying as if he had somehow spoiled their day, said, "Knives and—*how was this done?*"

"With an iron bar and a knife." At the kiosk, Constable Yan, watching Lee with the vet, began to walk over toward the two keepers to take their statements. The kiosk was in the shape of Noah's Ark. It sold soft drinks and ice cream for children. Feiffer said, "It happened during the rain. Nothing else had been touched except the animals and the locks on their cages." By the kiosk there was what looked like a white painted rock that was being removed a section at a time by chipping. He had brought his son here once. He knew what the rock had been. Feiffer said, "And the Wishing Chair has been smashed."

"It was the dog's area. It was where Wai the dog waited so children making wishes could pat him. 'Wishing Chair—Wai Will Grant Wishes For Good Children.' It's written on the sign." He asked, "Where is he? Where's Wai?"

"He's dead too."

Yat said, "He was a nice old dog. He was thirteen years old. He belonged to my two boys." His eyes were filling with tears. The pain in his stomach and behind his eyes was, somehow, getting longer and more exquisite: it was a pain that had nowhere to go, would not abate, and to which there would be no end. Yat said, "He lost all his teeth and he couldn't eat meat and he used to eat the soft sweets and sandwiches children brought him and—"

Feiffer said softly, "I'm sorry."

"Children made wishes on that chair! Most of the time—when you heard them whisper to their parents what they had wished for—they had wished for Wai!" Yat said, "He had no teeth! Someone—he would have come up to someone hoping for a pat and he—" Yat, his eyes staring, said in sudden English, "Who's done this? *Who's done this?*" Yat said, "They're not worth anything, the animals—they're just ordinary animals! They're tame. They just came up to you and they—" He saw his boys' faces. "It made people happy!" Yat said, "It made me happy! I was an accountant for a shipping company, I made a lot of money from it. I make nothing from this, but it—" Yat said suddenly, "Look! Those two keepers—they're not keepers at all! They're my children! I was an accountant! Now I work in a kiosk selling sweets and listening to wishes and I—" Everything, everything was dead. Yat said, "Look! Look!" He took Feiffer by the shoulder and turned him to look back through the trees in the main area down one of the walks, "That's the city! That's the city of Hong Kong! Look! Look at it! There are no trees or birds or animals or wishes there, all there are are accountants and companies and— People came here to be happy!" Yat said suddenly calmly, "I was an accountant before. Before, when my two boys didn't even know who I was, I was an accountant." He nodded, "Basic value of assets in zoo: sixty-four animals and birds, common species; buildings: various, no sale value; land: three and one-third acres: reclaimed from sea for parking area, found to be unsuitable for building without unacceptable level of capital investment; present value of business: nil; trained staff: none." Yat said softly, "I was a man making a lot of money." He looked across to his two sons. "I was dying little by little." He asked, not to Feiffer, but to the decision he had made a long time ago, "Who would have done this?"

"I don't know."

"Who doesn't have wishes?"

The vet, standing up, moved on to the gutted Shetland ponies by the donkey.

Feiffer said softly, "I don't know." He had been there with his son himself.

Yat was weeping, shaking. He had nowhere to look. He looked steadily at the silhouettes of all the buildings and the smog and slightly blue mist of the city of Hong Kong through the trees. Only the Wishing Chair had been smashed. All the animals and birds were dead.

WISHING CHAIR—WAI WILL GRANT WISHES FOR GOOD CHILDREN.

Yat said, "I'm sorry, I'm sorry." He was weeping, smiling, trying to apologize.

Yat said softly, apologetically, "I'm sorry, I'm sorry, I can't talk anymore. I want to be with my two boys."

Everything, all the wishes, were dead.

Still moving his hands in front of him, a short, balding man in his fifties, still trying to clap the air to make it all go away, still weeping, he began to walk slowly toward his two sons dressed up as keepers trying to think of what to say to them.

At the going down of the sun we will remember them.
You didn't have to. At the beginning of the day they were rising out of their graves to visit.

You couldn't have a haunted wall. Yes, you could. In *Poltergeist*, for God's sake, you had a haunted television set. In *The House That Dripped Blood* you probably even had haunted fuseboxes. In the

Detectives' Room all the phones were ringing. There was no one on the line. Oh, yes there was, but it was the wrong line. It was the line to The Pit. Down in the pit, in the wall, the pendulum with the scythe on the end—the one that took off Vincent Price's head in the last reel—was going, "Whoomp, whoomph, whoommp" as it swung slowly back and forth, back and forth, back and forth . . .

"RAAAHHGG!"

Something in The Pit didn't like it.

Or It did.

"—Wah!"

Yep, it liked it. It loved it. There was a cackle, a roar and then, as virgins' heads rolled like cauliflowers somewhere between the brick, the masonry, the plaster and the peeling green paint, there was a hissing sound, then a gasp and then . . .

All the phones stopped ringing. All the phones started howling.

"RAAH-HA!"

It didn't like it: it loved it. There was thumping, pulsing, roaring. Grabbing on to the side of his desk, waiting for the wind that would stick them both to the ceiling, Lim with his hand upraised in the traffic policeman's Number One Stop Signal, yelled, "Go! In the name of God and all the angels in heaven I command you to GO!" It didn't work. You had to be a Christian. He was a Buddhist. Lim, as the sound of a lost soul with a sledgehammer came banging off the wall, yelled to O'Yee at the top of his voice, "Sir, sir, you're Irish! Say something Catholic!"

O'Yee said, "Oh, Jesus—"

The Thing inside the wall said, "RAAH-HO!"

Lim said, "Say something else! You've got him on the run!"

The wall was dripping slime. It wasn't slime. It was still condensation. It was very slimy condensation. It fell onto the dead fly and made it glisten. There was a flash of lightning and the fly was luminous. O'Yee said, "Oh, God . . . oh, God . . ." O'Yee said, "I'm a married man!"

"Command it!" You needed a voice like Rod Steiger. O'Yee, his glasses fogged, had a voice more like Rod Steiger's cat. Lim, waving his arms around, thinking he was going forward, but in fact going backward, ordered the wall, "Be still!"

The wall ordered him back, "AAARRGG—wah!" The wall, getting hold of the pendulum and swinging it like an axe, went, "Boom! Boom! Boom!"

Lim yelled, "Sir!" Lim yelled, "Sir! Do something! A cross! Get a cross!" The Thing—The Force—was lifting Lim off his feet and then dropping him back down again. No, it wasn't. He was hopping up and down. Lim, hopping, yelled as the wall, moving onto higher things, began screaming at them like a woman having her throat cut, shrieked, "Sir! Mr. O'Yee, goddamn it— *you're the senior officer around here, not me!*"

"Boom, boom, boom, boom! Aaarrrgg—wah! Aaiiyaaa!"

All the phones started ringing again.

Herk, herk, herk . . .

The lightning flashed in the window and lit up the lucky dead fly.

"YAAASHH!" Flash. "Boom!" It was trying to tell them something. It was trying hard. "Naaarragg!" Maybe it was The Secret. Maybe it was— "Grr—rah! . . . creak . . ." It reached a crescendo. It made its point. It got their attention. It was the moment. The wall said clearly and distinctly, suddenly, "Twenty-eight! Twenty-eight! *Twen-ty-eight!*"

All right then. O'Yee, nodding, happy, said, "Anything you say."

"TWENTY-EIGHT!" It seemed content. It had said it.

O'Yee said, "Right!" He took charge. He knew what to do.

Like the wall, completely, utterly, totally, he fell deep-grave and white-haired, inanimately, frozen, stiff, dead . . . silent.

"Probably some sort of Malay parang or a machete—and the good old reliable iron bar." At one of the dead Shetland ponies, the government vet, Dr. Hoosier, pushing his glasses back onto his nose with a surgically gloved finger said softly, "Dead about four to five hours." The creature, fully grown but the size of a stuffed toy, had had roan markings on its flanks and legs. "You can see here on the skull where something was brought down across the area slightly above the right ear transversely over the skull and then skipped off onto the muzzle, removing the eye with a sharp edge." He pushed at the top of the skull. It was soft and broken. "And then a second blow coming directly upon the first, before the animal had time to move—shattered the upper teeth and knocked the creature toward the left onto its side. Then, as it was falling, the first of the incisions was made, badly, in a hurry, slicing the surface derma of the shoulder and then, when the animal was on the ground, the cutting and stabbing continued in the belly in a frenzy." Hoosier, running his fingers down the torn flesh and exposing a length of intestine, said, "It would have taken about ten to fifteen seconds. The first blow would have killed by impacting the brain against the hard interior of the skull and the secondary stabbing wounds—" He looked at Feiffer's face. He said formally, tonelessly, "—the secondary stabbing wounds were done after the bar was dropped and the second weapon drawn as an unstoppable reaction."

"Are you saying it was a psycho?"

"I'm saying it was done methodically, cage by cage, enclosure by enclosure." Hoosier said, "The animals and birds in the farthermost areas of the park were done first and then, judging by the fact that the stab wounds and the blows seem to increase in force as they get to this area, whoever did it worked his way systematically up here." He looked across to the donkey lying with its guts spilled out on the roadway like a hose. "The donkey was killed first because the blows and the incisions are still comparatively weak, and then—in my opinion—the frenzy took full hold until it culminated with the dog." He said, glancing up with no expression on his face at all, "The dog has no contusive wounds at all. It probably jumped up onto the person and was stabbed to the heart with a single thrust." He said quickly, "I doubt it attacked whoever did it. It's a Labrador of great age with advanced hip displasia and what appears from the joint swellings to be arthritis and, more importantly, it didn't have any teeth left." He was a tall, athletically built man with what sounded like the remnants of a Canadian or American accent. Hoosier said, "I've never seen anything like it." He said, "It was raining last night. I assume that the rain washed away anything that might be useful to you."

"Yes."

Hoosier said, "Whoever did it didn't get wet. They had an umbrella." He had something in a plastic bag in his hand. It was a scrap of what looked like umbrella fabric. Hoosier said, "I found it in the barn owl's cage. The owl must have been awake, it must have seen what came into its cage and tried to hit it." He handed over the bag. "Judging by the way it's ripped, I think the owl must have thought it was some part of its attacker's body and hit it with its talons." He said, again matter-of-factly, "The owl was cut in two. I'm only guessing, but I think its attacker put up his arm to ward it off with the parang or machete or whatever it was held parallel and the owl flew into it."

Feiffer said softly, "Thanks very much." He glanced back to Yat and his two sons and then to Constables Lee and Yan by the kiosk. They were all silent, like stone, looking away. Feiffer said, "Thank you very much."

Hoosier said, "I came here once or twice myself." He smiled an odd, thin smile, "—funnily enough in my profession, for the trees." He said, "And there's one other thing." It was next to his attaché case full of instruments. It was not in a plastic bag, but simply lay there. "I found this in the owl's cage too." He reached down and handed it to Feiffer with a shrug. "It's a feather. It isn't an owl's feather and it isn't from any of the other birds I've examined or any bird listed on the nameplates of any of the cages." He shrugged again. "It's a single wing feather from a bird approximately twelve to fourteen inches long showing no signs of violent removal." He handed it over. "It's a funny color. It looks, in its coloring, like nothing so much as a piece of burned, very dry wood." He said, "I think a bird expert would describe it as woodlands hot climate camouflage marked." Hoosier said, "I hate this. I'm used to dead animals and animals suffering, but, in a place like this out in the open, I hate it. I hate it because all the people who aren't used to it have to see it." He reached down and touched at the pony's mane and stroked it. Hoosier said, "Whoever did this carried an umbrella so he wouldn't get wet. I'm glad for him. Getting a cold after all this would be just too bad, wouldn't it?"

"What sort of bird is the feather from?"

"I have no idea at all." He was still stroking the pony's mane.

In Yat's Animal and Bird Life Park and Children's Zoo of Kwai Chung Street Feiffer said for the third time to the man's bland, expressionless face, "Thanks very much."

He looked down at the feather in his hand.

He wondered what ghastly awful thing had happened here during the night and the rain.

He wondered about the Wishing Chair.

It was only 8:36 A.M., only the first beginnings of the day.

He wondered what sort of creature the odd, burned, camouflaged feather had come from.

It spoke English.

It hadn't said in Cantonese, "Yee shap pàrt," it had said "Twenty-eight."

The wall in the Detectives' Room, for better or worse, spoke English.

8:36 A.M. In the sky, everywhere, there was lightning.

3

Well, it was too late to give up smoking today.

One cigarette wouldn't make any difference. He needed it to calm his nerves.

Spencer had taken them and put them in the car with his gun. He had also taken the keys to the car. Enough was enough. Auden, like the barons at Runnymede, starting to complain, said under his breath . . .

Auden said, *"Oh my God!"* King John had gotten word and he had gotten Merlin—

Wrong king.

—or Nostradamus, or—

Wrong country.

—or John Dee.

Wrong century—

He had gotten his magician to shoot a bolt of lightning down the street toward the bank. It was the Tibetan Tornado. Auden said, "Oh my God, oh my God, oh my God—" There was a man dressed in a light summer suit at the autobank, pulling his money out of the slot. It was a lot of money. Auden read on the side of the bank RUSSO HARBIN HONG KONG TRADING BANK, AUTOBANK. The man was wearing a light summer suit. Coming toward the man at the speed of sound there was a blur, a flashing, a spinning circle of running legs. The legs belonged to the Tibetan. Auden, his mouth hanging open, still framed in the first syllables of, "Give

29

me the keys for the car—" said, not through his mouth, but in a direct line from his speech center, bypassing the mouth to every atom of his body, "Oh my God!" The Tibetan had a face and a body: you couldn't see it in the blur. The man in the summer suit was looking down the road. His coat was flapping as the air around him was sucked up around the Tornado and slipstreamed back past his piston pumping arms.

"PHIL!"

Auden said, "Who?" His mouth was still dribbling on about a cigarette. Auden said, "Oh." He thought it took a long time. It didn't. The words didn't make it. His brain had locked in the job of keeping him upright on the pavement. It was a full-time job for his brain. Auden said, "Oh." *Phil*. That was him. A Wang! That meant something too. His brain just didn't have the time to waste on trivia. Auden, as the Tornado, gathering speed, outstretched his hand like some sort of stiffened battering ram on the castle door that was going to go like matchwood, said to Spencer, to his brain, to anyone who might listen, "I'm—I'm—" Auden said, "Ohh!"

He wasn't moving. He was biding his time. Spencer, reaching for his stopwatch as the Tornado covered the last six feet between him and the man at the autobank in less time than it took to think about it, yelled, "Good! Good! Wait for him! Use strategy! Good! Good!"

The Tibetan hit the man at the bank. The man at the bank didn't know what hit him.

Spencer screamed, "Two seconds! It took him two seconds to cover the—" Runners, like race car drivers, weren't morons: they needed to know scientifically what they were up against. Spencer, holding up his stopwatch to show it was no wild guess, yelled, "Good! Hold your ground until he—"

The man wearing the light suit at the bank shrieked, "MY MONEY!"

He was holding his ground all right. He couldn't move. Somewhere there was the vague memory of having agreed to something, but his brain must have decided he had done it when he was drunk or incapable and, busy with its own problem of wondering why his body wanted to fall down, it had filed it away in one of the synaptic backwaters and forgotten about it.

Auden said, "Ack . . . ack . . ."

". . . and GO!" He had underestimated Auden. He was good. He was standing his ground looking relaxed with his mouth held slack and he was simply watching the Tornado come toward him

and there wasn't an ounce, not an iota of nervousness about him.
Bannister, Landy, Zapec—all of them, they had that greatness
about them, that cool, calmness that— He was going to move,
wasn't he?

The man at the bank yelled, "MY MONEY!"

Spencer yelled, "*Phil!*"

He was grinning. He was a thin little man in a khaki shirt and
khaki shorts and no shoes and he was grinning. Auden stared at
him. He was coming like a whirlwind. He had good teeth and
short, wavy hair. Where his legs should have been there was a
sort of spinning thing. He was a Tibetan. You could tell he was a
Tibetan because he looked . . . Tibetan. Well, that solved that
one. Auden, his brain happy, going back to its main work of
getting his heart to keep working, said, "Right." The Tibetan was
almost upon him. It would be nice if he said hullo in Tibetan as he
went by because that would settle it once and for all and he could
put in his report *Tibetan*. Well, that solved it. Auden, thinking his
body was turning around to go back down the lane to have a bit of
a rest after all that hard work and not moving an inch, said
somewhere in the dark busy brain recesses, "Good."

"*PHIL!*"

Auden merely smiled at him.

The Tornado reached him in a sonic boom that swayed him.
Auden, staring at him wide-eyed as he went by, said pleasantly,
"Um—"

"MY MONEY!"

Auden said, still smiling, "The Tibetan's got it." He looked for
the rockets on the Tibetan's feet.

"THAT'S HIM, PHIL!" Spencer, aghast, shrieked as the Tibetan
passed on his way to the hill and Auden merely nodded
knowingly at him, "Phil, don't be sporting! Don't give him a start!
Get him now!"

It wasn't whether you won or lost, it was how you played the
game. He had heard that somewhere. He couldn't think where.
He tried to think where. His brain couldn't be bothered. Auden
said to his brain, "No?" and his brain said back, "No." Auden
said—

"A Wang! A Wang!"

It was Spencer. Auden said, still smiling, numb . . .

The Tibetan going past in a blast of air that hurt his ears,
shrieked in English, "Number One! Number One hill climber!"
He was going for the ninety-degree barrier of stone and brick at
the end of the street that masqueraded as Sagarmatha Hill. The

Tibetan, chortling, yelled, "Number One dumb cop scarer!" He had the money gripped in one of his pistoning hands. The Tibetan yelled, "Fat, useless European!"

Auden said, "WHAT?"

"Phil! Phil! RUN!"

Auden said, "WHAT!"

His brain, unused to all the concentrated work, went *bang*!

Auden said, *"Fill your hands you sonofabitch!"*

Spencer shrieked, "Phil! *Run!*"

By God—

By God—

The Tibetan, going for the hill, called back over his shoulder, "Ha, ha, ha, ha! *Fatso!*"

By God—

Auden yelled to his brain, "You!" His brain went *pop*! He called on his body. It was there.

Auden yelled, "By God—"

Spencer yelled, *"Run!"*

By God, in that instant, Auden—

By God, he—

With the Tibetan traveling away from him toward the hill at something approaching Mach One, Auden, only waiting for the right moment, biding his time, Auden the Great, Sir Phillip Auden Coeur de Lion, Auden the Magnificent—Auden the *Mortified*—ran!

Far out over the harbor there was a single bird wheeling and hunting above the shoals of fish moving to deeper water on the changing tide. Sailing and then turning to gain height, then stalling and circling over the water, it was a silhouette against the glittering morning sun on the water, at that distance too far away to identify. On Beach Road, traveling east, Feiffer saw it execute a thirty-degree roll on soundless wings and side-slip down, then, missing something or not seeing something it has seen from higher up, slide out of the roll on an invisible rising current of air and flap to catch another current.

Often, watching the birds, he had merely watched the birds. It was the Bambi syndrome, the legacy of Walt Disney anthropomorphic pretenses that little lambs and birds and baby animals had names and lived, like Badger in *Wind in the Willows*, in little underground houses with their tweed jackets and hats on pegs behind their armchairs as they sat reading the Sunday paper. It was the pretense that the family cat could be spoken to like a baby and did not, at night, kill and slash and torture anything it caught for the sport of it.

He watched the bird. It was out there not sailing for the comfort of the human heart, but for killing, for food. It was a bird. It saw itself as a bird, not as a symbol, and the fact that it was free and loose and wonderful was only something that men thought. Out there, it was merely hungry and was looking for something to kill. It was a sea gull, nothing else, merely a bird at work for its food.

It was more.

On the seat next to him, in a plastic envelope, there was the strange, gray-black tawny feather. He had no idea at all what it was.

Everything in the place had been dead.

It was a feeling he had never had before. He could not put a name to it.

It was the Bambi syndrome, brainwashing.

It was something else, more.

Whatever it was, it had no name.

He wondered.

Passing a garbage truck at the corner of Beach Road and Wyang Street he made a left to change lanes for Queen's Street to go north, still glancing at the bird wheeling in the free, still, rising air above the harbor.

The truck had stopped for a pickup at one of the litter bins. In the bin, wrapped in newspaper, there was a broken umbrella with a name engraved on its handle and, put down inside it, out of sight, a heavy iron bar.

It was 8:42 A.M., too early to worry about plunder, and the trashman following the truck emptied the contents of the bin into the back of the truck without looking at it.

Briefly, as he pulled the empty bin back from the apron of the truck's disposal unit, he saw something dark and weightless flutter from the mess, but it was only a feather and, giving the bin a bang against the lip of the apron to make sure it was empty, he took it back, clipped it onto its post in the street and, making a sniffing sound, began jogging after the truck as it moved off again for the next collection.

Out there in the harbor, in the lightning, the bird was wheeling and turning above the water.

The trashman had a job to hold down.

He looked across to it not once, not at all.

* * *

In the Twilight Zone it must have been time for a commercial break. The phones were working. At his desk, gripping the receiver for dear life, O'Yee said, "Inspector Hurley?"

"Hullo . . ."

O'Yee said in a rasp, "Inspector Glenn Hurley . . . ?"

Hurley said in a whisper, "Yes."

O'Yee said, "Christopher O'Yee, Yellowthread Street."

Hurley said, "Ah."

O'Yee said, "I just wanted to know if we'd beaten anyone to death in the cells here in the last few years."

Hurley said, "No." Hurley asked with interest, "Why? Do you think you're about due?"

O'Yee, clearing his throat, went, "Harra—hem!" He looked at Lim. Lim was looking at him. O'Yee said, "No, why I—"

"I can send you a form."

O'Yee said, "I'm just checking. This is an official police investigation and I'm directing an official police enquiry to you for which I require assistance and I—"

Hurley said, "Anything I can do to help."

"You're writing the official history of the Hong Kong police— how many people would you say have met violent externally induced ends inside the precincts of the—of the precinct station or, indeed, self-induced deaths inside the—" O'Yee said, "Here."

Hurley said, "If it's an official police enquiry I'd have to go downstairs here in Headquarters and dig out all the records going back for the last hundred years, cross-index them with coronal proceedings and departmental enquiries, then with actual trial records and then, to give you the exact, precise figure—"

"Just give me a rough estimate."

Hurley said, "Roughly—none."

"Somebody must have hanged himself from a steam heating pipe at least once in the last—"

"If someone had hanged himself more than once, then the first hanging wouldn't have gone in as an accidental death because, obviously, he was still alive to try it the second time." He had a degree in sociology. Hurley, being helpful, said, "There was one guy a few years ago who tried to fast himself to death in one of your cells—"

"He was an Indian fakir. Fasting was what he did for a living."

"Then none." All he wanted was a nice secure job in an American university museum somewhere working on rice husks and flint forks from a prehistoric cave find. What he had was a junior honorary inspectorship in Hong Kong working on guns, knives and corruption. Hurley, sighing, said, "Your station has a reputation for incorruptability."

O'Yee said, "Right." O'Yee said, "Twenty-eight."

"Mind you, it's only been a police station for about sixty years and even then, during the war, it was—"

O'Yee, subliminally, said, "Twenty-eight." He saw Lim cringe.

Hurley said, "Pardon?"

O'Yee said, "Nothing."

"You haven't actually killed someone in the cells today have you?" Hurley, sounding anxious, said, "Look, if you've killed someone there today past statistics aren't going to be of any assistance. I'm not going to be of any assistance." Hurley said, "Joke though it is, I'm still nominally a cop, an officer of the law, and if—"

"We haven't killed anyone!"

"Half killed them?"

"No!"

"Then if you're considering—"

"There isn't anyone in the cells! What there is is in the walls—" O'Yee said, "Twenty-eight! Twenty-eight! *Twenty-eight!*"

Hurley said, "Oh, God."

"What do you mean, 'Oh, God'?"

"Nothing! Nothing! Nothing at all!"

"Yes, you did! You meant something! What did you mean?"

"Nothing! I didn't mean anything!"

O'Yee said, "I'm not crazy!"

"No, of course not." Hurley, sounding as if he was talking to someone crazy said, "Well, I have to go now—"

"Someone, somewhere, sometime must have been beaten to death in the cells or no man ever loved or I never wrote!" He was going crazy. O'Yee said, "Then how about beaten to a pulp? Beaten to a near pulp? Badly frightened?"

"In nineteen twenty-eight?"

"Why nineteen twenty-eight?"

"You said twenty-eight. I assumed you meant—you know, twenty-eight with an apostrophe in front of the twenty, like, you know: 'twenty-eight . . .'"

"What happened here in nineteen twenty-eight?"

Hurley said, "Nothing."

O'Yee said, "The walls have ears." They also had a mouth. Behind Lim the wall was beginning to creak. There was static starting in the phone. There was a grinding noise. O'Yee said, "I mean, I mean that psychic events can be imprinted on walls as if they were screens for a projector and if the projector is projecting things that the wall saw—" O'Yee said, *"What the hell happened here in nineteen twenty-eight?"*

"Probably a little man with a surveyor's theodolite said to another little man holding a measuring rod, 'Back three feet or so.' "

"You mean the station wasn't even built here then?"

"No, it was built in the nineteenth century as a police day post." Hurley said, "It was extended as a full station in about 1929 on the site of the old settlement."

O'Yee said, "What old settlement?"

"The leprosarium, and then it came into full twenty-four-hour operation and first appears in the police crimes returns in nineteen thirty-one." Hurley said, "Architecturally, it's an expression of the late Victorian tomb school of redbrick design that persisted well into—"

O'Yee said in a whisper, *"Leprosarium?"*

"Well, no, more the lazar house for the leprosarium a little way up the street—"

O'Yee said, *"Lazar house?"*

"Death house, you know. But it didn't last long because of the bad joss the Chinese lepers associated with it because it had been the site of the old gallows in the last part of the century."

O'Yee said, *"Gallows?"*

"It was a convenient site because, traditionally, long before the Opium Wars in the mid-eighteen-hundreds, the Chinese had used it for their execution ground and the continuum, you know, in the locals' minds of beheadings by the old regime and neck stretchings by the new—by the British . . ." Hurley said, "Well, it had a certain neatness about it."

"Beheadings?"

"Yeah." Hurley, becoming interested said, "There are some old photos and prints of some of them on file. If you like I could—"

O'Yee said, *"Hangings?"*

"Oh, and a few shootings in the back of the neck, but that was mainly reserved for rapists caught in the Chinatown section where the Imperial Government still had some authority—"

"Shootings?"

"Yes, they had a hell of a time digging up all the bodies and heads and twisted hangman's ropes when they laid the foundation for the extension and the cells." Hurley said, "No one ever asks me about history. It's really most interesting to—"

"Hangman's ropes?"

"Yes. Even the Japanese during the war got a bit pissed off when they were there because of all the bits and pieces that kept coming up to the surface."

"The Japanese had the station during the war?" Lim had goggled out. He was walking up and down, then round and round making funny little gurgling noises. O'Yee said in a fury, "And what the fuck did they use it for if they didn't kill people in the cells—*a goddamned preschool crèche*?"

"No, a torture chamber."

"A *WHAT*?!"

"A torture chamber." Really, the ignorance of some people was appalling. Hurley, sighing, said, "It wasn't taken over by the Imperial Japanese Army as such, it was taken over by one semiautonomous branch of it called the Kempeitai. The Kempeitai was the Gestapo of the East—"

"I know who the Kempeitai were!"

"But I don't think they actually killed anyone in there. At the end of the war during Liberation it was said that one of the Chinese secret societies caught the torturers and hacked them all to pieces, but I think that may have been outside on the grass—"

"Outside, there isn't any grass!"

"There was then. It was, of course, where the old typhoid pits had been in—"

"OH, GOD!"

"—the great epidemic of—"

"Herk!"

"What was that?"

"Herk!" THEY had control again. The phone, as a sheet of lightning exploded against the window and lit up everything in the room, went "Pzzt!"

"Herk! Herk! *Herk!*"

Hurley said in alarm, "Hullo, are you still there?"

The wall shrieked, "YAR—RAAAGGHHH!"

All the phones went dead.

He rose up. He ran. He flew. He had lift-off. He was up off the ground flying, turning into a blur. Auden's brain said, *"My God, he can do it!"* He didn't need his brain. His legs had turned into flywheels. They were flying. No, they were not sparks: it was the metal eyelets in his shoelaces—they had turned into sparks. He was glittering in the sun. Auden said, "My God, I can do it!" His feet were not touching the ground, they were hydroplaning. He had reached bow wave speed and only the minimum keel was on the surface and to the accompaniment of swelling music *PT 109* was up off the water with all guns blazing shooting torpedoes as it went.

Spencer shrieked, "You can do it!" He could. Spencer shrieked, "You can!" Spencer shrieked, "GO! GO!"

He was going. The Tibetan, making for the hill with a fistful of money, looked back to sneer. He saw something the size of the Incredible Hulk moving at the speed of The Unbelievable Blur and he didn't sneer. Faster than a speeding bullet, more powerful than a locomotive— The Tibetan, turning, still running, did a sort of trip-skip, then a hop to recover, opened his mouth, closed it again and *ran*.

Huh, huh, huh, huh! It was a tea kettle steaming up getting ready to blow the lid off. He heard the crowd start to roar. His feet didn't belong to him anymore, they belonged to posterity. He heard posterity roar: the crowd, the fans, the blurred faces in the stands on their feet shouting. Auden, running, no longer running, reaching Zen, passing enlightenment, unstoppable, unstopping, hit the first pain barrier at the fifty-yard mark.

The first pain barrier at the fifty-yard mark was as nothing. His brain, astounded, said to the first barrier at the fifty-yard mark, "Ha, ha!" The barrier came and went. It was still there as a faint twinge in the region of the left ventricle. The left ventricle was as nothing. All the people and traffic on the street were going: they were fading, doing a dissolve. The music in his ears was swelling. The music he heard was *Chariots of Fire*. He was going so fast that he was traveling in slow motion. Time for important flashbacks in his life—God, he could hardly wait for the movie! Auden, talking to his brain, said, "Flashbacks!" He hit the pain barrier at the seventy-five-yard mark and his brain said, "Aghhh!"

"GO! GO!" It was Spencer shouting, jumping up and down clutching his stopwatch. He saw the Tibetan weave his way in and out of a crowd of people standing there watching like hurdles and then Auden, not weave at all, but cleave through them like a dreadnought. Some dreadnought. If they had had dreadnoughts like that at the battle of the Dardanelles the fleet would have been in Constantinople for breakfast.

Seventy-five-yard pain barrier nothing. He had not even worked up a healthy sweat. Auden, traveling on winged feet, the air whistling cleanly in his ears and blowing out wax and all his inferiority, yelled to the Tibetan *with no breathlessness at all*, "Give me a race! Run faster! At least make a contest of it!" His brain was working overtime keeping his lungs supplied with air. His brain yelled at him, "Don't waste time with useless taunts!" So much for his brain. Useless taunts were what raised man up from the animals. Auden, as the Tibetan reached the bottom of the ninety-degree hill and turned back to glance at him with fear on his face, yelled, "Sagarmatha Hill—think you can make it?" The Tibetan went up the hill like a mountain goat.

Auden the Magnificent, laughing gaily, was a second behind him like an enraged yeti. By God, Errol Flynn had had it right in moments of triumph. Auden the old swashbuckler, wishing only that there was a dewy-eyed girl to fall into his arms panting at the top of the hill when he triumphed, when he ascended, when he charged, when he came through, yelled, "Ha, ha, ha, ha." It was the old sword-fighting with the Sheriff of Nottingham laugh. Auden, his brain still protesting—Auden yelled to his brain, "*Shut up!*"—yelled with a flick of his head, "Hee, hee—ho! Ho!"

He reached the eighth step and his legs gave up. The ninth step and his legs came back, the tenth and the legs gave out. Will-power. The conquest of the flesh. Auden, accelerating, forgetting it was a hill, deep in psychic running, running for nothing, but running, running *through*, yelled, "You're done! You can't make it!"

The Tibetan yelled back, "Slob! European slob!" He was scampering up the hill, but *not in a straight line*.

Auden shrieked, "Tactics! There's more to success than brute force!" He was gasping. It was his brain complaining again. Auden, turning red, sucking in air wherever he could find a bit, yelled, "Never underestimate a European!" The Tibetan still had the cash clutched in his hand. Venality, it was always your undoing. It was the sport of the thing, the amateur triumph. Even as they begged him, Auden the Fleet would never turn professional: it was something deeper than mere cash—it was the triumph of the will. He heard the crowds at Nuremberg roar. He heard the people on the street looking up, gasp, he heard—

He heard Spencer shout, "Phil! Phil! I've got Wang's pension on you at twelve hundred to one!"

He was gaining on the Tibetan, inches away. He put out his giant, great glistening hand to grab him by the scruff of the neck. He looked down. He looked back. He was halfway up the sheer face of a mountain. Auden's brain said, "Shit—!" Auden said, "Shut up!" The Tibetan, in terror, said—

The Tibetan said, "Ow-wah!" and staggered. A tenth of an inch—a single lousy, miserable tenth of an inch from him—

Auden saw his hand fly up and the money cascade into the air. He saw the Tibetan turn and look shocked. The Tibetan said— Coming a second after, Auden heard the sound. It was a popping sound. It echoed. The Tibetan said, "I've been shot!" He looked hurt. Auden, wavering, going down a few steps with the momentum, said, shaking his head as the man looked at him, "No . . . No, it wasn't me . . ."

He saw Spencer looking up with something in his hand. Auden shrieked, "You shot him!"

"I didn't!"

"You did!" Auden, only mouthing the words, mouthing with no air left, his legs all stilled and stopped and hurting like hell, shrieked, *"You shot him!"*

There were people running up the steps. They were after the falling money.

Auden, aghast, shrieked, "You— That wasn't fair!" Spencer yelled, "I didn't!" What he had in his hand was his stopwatch. Spencer yelled, "I didn't!"

"That wasn't sporting!" He never thought he'd live to hear himself say it. Auden, hopping up and down on the spot like a grasshopper with hemorrhoids, yelled with the minuscule amount of air his brain, getting even, allowed him, "YOU SHOT HIM!"

"HE'S GETTING AWAY!"

"YOU SHOT HIM!"

"I—" The Tibetan had reached the top of the hill, hobbling a little. Then he was gone. Spencer, shaking his head yelled, "IT WASN'T ME!"

Wasn't it?

No, it wasn't.

Spencer, ever mercenary, yelled, "GET THE MONEY!"

Auden reached down to get the money.

And something odd happened. Someone, somewhere, some-how . . .

. . . shot him too.

The door to the Detectives' Room flew open. Framed in the doorway, a vision of mirrors, trigrams, amulets, charms, lo pans and determination, was not the Assistant Feng Shui Man, but the ultimate, the great, the Master Feng Shui Man. They were playing in the big league.

The Master Feng Shui Man, the Clint Eastwood of the spirit

world, said, "Huh." God, he was magnificent. He glittered, he glowed, he shimmered. A vision of light from his mirror-spangled singlet to his mirror-spangled shorts and polished knees, he turned slowly in the doorway cascading light and hope and determination. His lo pan was no second-rate piece of baked clay: it was gold, carried low in a tooled leather holster.

Constable Lim said in a whisper, "Wow . . ."

"Huh." Tight-lipped, hard-faced, taciturn, the Master Feng Shui Man, narrowing his already very narrow eyes, said in a rasp to the wall, in some secret magic language, "Go ahead. Make my day." (It had to be that. What else could it have been?)

Constable Lim said in a gasp, "Whoosh!"

The wall said, "AARRGGHH! Wah! HAAAA!" The entire wall, lit up by a sheet of lightning at the window, vibrating, said in a sound that pealed like the clappers of doom, "BOOOOMM!"

O'Yee shrieked to the Master Feng Shui Man as the door flew open again, this time, the Master Feng Shui Man not coming in, but going out, "Herk! Herk! Herk!" It wasn't the phones. It wasn't a Heavy Breather. It was *him.*

O'Yee, finally, desperately, as his last word on the subject, said, shaking all over, "—Herk!"

Auden, grabbing for the falling money, losing it, sending it up again into the air in a cascade as the crowds toiled up the hill with their hands outstretched and their eyes full of pillage, yelled down to Spencer, "Ow-wah!"

He saw the bullet lying on the step near his foot. It was a .177 round ball from an air rifle. He saw the hungry hordes coming for the money. He saw—

He saw—

He saw . . .

Phillip John Auden in today's extraordinary race from Marathon to Mount Olympus, in the Errol Flynn–John Wayne Self-Respect Stakes at 8:45 A.M. also ran . . .

All that was left were just the last few final syllables before the movie ran out, the lights came up, and all the people staring goggle-eyed at the flickering images of heat and dust, drama and passion went home. He rubbed at his arse.

Auden, still rubbing, said softly, "Aw . . ."

"Aw, Gee . . . !"

If he could have, he would have sat down on the step and wept with disappointment.

4

There had been no sexual assault. They had merely been killed. In the emptied-out kiosk, the government vet, Dr. Hoosier, closing the sternum-to-groin autopsy incision on the dog with number eight thread, said softly to Constable Lee watching him, "'Thou met'st with things dying . . . I with things new-born.'" It was from Shakespeare's *The Winter's Tale*. He had seen it the last time he was at home in Toronto.

The dead creatures were everywhere in the room. The counter flap was open, but it did not dispel the smell.

The man obviously did not understand English. He looked down at Hoosier working on the ground with his instruments and had no expression on his face at all.

The man Feiffer had had the same look. There was only the faintest tightening of the muscles at the corner of Lee's mouth.

Hoosier, finishing the suturing and sliding the dog to one side to gut one of the peacocks, said quietly, "'I am a feather for each wind that blows.'" That was also from *The Winter's Tale*.

He saw Lee redden a little.

Hoosier asked, looking up, "Do you speak English, Constable?"

He did. He wore a flash on the shoulder of his khaki uniform to show he had passed a course and spoke it fluently.

Lee said, "No." He looked down at all the dead things on the floor.

He stood watching, unchanging, unmoving, with no expression on his face at all.

He was the modern equivalent of Nam-mo-lo, the sorcerer ancient Chinese fishermen employed to keep their boats safe from evil spirits and influences. He was the Double Flag Man, the fishing junks' registration documents issuer. He provided the Communist flags and registration papers the Hong Kong junks used in Communist Chinese territorial waters and the Hong Kong flags and documents they used when they left them. He provided the Hong Kong flags and documents the Communists flew in Hong Kong waters and the Communist flags they flew when they went back home with their catch. He kept everyone's hold full. Somewhere, to someone he was probably liable for taxes. No one ever asked. He was some sort of Communist the Hong Kong fishermen could deal with on a friendly basis and, to the Communists, probably, equally some sort of not-too-bad capitalist. He was a commission agent, a shroff, a compradore. He had been in prison in China for displaying revisionist tendencies and, in Hong Kong during the Cultural Revolution riots, he had been in prison as a dangerous radical. In Hong Kong, in Stanley Prison, he had kept birds. In the Hong Kong–China Dockyards off Beach Road, George Su, dressed in singlet and shorts, grimy, fiftyish, peasant-faced and with manicured fingernails and soft hands, said from his desk without looking up, "It's a primary plume from the left wing of a large woodland bird. Technically the feather is called a remex. The color—the look of a burned and blackened tree—means it's from a hot, woodland area of the world." All he had for his office in the dockyard was his desk. It looked like the sort of government-issue desk you saw in prison cells. It probably was. George Su, turning the feather over in his hand and glancing across past the rows of moored junks and sampans in the dock area toward the sea, asked Feiffer in Tanka, the language of the boat people, "What I heard about Yat's—is it true?"

"Yes, it's true."

Past the moored boats there were knots of people waiting to come forward and speak to him. George Su, shaking his head to them and changing from Tanka to Cantonese so they would not understand, said, shrugging, "Plumage is the coat which covers birds against the elements just as fur covers animals." He looked down at the feather and then back up to Feiffer. "The number of plumes, secondary, primary and the rest of it including down can range from about a thousand to twenty-five thousand depending on the needs of the bird." He was quoting it from somewhere, from a book he had read in prison or, like Robert Stroud, the Birdman of Alcatraz, maybe one he had written. "Basically, as well as giving lift for flying, feathers are a form of insulation or waterproofing depending on whether the bird is a land or a sea creature. In this case, it's camouflage." He asked Feiffer directly, "Is this all you've got?"

"Yes." The piece of black umbrella fabric was nothing. It could have been from any of the fifty-three million black umbrellas manufactured in Hong Kong every year. It had been raining: that was the only reason the umbrella had been there. Feiffer, sitting opposite Su at the plywood desk and trying to see the papers the man had turned facedown when he had seen him coming, asked, "Is it a local bird?"

"No."

"How about China?"

"China is local." Su, smiling, said without force, "Hong Kong is part of China. When you ask if it's local I assume you mean regional. China isn't in the region of Britain, it's in the region of China." He was a man who supplied flags. Su said, still smiling, "Thank God, Harry, we're all peaceful realists these days." He held the feather up for Feiffer to see, sliding his fingernail down its length and, somehow, opening it up. "It isn't a bird from anywhere around here." He slid his fingernail back up the length of the feather and, somehow, closed it again. Su said, "The ornithological zip-fastener. That's what birds are doing when you see them preening. Each main feather is held in shape and in place by a series of little hooks and barbs to give elasticity when the bird flies. Sometimes the hooks become undone and the bird has to run its beak along them to zip them up again." He looked up to see Feiffer's face. "Didn't you know that?"

Feiffer said, "No."

Turning the feather quill point-on, Su said, "The little hole running up the calamus—the shaft—is for blood to carry nourishment to the feather." He asked, "Don't you ever watch birds?"

"Can you help me with anything, George? Anything at all?" Su said, "It's a feather. It's from a bird."

"Someone dropped it."

"Did they?"

"Well, did they?"

He had been in prison. Su said, "How do I know? You ask and I reply."

"Can you speculate?"

"On what?"

"*On what the hell it is!*"

"It's a feather. Go ask an expert."

"You are an expert! I'm asking you!"

"I'm a man who kept birds in prison!" Su, looking up suddenly as the sound of his voice made all the people waiting for him tense, said, "What birds may mean to me probably means nothing to anyone else except me! I'm a Communist: a New Man—an organized, majority-respecting and self-denying New Socialist whose life is ordered and organized and set and fixed and predictable! The gaps in my existence birds may fill—"

"Is that what they fill?" Feiffer said quietly, "I watch and see them in the skies sailing and I—" He was leaning forward, his finger pointing at the feather on the table, almost touching it, "—And I don't know what I think."

There was a silence.

Feiffer said without tone, "I've never been in prison."

Su looked at him. Su said after what seemed like a long time, "Yes, you have. Yes, you are. Why else would you stop and look at freedom if you didn't covet it?" He saw Feiffer looking at him. "Dreams, Harry—" He touched at the feather, "This is a night bird. It hides during the day with its camouflage: it answers to no one, considers no one, doesn't hide in the darkness but is most free in it, and—" George Su said with a faint, soft smile on his face, "At night, in prison, before I got permission to keep just a few finches in my cell, at night, in the darkness, in the silence, I could hear the great birds and the swift birds and the birds over the sea wheeling and soaring and calling, moving across a sky I knew nothing about, seeing even my own country from a view I had never seen—a view no one, not even our great leaders had ever seen—and sometimes, I imagined, I thought—" He stopped. He said abruptly, "What there is when you stop to watch something high up in the sky, alone, moving without effort— free—that thing has no name. That thing is dissatisfaction." He said tightly, "That thing—looking, watching, wondering, want- ing—that thing put me in prison in China." He looked, not at Feiffer, but at the Tanka-speaking fishermen waiting to see him and addressed them histrionically in the language he knew they did not understand: "All birds and creatures of the wild in the perfectly ordered and well-run modern society, be it socialist or capitalist, should be instantly removed from the sight of the workers lest they interfere with production levels!" He was the Double Flag Man. Somewhere, to someone he was probably liable for assessment. He had been assessed, twice. Twice, he had been found liable. Su said, standing up, with the feather a little from his face, "Plumage. It insulates, protects, waterproofs—that's all. It isn't a hue a man puts on to keep himself safe through life, it is merely a matter of necessity, camouflage."

Feiffer asked, "How big was the bird, do you think?"

"Big. At least eighteen inches, maybe two feet long." Su said, "It isn't from around here." He asked, smiling, "Am I making you uneasy?"

"I don't know."

Su said, "Smell it." He handed over the feather. There was the faintest odor about it, emanating from the point, from the calamus, the blood hole in the shaft. Su said, "Carbolic acid." Su said, "I don't see birds as objects, as possessions—"

"Are you saying it came from a caged bird?"

"Carbolic is sometimes used to clean metal cages. Yat's would have used a high pressure hose." Su said, "When I left prison I let all my birds go. I don't own birds anymore and maybe, I never did, but whoever dropped this—"

"Are you saying someone carried a caged two-foot-long bird into Yat's and then—" Feiffer said, "It was in the umbrella! It was caught in the umbrella and then when the owl ripped at it it fell out and—"

"—and it could have been in there for years. Or if it started raining and the umbrella was simply found in a trash can or in the gutter or—"

Feiffer said, "It was raining before the killing started. It was raining before whoever did it left home." He turned the feather over in his hand, *"What the hell is it?"*

George Su said softly, "I don't know." There was still that faint half smile playing about his lips. It was not sadness, it was something else. The Double Flag Man said, shaking his head, "I don't know. All my life I seem to have been saying the same thing to different people. I watch birds. They do something to my soul, but what it is, I don't know." All he had in the world was his table and his flags and something, all his life, he had never been able to put a name to. Su said, shrugging, "Once, in China in prison, one of the guards threatened to have me deafened so I couldn't hear the birds anymore." Su said, "But I hear them. Some of us—including you—always hear them." He raised his hand for the knot of fishermen waiting for their documents and flags to come forward. Su said, "I'm a busy man. It's a feather. What else do I know of scientific value? Nothing. Nothing at all." He saw Feiffer carefully slide the feather back into its long glassine evidence bag.

The Double Flag Man said a moment before the fishermen reached him to get their documentation and their flags and to plead their cases, "I'm sorry. All I am is a man who, when he has the time, watches birds."

What if you leaned against the wall and it opened up and you found yourself in 1786?

$E = mc^2$. There was something in there about things like that happening.

$E = mc^2$. Knowledge gave you power. So did a short-barreled .38 Special Colt Airweight in a Berns-Martin upside-down shoulder holster.

But not much.

What gave you knowledge and power was decisiveness.

He decided.

In the Detectives' Room, the strongman armed, O'Yee, holding Lim's eyes with his own in a glittering stare, said in a voice so faint Lim had to come forward to hear, "Well . . . um . . . what do you think?"

All the man Feiffer had was a feather. In the emptied-out kiosk, Dr. Hoosier, with Lee still watching in terrible silence, began to work on the owl.

It had been decapitated.

Kneeling on the stone floor with a piece of plastic sheeting under his knees, drawing a breath, he reached simultaneously for the two sections of the owl—head and body—and drew them together so he could work on them to what point God only knew with his knives.

It was nothing.

"I am a feather for each wind that blows."

It was only a feather.

Probably, evidentially, it was nothing at all.

In the Russo Harbin Hong Kong Trading Bank, the chief teller said nodding toward the rear wall behind the counters, "Mr.

Nyet." What he was nodding at was a dusty portrait of a man wearing what looked like a batwing collar and an expression that turned widows and orphans awaiting eviction from the bank's property to jelly. He wasn't. He was nodding to a sign in English and Chinese next to the portrait. The sign said IN THE EVENT OF A ROBBERY ATTEMPT STAFF ARE OBLIGED TO LAY DOWN THEIR LIVES IN DEFENSE OF THE BANK'S MONEY OR FACE INSTANT DISMISSAL. He wasn't nodding at either of them. He was nodding at the invisible speak balloon that ran from Mr. Nyet's set, closed mouth to the sign and then back again. The chief teller said, "We're a small bank, we don't have a guard."

Spencer said, "Right." He had a wad of money in his hand he had picked up at the base of Sagarmatha Hill. He glanced at the brass-plated plastic nameplate behind the chief teller's section of the counter and read his name. He was a full-blooded Southern Chinese wearing a white shirt, dark tie and dark banker's trousers. His name, according to the plate, was Ivan. Spencer said, "Right, Ivan." Contrary to popular belief, all Chinese didn't look the same. In the Russo Harbin Hong Kong Trading Bank all the Chinese looked the same.

Ivan, nodding at them as they stood at their section of the counter watching, said to introduce them, "Sergei, Igor, Nicholas and Natasha." They nodded. Spencer looked to see which one was the girl. Ivan, still nodding, said, "The bank feels Russian names give a certain feeling of Zurich bank vaults to a small bank." He asked, "How's Mr. Auden?" He had redeemed the customer's lost money from the autobank. He began counting what was left. There wasn't much. Ivan, glancing over at Auden sitting in one of the chairs by the deposit and withdrawal form counter by the door, said in a whisper, "If Mr. Nyet were here, he'd fire me for saying it, but I went outside after the hit and saw the race." In the chair, Auden had his shoes off and was looking at his socks. They seemed to be making pulsing whoom, whoom noises. From the look on his face, he seemed to be thinking as he looked. Ivan said, "He must have feet made of pure rawhide."

If he hadn't, he did now. Auden, looking up at the sound of a human voice, said, "Hee . . ." His shoes were laid out side by side on the floor next to him. He looked at his feet and thought he would have to get new shoes. His shoes seemed to have shrunk. Auden, with a strange, odd, funny sort of totally destroyed feeling that, in its own way, had a sort of sensuous glow about it, said to acknowledge the presence of the voice, "Ha . . . he . . . ah . . ."

Spencer said intimately to Ivan, "He's in a bad way."

"He almost got him."

Spencer said, "Yes." He felt responsible. Spencer said with what he thought was a Russian accent, "The nature of man is to suffer." It was Tolstoy.

Ivan said with another nod, "Then you've come to the right place." The whoom, whoom pulsing sound was getting louder from Auden's feet and there was a peculiar reddening coming to his face. The man just sat there rubbing, staring at his shoes and making occasional pee-wit sounds. Ivan, finishing counting, said, "According to the computer, the Tibetan got away with three thousand dollars of our customer's money. You've recovered just over two thousand." He looked across at Auden and said on behalf of the absent Mr. Nyet, "Well done." Judging from his portrait, it wasn't what Mr. Nyet would have said at all. Ivan, glancing to Natasha to offer the bank's full hospitality to one of its most favorite sons, asked Spencer, "Do you think he'd like a glass of water?"

Auden said from nowhere, "You're not Russians! You're Chinese! I thought the Chinese had broken with the Russians and they were pursuing their own brand of Communism!" All he got from the outside world through the pain was a hazy red blur. Auden, letting go of his foot and looking worried, said anxiously, "Bill? Bill, are you there?"

"It's all right." Spencer, going over and laying his hand gently on Auden's shoulder, said, "Don't worry." He smiled back at the androids behind the counter. The androids were all looking at Auden and looking worried. Spencer said gently, "We're back in the bank now. The bank has redeemed the customer's money and what we're doing now is counting it so the bank can make the adjustments in its bookkeeping and—"

Auden said, "It blew away. It blew away and then there were lots of people grabbing at it and then—" Once he'd built a railroad—he'd made it run. Auden said sadly, in tatters, "I almost did it. I was close. Just an inch or two more and I could have—" He had Spencer by the coat lapels. He pulled him down. Auden, lowering his voice, said as the greatest secret of the twentieth century, "I could have done it. If I'd had the breaks I could have done it."

"You were great."

"I was." Auden, rolling on the chair and almost toppling off, said, "I was." All the Chinese looked the same. Why were they

Russians? Maybe he was dead. He was staring at a portrait of someone who looked like God. God had a batwing collar and mustache. He looked like Simon Legree looking like God. Auden, moving his hands in front of him to clear the red haze, said, "I did it for Wang!" He had to concentrate to make out what he was saying. He asked himself, "Who's Wang?" Maybe Spencer was dead too. He was there. The picture of God kept blurring and moving in and out. It wasn't a picture of God, it was a picture of his Uncle George. He was back home rooting around in the cupboard under the stairs. Auden, looking disappointed, said, "I scribbled a dirty word on the back of the frame. It wasn't me, it was Robert Phillips down the road!"

"It's all right, Phil."

Auden said, "And I got my shoes all dirty on the way home from school and now everyone's going to be cross with me." It was odd the way his body felt. It wasn't as if his body was going to pack up and die, it was as if his body was overpacked, like a suitcase. The connection between his mouth and his lungs had gone—well, that had gone in the first few moments—(Auden's head thought, "In the first few moments of what?")—and now . . . Auden said, "Why aren't I sweating? In the gym I sweat. Why aren't I sweating?" He looked his body up and down. His body didn't mind: it was past caring. Auden said, "I'm not sweating at all!" Auden said, "I'm pulsing! I can hear myself! I'm *pulsing!*" He had tried to watch Carl Sagan's *Cosmos* on television one night and got the episode about stars turning into black holes. Auden, collapsing in on himself, becoming a vacancy in the universe, said in a panic, "I can't feel anything! I'm not in any pain! I'm on the outside looking in and I'm a physical wreck and I'm not fit at all!"

Spencer said gently, "You went beyond the pain barrier, Phil."

From the counter, Ivan said, "Well done, Mr. Auden!"

Natasha—which one was Natasha?—said in a girl's voice, "You were wonderful!"

Auden said in a whisper, "Which one's the girl?" He saw Spencer shake his head. Spencer didn't know either. Auden said, suddenly desperately, "*I was shot!*" He said staring at the picture of God and the anteroom to heaven where all human failings were gone and you were totally aware and all-knowing and you couldn't even tell the difference between the girls and the boys, in horror, "I was shot dead in the street!"

"It was an air rifle pellet!"

"I was shot!"

"It was a tiny little .177 caliber air rifle or pistol pellet. It hit you on the—" Spencer said, hesitating, wondering how the man continued to sit happily in the chair contemplating his socks, "In the rear and it—"

Auden said, "Someone shot me!" Auden, grasping Spencer hard by the arms and pulling him into the foxhole to say a few dying words in the midst of the barrage in close-up, said, "Bill, Bill, tell—" He pulsed out. Auden said suddenly, smiling sadly, still building railways, "Once, once, Bill, I was good . . ."

Spencer said, "You were shot on the backside. It didn't even break the skin."

". . . it was me. It wasn't Robert Phillips. I wrote the dirty word on the back of . . ." He pulsed back into his body. He stopped pulsing. He began to sweat. He stopped being dead. He began being alive. He stopped not feeling. He felt. Auden said as all the feeling came back into his body, "AARRGGGHHHHG!" He jumped up out of the chair to protect his stinging arse and came down on two raw hamburger steaks attached to the end of his ankles. Auden said, "ARRGGGHHH!" Auden said, "Bill! Bill! *Someone shot me!*" He had been chasing the Tibetan. "And him! Someone shot him too!" He thought now that he was back from the dead all the Chinese in the bank would look different. They didn't. They all looked the same. IN THE EVENT OF A ROBBERY ATTEMPT STAFF ARE OBLIGED TO LAY DOWN THEIR LIVES IN DEFENSE OF THE BANK'S MONEY OR FACE INSTANT DISMISSAL. He was still staring at the picture of God dressed up as a batwinged, black-eyed, bitter Kaiser Wilhelm in a striped tie. It was too much.

He hurt.

He hopped.

His brain gave out completely and went *pop!*

Auden, hurting, hopping, popping, pulsing, yelled in utter, complete, lost, hopeless panic, "Bill! Bill! Bill, *why is this happening to me?*"

He glazed out. He became stone. He said in a sort of thin bubbling sound between his set stone lips, ". . . bibblebip . . . burb . . ."

He seemed happy. Sometimes, as his lips moved from side to side and dribbling noises came out, it seemed almost as if he was smiling . . .

It was the aloneness of the bird over the harbor that had

fascinated him: the total, complete self-containment that over and over had sent it wheeling and climbing and riding the currents of air.

If there was no hunting or watching and their bellies were full, why did they do it?

They did it because it was their pleasure. There was no other reason. Maybe that was why people watched, why, when they watched there were no thoughts to it, but only the watching. Maybe it was something too simple to be thought of or a hunger too deep to be recognized. Maybe it was simply the pure beauty of what birds did, what they were designed for and nothing else, or just the pure pleasure of what they were that the person watching was not and never would be.

When he watched birds high and silent in the air, he—perhaps like the birds themselves—had no thoughts except the thoughts of the stillness and the air.

It was not the Bambi syndrome. The Bambi syndrome meant that the birds never killed or tore their prey apart with their talons or beaks. They did tear their prey apart with talon and beak. That part of them, the killing, was not part of their pleasure, but merely a necessity.

They were the things of dreams, high, silent creatures in the air, looking down.

All he had was a single, unidentifiable feather.

On the steps of the Hong Bay library on Aberdeen Road, waiting for opening time, Feiffer watched the birds high out over the harbor.

He had in his pocket the address George Su had given him. Watching the birds, he touched at it with his hand to check it was still there.

He looked at his watch.

In Yat's, someone dreaming, perhaps for a long time, had awoken.

Far out to sea, there was still lightning from the typhoon on its way to Taiwan.

The dreams were of chaos and mutilation and death. Now, awake, they were no longer dreams.

He saw the birds wheeling and gliding and wondered what he thought.

He wondered what whoever it was who had suddenly awoken —he wondered what, now, at this moment, he was thinking of.

5

Behind a garbage skip in Annapura Lane off Old Himalaya Street, Spencer, scuffling around in garbage no one had bothered to put in the skip, said definitely, "He fired from here." He had the two squashed .177 caliber pellets from Sagarmatha Hill in a glassine envelope and he held them up and tapped them at the side of the metal box. "It was an air pistol"—he was stepping back, going through aiming motions against the side of the metal judging the height—"Not a rifle. He rested the barrel against the skip here to keep it firm and he swiveled it against the corner, bending down a bit to follow the moving targets."

One of those moving targets, Auden, looking not at the garbage around the skip, but at the hamburgers at the end of his ankles, said, "Hmm."

Spencer said, "See, here." There were two little splashes of what looked like vaporized oil on the gray metal of the skip. "Yeah, it was definitely an air pistol. He dieseled the weapon with a drop of oil in the breech to give it more range." He wondered if he had Auden's full attention. Auden was mouthing something out of the corner of his mouth. Maybe he was just taking in the information. Spencer said, "Actually, to say you 'fire' an air weapon is totally wrong. It's like a bow and arrow: you don't actually fire an air gun or a bow and arrow because there isn't actually any fire—what you do is *shoot* it." He leaned against the side of the skip and shot his finger in the direction of the hill. Spencer said, "It was a shot of almost forty yards, the one that got

53

the Tibetan, and you, you were almost thirty yards——" He saw Auden about to say something. Spencer said quickly, "No, farther. You almost had him, Phil, so the second shot must have been almost forty yards too." He said, deciding, "Say thirty-eight yards." Spencer said solicitously, "It doesn't still hurt, does it?"

Auden said, "Yes." Auden said, "If there are guns around—if people are bloody shooting or firing and dieseling or whatever the fuck they're doing, it's time to call in the SWAT team and kill them." The Tibetan needed killing. Auden said, nodding up at the hill, "SWAT can lay in a sniper with a Remington bolt action and when the bugger gets to about step number sixty-five——"

"The Tibetan didn't shoot you!" Spencer, coming forward and pushing Auden hard on the shoulder to bring him back to reality, said, "The Tibetan——"

Auden said, "Ow!" He staggered. He limped.

Spencer said, "Phil, the physical exertion, I know——"

Auden said, "I put my shoes on!"

"It's best. If you don't, your feet will swell up." Spencer, trying to take his mind off it, said, "Dieseling: that's where, in order to increase the range of an air weapon, you put a little drop of light oil behind the pellet in the breech and then, when the blast of compressed air hits it, the speed of the pellet leaving the barrel is increased by the explosion of the oil." He said thoughtfully, "So, I suppose, in this particular case you could say he *fired* an air pistol."

In this particular case you could say he was about to fire a partner. Auden, still wincing, said, "You were down here. You should have heard it."

"An air weapon, especially one leaning against a metal object for steadiness, doesn't make a bang, it makes a——" He leaned down again. Spencer, pointing his finger and going "poof" to prove that fingers leaned against a metal skip made only a poof! noise said, "He must have allowed for the wind——"

"There wasn't any wind!"

"Well, he had to allow for that too." Spencer, still with the finger, said, "Pooff!" He looked at Auden, smiling.

Auden said, "I could have got him! If I hadn't been shot, I could have got him!"

There were two pellets in the envelope. Spencer, nodding with a total lack of sincerity, said, "Sure."

"I was inches away!"

"Well——" Spencer said, "Well, a few inches anyway." Spencer, tapping the pellets in the envelope, said, "You have to remember that the Tibetan was shot too."

"He was shot higher up than I was! He was shot five steps away—" Auden said quickly, "Four steps away and he was shot somewhere in the back! I was shot in the arse! I was in mid-stride." Auden said, "He was shot in the small of the back as he was turning around to give up! I was on top of him!" Auden said suddenly, mystically, "Bill, I *flew*! I was *flying*! You know all that Zen stuff about becoming the object and the action and—that happened to me! I wasn't running, I was the running. I wasn't chasing the Tibetan I was the Tibetan being chased!" His feet, suddenly, in line with his enlightenment, stopped hurting. Auden, starting to hop up and down, to flex, to exercise, to work out, said without room for argument, "I did it! All that Om stuff! I became *Om*!"

Spencer said softly, "Poor old Wang."

"To hell with Wang! I did it for Wang at the beginning, but when I started running, when I hit the hill, when I was *ascending*—" Auden, coming forward and taking Spencer hard by the shoulder to put his face an inch from Spencer's nose, said in a hard whisper, "Bill, when all that happened, I became *One*!"

Well, Half anyway. Spencer, releasing himself from Auden's grip, said looking up toward the hill and then down at the two diesel marks on the side of the skip, "Well . . ." Spencer said, "You're right. Let's call in SWAT and have everybody killed."

"What about Wang?"

Spencer said, "To hell with Wang." Spencer said, brushing the thought away with his hands, "There are worse things in the world than a massive coronary at twenty-three years of age." Spencer, looking down with friendly concern at the two mis-shapen blobs of flesh stuffed into Auden's shoes at the end of his legs, asked, "How are your feet?"

"My feet are fine!"

"You said they hurt."

"I can rise above hurt." The hill also rose. It rose almost straight up. Well, if it hadn't where would have been the triumph? Hill, where was thy sting? Where the hell was his victory? Auden, looking desperate, said, "Make another bet! I'll take any odds you can get! Make another bet and this time I'll do it!"

"Phil, I couldn't promise you'll hear the gunshots. In all the noise—"

It was the noise of the cheering. Auden said, "If you close your body to all the assaults of the world, Grasshopper, how can death come in to claim you?" He remembered it from a kung fu movie on television. It must have been written by someone who had a deep knowledge of Zen. Or maybe who jogged a lot. Auden said, "I can do it! Give me the chance and I won't let you down! Give me a chance! A shot at the title!" Wrong movie. Auden, getting desperate, said, "What sort of fucking bookie gives an out-of-condition aging European odds of twelve hundred to one to catch a flying bloody Tibetan mugger on Sagarmatha Hill *on the first attempt*?" Auden said, "It was a practice run! I was just walking the track! Even bloody racing drivers get a practice run!" Auden said, "I qualified! I made the time! I'm in the big race!"

"What about your feet?"

"My feet are merely vessels in which I place my—" Auden said, "My feet are okay." Auden said, "How many shots did your bookie give me? Really?"

Spencer said, "Five." He tapped at the diesel marks with his knuckle.

Auden said, "Quite right too."

Spencer, smiling, said in a whisper, "Phil, you were magnificent . . ."

Auden said, "Damn right I was!"

Spencer said tightly, "A Wang! A Wang!"

Auden said, "Right!" His feet hurt like hell. He looked across the road and saw the entire staff of the Russo Harbin Hong Kong Trading Bank standing outside their glass doors looking over at him. Auden shouted, "We're not done yet!" Auden, starting to do little running-on-the-spot exercises to limber up, shouted, "Bring on the Tibetan!" He wondered which of them was the girl. Auden shouted, "The bank's money—I'll defend it with my life!"

He was running on the spot on some garbage people were too lazy or too stupid to put properly in the skip. It felt like he was running on squashed hamburger meat. He wasn't. He was running on his feet.

Auden, to no one in particular, said, "Damn right!"

His brain never let him down. Coming on-stream, his brain took one look at his feet and, going *bang!*, made him go numb all over.

Outside the bank they were cheering.

Auden said, "*Yeah!*"

They all loved him.

He wondered, in the line of happy, cheering, waving fans, which one was the girl . . .

In the Hong Bay reference library reading room, Feiffer, with a pile of books on the table in front of him, said softly, "Shit . . ." It was hopeless. He had never known there were so many species of birds in the world. None of the books divided into birds of hot woodlands countries or dry, burned areas, but, rather, by the species themselves. All the names of the species were in Latin: the Latin, like the birds, like the climatic regions in which they lived or to which they migrated or from which they bred, crossed over and became nothing but an unending mass of lines of movement and distribution that told him nothing.

He was getting nowhere. He had the address George Su had given him in his pocket, but before he used it he had to have something.

He had a single feather.

He could not even understand the Latin names.

He had nothing.

He kept stopping in the books at the pictures of creatures so beautiful they took his breath away: birds of paradise, the Fairy Pittas, the birds of the deep forests of South America, the hornbills, great and elf owls, and all the eagles, hawks and ospreys that sailed high in mountains and above harbors. There were things he had never heard of: trogons, mousebirds, tanagers, bellbirds that made sounds in the trees like carillons of glass bells and birds known only by the sounds they made: the go-away bird, wait-a-while bird and even a gray crowned gregarious almost shot-out Australian bird that, over and over, made a sound like a Swiss goatherd or shepherd yodeling across mountains.

Once, in the early years of the century, in America, there had been millions of meat-bearing birds called passenger pigeons. They had been hunted for that meat.

Now, there were none. They were all dead and the species totally extinct.

In Yat's, everything there was also dead.

He knew the names of almost none of the birds in the books. Through all his life, the birds had been there all around him and he had seen none of them, bothered to learn nothing, and he knew almost none of their names or what they were.

Outside, seen in flashes on the windows of the library, there was still lightning in the sky.

He looked at his watch.

10:00 A.M. exactly.

In the books, it said, now, most of the birds of the world were fully and totally protected.

There was no one else in the library so early.

With the sound of his footsteps echoing in the empty, book-lined reading room, he went toward one of the corridors toward the index files by the enquiry desk at the main entrance of the place.

There was no natural history museum in Hong Kong. He had only what he could find himself.

He had only the books he could not completely understand or even find properly.

He had, in Yat's, something so awful he could not even find a name for it.

He had the address Su had given him.

He had a single feather.

10:00 A.M.

In the library his step rang in the empty room as the lightning, silently, persistently flashed at the windows.

Outside the window of the Detectives' Room, in the street, there was a little girl in a cotton dress on a bicycle pulling petals off a flower.

At the window, O'Yee said with tears in his eyes, "Oh . . ."

She had a Band-Aid on her knee.

O'Yee said, "Ahhh . . ."

He looked farther. There were cars, people, folks greeting folks, hot-chestnut sellers with hot chestnuts roasting on an open fire, smog, noise, stench, all the old familiar places . . .

O'Yee said, "Phew . . ."

. . . that his heart embracèd. O'Yee said, "Aaahh . . ."

His heart embraced her. She was a skinny, knobbly-kneed, almond-eyed Chinese with gaps in her teeth. The flower she gently de-petaled one by one, singing her little soundless rhymes, was a plastic pansy.

Innocence—he remembered what that was. That was what little girls on bicycles were for—to remind you of it. O'Yee said firmly over his shoulder to Lim, "Did you ever see that movie *Frankenstein*? Did you see the scene where the monster with the skewer in his neck comes up to the little girl?" He didn't look back over his shoulder. O'Yee said, "She was playing with a flower too. This thing shuffles up to her going Rah! Rah! and looking like death and what the hell does she do—she gives him the flower!"

"And then he kills her. Right?" He hadn't seen the movie.

"No, he doesn't kill her! He realized that even down there in the depths of hell life is still beautiful and there's good in the world and he sits down there with her and smiles at her!"

Lim said, "It must be an old movie." He looked at the wall. The wall was silent.

"There are certain elemental truths in the world! One of those elemental truths is that little girls fall down and scrape their knees and that little girls gently take the petals off flowers! It's a reflection of a hidden truism that the world still retains some semblance of predictability and peace and comfort and—" O'Yee said something he had read in *Readers' Digest*, " 'Everything in the real world can be understood by reason, the other world—the next world—requires only love.' " O'Yee said, "This isn't happening. If it is happening it's something ordinary and because we're both so far from the basic elemental truths in the world that every little girl with a Band-Aid on her knee and a flower in her hand knows from birth we're running around frightened and confused." That was why he was a senior detective inspector: with age and travail came a wisdom no police training manual ever taught. O'Yee said, "No unearthly power can stand up to the light of innocence and love." It was true: he had never won with his own kids. O'Yee said, "You watch, I'll open the window and that girl will smile up at me and, just like that, there'll be a flash and everything will return to normal!"

It must have been one hell of a movie. Lim, glancing back at the wall, said, "Yes?"

"Absolutely." O'Yee, turning to lay his hand gently on Lim's shoulder, steering him to a view of all that was honest and pure and true in life, said gently, "Have you ever seen a ghost story that had an ending you believed in?"

"No."

O'Yee said, "That's because there isn't any ending because there aren't any real ghost stories!" He was getting there, he could feel it. O'Yee, reaching for the window, said in full throat, "There are no sounds coming from the wall! There is no headless ghost! There are no mutilated spirits haunting this station! There

are no psychic disturbances! There is no danger! There is only—"
He opened the window and called out to the girl, *"Hey!"*

"AAARRRAAGGHHH! Twen-ty-eight! Twen-ty-EIGHT! NAARRINGGAHHH! *BOOM!"*

Or, on the other hand—

O'Yee, leaning out the window shouting after the fleeing girl at the top of his lungs, the skewer in his neck starting to hurt like hell, yelled, "Hey! *Hey!* You've forgotten your bicycle—!"

. . . the girl was the one who fawned. In the street, Natasha in white shirt, brown tie, brown slacks and with bobbed hair, said in Cantonese in a voice that turned him to vanilla, "You were so brave, Mr. Auden. For a man of your size to chase up that hill like a man carrying no muscle on his bones—like a mere Chinese— that was what won the Empire for you English." She, like all the other tellers in the bank, was about five foot two. She came up to Auden's bicep.

Auden flexed it.

Natasha, gazing up at him and seeing the firm set of his jaw, said in admiration, "If we had someone like you in the bank not even Mr. Nyet could push us around." Was there a tear? Natasha, putting out her fingers gingerly to touch the mighty frame and then pulling them away out of maidenly reserve, said, "You carry all your muscle and sinews like a dancer, so gracefully." She gave him a modest smile.

Ah, it weren't nothin'. Auden said, staring above her and out to the far horizons, "A man has to do what he's capable of."

"You are light and freedom to us in the bank."

Auden said, "I try."

"You are the spirit of the wind."

"Banks are important too."

"Not ours."

Auden said encouragingly, "Oh, yes. Commerce is important too." He gave her his Errol Flynn smile, "Not everyone can go haring about up impossible hills—"

Natasha said with a gasp, "Chasing impossible dreams . . ."

Auden said, "Climb every mountain!"

Natasha said, "Keep right on till the end of the road."

It was so nice to meet someone who wasn't a Communist. Auden said, "A man must dream." Once you got close to her you noticed she was a girl. You could tell by the way the front of her shirt rose and fell. You could smell it. It was perfume. It wafted. It rose from her five foot two about fourteen—well maybe twelve—inches upward and came in zephyrs and— Auden said abruptly, "Business before pleasure."

Natasha said with the tear still glistening, "The bank is a terrible place to work, Phillip." She asked, "May I call you Phillip?"

Auden said, "Sure." For a man of muscle and sinew the voice came out as fast-melting butter. Auden, clearing his throat, said, "Sure!"

"We have no happiness in our lives in the bank, only drudgery and the dust of shattered dreams. Shattered by Mr. Nyet." Natasha said, "He's away at the moment." She said with what looked like a sneer, "He knows better than to be around when great things are happening!" Natasha said, "I'm an athlete myself. The bank staff and I, we all planned to represent the bank this year in the Pan-Asia Bank Officers' Games in Bangkok, but Mr. Nyet—" She sniffed, "Mr. Nyet refused to sponsor us—"

Auden the Magnificent asked with interest, "What sport do you play?" Maybe he could give her a few tips.

There was a silence. She gazed up at him with almond eyes. How anyone could fail to see she was a girl was beyond him. Auden, leaning down to catch her sweet and low voice, "Hmm?"

Natasha said, "Indoor games, Phillip."

Auden said in English in a whisper, "Oh, boy . . ." It sounded as if he was practicing his fast breathing for the next run. Auden, looking around, wondering where the hell Spencer had gone, said, "Oh." Auden said, "Ah." Auden said, "Well . . ."

". . . Phillip . . ."

". . . Natasha . . ."

"Thank you, Phillip, for showing us all that there is a way to rise above all of life's hard blows, that there is Hope." Natasha said, "And you do all this for the love of a friend, for poor P.C. Wang—"

Who? Auden said quickly, "I do."

"Phillip . . ."

Auden said in a tiny voice, "Natasha . . ." Auden said, "Natasha—"

Natasha said, "Yes?"

Auden said, "Um." He looked at his watch. It was working, going around: both hands, the big hand and the little hand. Auden said, touching her gently on the shoulder with his mighty mitt—like all powerful hulks gentle to a fault, "Just—just stand clear when I go." Auden said, "Just—just—" Auden said, "This time, I'm going to go full speed!"

"Oh!"

"Oh . . ."

She was a girl. He could tell. His legs, as she brushed against them to give him room to move, turned quiveringly, completely—to jelly.

"Twenty . . . *eight*!"

"Aw—SHUT UP!"

Enough was enough.

He was, after all, the officer in charge.

He took charge.

"AW, SHUT UP, WHY DON'T YOU!?"

In the Detectives' Room, O'Yee, getting madder'n hell, slammed the window to the outside world with a bang.

They were forming. All up and down the street to the base of Sagarmatha Hill, people were forming. Natasha had gone back into the bank. Auden had stopped saying, "Oh . . ." They were forming to catch some of the money when either he or the Tibetan dropped it when they were shot. Auden said, *"Hell!"* Maybe he was hiding behind the trash skip. Auden, not turning around, his eyes glued to the waiting multitudes, said out of the corner of his mouth, "Bill?"

He was nowhere. He was gone.

All the multitudes were fit young men wearing singlets and shorts. Some of them looked like rickshaw pullers: they had muscles in their legs like oak.

He looked at their feet. They were all bare. They looked like Frisbees. Auden said, *"Hell!"*

He waited, calm, unruffled, by his demeanor and his grace the undisputed, the favorite, the Olympian. Auden said with a sneer on his face to the waiting hordes, "Huh!"

Auden, out of the corner of his mouth, so imperceptibly that it looked merely as if his lip muscles were doing warming-up exercises, said, "Bill! Bill! —*Bill!*"

He was never around when you needed him.

Auden, in his last final gasp before he crouched down on his starting blocks and waved across to the bank to where Natasha watched from a window, said for one last time, "—*Bill!!*"

* * *

He wondered.

In the library with a book in front of him opened to pictures and drawings of all the birds, he wondered.

By now, everyone would be finished at Yat's.

He wondered why, of all the buildings and cages and kiosks at Yat's, why only the Wishing Chair, why only that in the midst of all the terrible slaughter, had been smashed.

In the empty, silent library, Feiffer, touching his hand to his face, said softly, "Christ . . . !"

He wondered why any of it had been done.

It had been done with a machete. In the night, its edge, coming down, had glittered like lightning and then it had been gone.

"More pork, more pork, wide-awake, wide-awake!" They were the sounds of the birds in the books, sounds like bells, like music, calls, carillons, rolls, whiplashes, reprises over and over in the stillness.

In the library, there was only the stillness.

In the lightning, in the stillness, in the grayness and the pictures in the book in front of him, he wished he could hear the sounds of birds.

There were so sounds.

He wished he were someone else.

He wished, someone suddenly frightened in the big, empty room alone—

He wished—

He wished to God it had never, never happened.

6

Solipsism. It was a word. It was the last word left. It meant the belief that all things in the external world were only the imaginings of the last, the only mind, left on earth—that the earth itself was only the imaginings of the last, the only mind left on—left inside the cocoon of redness.

It was true. The word was the last word left in a world in which all the words had gone. Maybe it was no word—maybe it was only a sound, what things were, not a word at all, but only the awareness of the red. The redness was a veil, it was spinning, opening and closing in slits and buzzing without sound.

Solipsism. The street, through the slits, was yellow—there was a car, a mailbox—they appeared as objects in the redness, free-floating, passing by, entering the redness, sailing through it in colors and then, halting for a moment in the cupola of red, floating out again. The objects, the streets, Hong Kong came into the cupola disconnected, rootless—the car passed through a slit in the cocoon—it was black, a taxi, with the driver, openmouthed and shouting without sound—and then—then it was gone.

All the birds and animals had died. They had come into the cocoon like owls on silent wings, seemed suspended on wires and then, their heads coming loose and floating away, they had begun to spin, to fall out of control with dark liquids falling away from them like vapor trails; they had struck a part of the redness, the veil, the cocoon, and then had passed out, gone over, ceased to be. They had been wet. It had been raining. An umbrella, like an ectoplasm, had hovered there above the roof of the cupola. Beneath the umbrella and the cupola, the blood vapor trails had spun and turned and twisted and gouted in slow motion, splashing, passing through and out of the redness and there had been no sound at all.

Things had come halfway into the redness—the stomach and paws of a dog, the head of a crocodile, dreamthings: they had been pulped into blood and slashed to entrails.

And then they had gone again.

The street passed in through the cocoon, not at its base, but at chest height as a long, unwinding yellow strip with black lines on it where the paving stones were, then, a moving image on a racing-driver computer game, it was swallowed up into nothing and was gone again.

The red cocoon was expanding, contracting, pulsing, shimmering, opening and closing without cause.

Something on the yellow street—part of the yellow street— something following the yellow street came in—something— objects—black and stark white and bright blue and black, and then they were gone again.

There was a buzzing starting, getting louder and louder.

The objects in the cocoon were dreamer's pictures, the pictures of the sleepless. *Solipsism*: it was the thought—the last thought, the only thought in the cocoon that all there was was the cocoon. The red cocoon covered, enveloped, was the person inside it. The person reflected, was the reflection of itself, was only the image in a mirror with the form of the cocoon. The person's name was Jakob. It was a small, brown-faced old man.

The dreams, the objects came in and out of the red cocoon like pulsings of sleep, like the world seen in and out, sharp and blurred like spectacles taken quickly on and off.

There was a buzzing.

There was a sickness.

It was the sickness of the spectacles taken on and off, of the queasy loss of balance, of nausea, of trying, failing, to fix on a single object.

Through secret, different streets, like the birds traveling on different, invisible currents and along arcane, unknown, unknowable roads in the air, the person inside the cocoon traveled in another dimension, in another time, toward another destination.

Jakob. He was a small, brown-faced old man with a soft, almost whispering voice.

There was only the buzzing getting louder and louder.

It was not true. If there was any external reference to truth, to the world as it was, it was not true at all. It was a trick, a device, a secret.

. . . Jakob. He was a small, brown-faced old man with a soft, whispering voice.

It was camouflage.

It was a trick.

The machete, like lightning, had killed everything that had come into the cocoon and disemboweled it.

The person inside the cocoon, moving through secret streets to a secret place, like the birds of the night seen during the day, held up to the light, looked nothing like that at all.

He had cold, dead eyes, the small brown-faced man with the whispering voice.

His name was Jakob.

His last name did not matter in the least. No need for a last name.

He existed through the shimmering red cupola that only he—the last thought on earth—ever saw. He was God.

He killed things.

They came into the red, pulsing cupola and he killed them.

10:33 A.M. It was red light inside the cupola, the cocoon. Like a submarine, closed in and without windows, it passed through seas it never saw, never touched.

It was merely there, passing. The cocoon, like the hull of the submarine, was hard, enclosed, impermeable, without light other than the red light of depth and dark places.

It traveled invisibly, unseen in the places of the night.

10:33 A.M. In Icehouse Street, Hong Bay, Crown Colony of Hong Kong, as it passed by, like a memory, a thought, a secret held tight-lipped silent, no one knew it was there.

Jakob . . .

There was no Jakob.

What was inside the cocoon, hidden, invisible, hiding there, was merely a reflex, an amoeba. It was merely a mechanism that killed.

There was only the buzzing.

In Icehouse Street, only the person inside the cocoon, the person who was the cocoon, heard it.

Buzzing.

Jakob.

—it was very important that, methodically, in order, following a pattern, one by one at the right time and place, he, without mercy or thought, killed things.

There was no light in the dead, cold eyes as they walked. The dead, cold eyes saw only the redness.

7

"That's a peregrine falcon." Dead, mounted on a stand made of a broken tree branch set in stones and grass to resemble some sort of natural perch, it was a beautiful, multicolored bird of prey that looked like a small eagle with a beak like a razor. In his little, unpainted workroom and living area on the second floor of Number 83 Generalissimo Chen Street, Chao, touching it reverently on the head with the gentlest of touches from his long delicate fingers, said, "It comes here to Hong Kong very rarely from the high, wild places in China. Tell me, what would you do if you saw it lying dead on the road?" Everywhere in the little room there were stuffed and mounted birds, eagles, hawks, owls, in the corner what looked like a small collection of Chinese pheasants, finches, a kestrel about to take wing on a papier-mâché rock, even tiny bee eaters and hummingbirds. Chao Kai Sun, touching the wing of the falcon and stroking, asked, "Well, what would you do?"

"All these birds you have in here are on the list of endangered species."

"All these birds I have in here are dead." He was a small birdlike man himself. His eyes were bright and sparkling as if he lived some sort of intense inner life. It made his age hard to guess at. He could have been anywhere from twenty-five to forty-five. Chao, waving away whatever thoughts about him Feiffer was having, asked, "Well?"

"I don't know much about birds—"

"You know enough to know that all these—the hawks, and the falcons and the owls are endangered." He seemed to hop across the room to a workbench and return before he had even gone. "So is this. This is a common sparrow at first sight. In fact, it's a particular subspecies of sparrow that—"

Feiffer said, "Do you know what bird this feather came from?" He had it in his hand. He had offered it to Chao twice, but the man had not touched it. He didn't need to touch it.

Chao said, "Yes, yes, I know." He said tightly, "You haven't answered my question."

"Are all these birds illegal?"

"Yes!" Chao, looking happy, said, "Yes, every one. They have all been killed by the most effective and wholesale killer of flying birds in the world—the car aerial." The door to the next room was ajar. From it, Feiffer could smell the smell of formalin and preserving fluids. Chao said, "And I killed not a one. Each one of them, at one time, lay dead on the road or in a field in the New Territories or in a dirty gutter waiting to be eaten by rats or carrion and I, personally, killed not a one." There was something he wanted. It could have been absolution. Chao, his voice going up, said, "If you arrest me and I argue my case in court, the letter of the law says that possession of endangered species is as much a crime as the possession of a deadly weapon—if I go to court I will go to jail."

"And what will happen to your birds?"

"There is no natural history museum here in Hong Kong so there are no dusty storerooms or drawers in which to store them for the mice, so they will all be destroyed." He touched the falcon. "This was found on a rubbish tip in Icehouse Street." He tapped at the glorious bird's sternum. "It was almost cut in half by an aerial after high winds had forced it into the city and then heavy rains had forced it to come down onto the roadway to hunt in the light of a streetlamp." Chao said, "What was I supposed to do? *Let it rot?*"

"What are you doing with it now?"

"It is an endangered species." Chao, pleading his case to someone, not Feiffer, said, "Each new area of agricultural land that is rezoned to industrial or residential use slaughters more birds in a moment with the destruction of trees and habitats than a dozen men could do with shotguns in a month!"

"All your birds are dead!"

"If they were alive there would be no need to protect them."

"You're not protecting them. What you are doing is making decorations for drawing rooms—"

Chao said, "You've read a book on taxidermy."

"Every museum curator says that private—"

"There is no museum here in Hong Kong."

"You are not a museum."

"If a museum is ever formed in Hong Kong I will run it."

Feiffer said tightly, "Do you sell these birds you collect?"

"I do not." Chao said, "Once, the famous example, there were dodos in the world—large stupid birds like the mutton bird and now—"

"Like the passenger pigeon."

"Yes." He stopped. He seemed to soften. Chao said, "Look, listen: all the wild places where birds lived—where they bred and were free and high—all those places are going. They are being forced down to us, to civilization because all those places are gone—" Chao said suddenly as if in answer to a question that had not been asked, "I would never trap a bird! All the birds I have here died in the city and were brought to me by people who saw their beauty about to be turned into—"

"What people?"

"I never pay them. They know about me and they—"

"People like George Su?"

"This is his falcon." Chao, smiling, said, "And although you do not know me, you know George Su. You know what sort of man he is. You know that he—"

"I know that he's been in prison twice." It was no good. It was only the letter of the law. Feiffer, feeling like a policeman, asked, "What do you want from me?"

"I am committing a crime."

"Do you want me to issue you a *license* or something?"

"There is no license."

"Museums can get them."

"I am not a museum."

"Then as a recreational exhibit."

Chao said, "I show no one. The birds are not for show—they are dead! They are not birds anymore, but chemically preserved carcasses! They are nothing to see! They are no substitute for seeing the real thing or even seeing a photograph of the real thing in a book—they are not the real thing: they are dead corpses preserved like Egyptian mummies!"

"Then why the hell—"

"Because when all the real, free, living birds are gone—destroyed, shot, cut in half, turned out from their places, reduced to memories, this may be all we have left!" Chao, never a museum curator, said with vehemence, "Do you think a few jade baubles and amulets and scrolls hung on a wall reflect the true, the real glory of the ancient civilization of China—in a museum? Do you think they bear any resemblance to what was real and living then?—Do you? Do you think that these poor dead things resemble—at all—the flight of a bird in the sky or the feeling a man gets when he sees it?—*Do you?*" Chao said, "In the end, like the scrolls and the baubles and the amulets and the dust, this is all we may have left one day!" Chao said, "They lie dead on the road and they are picked up and brought to me. No one is paid for it and I do not sell them or give them back! The people who bring them would not want them while there is a single living bird left—what I do is store them up like some sort of survivalist against the day when everything is gone and all that is left is ashes."

"I'm not going to arrest you."

Chao said intensely, "Think. Think. If you are learning about things, if you are reading books about things—think!"

"There are millions of birds in the world!"

"Are there?"

Feiffer said sadly, "No."

"Think . . . Harry?"

Feiffer said, "Yes."

"Harry . . ."

He could smell the formalin. In the next room, like some sort of ancient Nile priest, he embalmed the bodies of something sacred, something that would never come again. In the main room, there was only his single bed, a gas stove and an old refrigerator and, everywhere, everywhere, the birds. Feiffer said, *"Who the hell are you?"*

Chao said, "Chao Kai Sun." He had a strange, otherworldly smile on his face. "I'm a policeman. Like you." Chao said, "I'm a detective senior inspector stationed in the New Territories on the border at Lo Wu." He took the feather in its glassine envelope and looked at it, then looked up again. Chao said, "You asked me what I wanted from you—"

There was a silence.

Chao said softly, "Harry, if you see any birds—any wonderful or strange birds—dead on the road, over the years . . . would you bring them to me?" Over the harbor, the bird had sailed and risen on currents of warm air, not hunting, not even reconnoitering, but merely sailing in the warm air. It had been doing it simply because it liked it—there was no other reason or explanation. Chao said, "Because one day, all the birds will be gone. Like coal and oil and things from the earth. Coal and oil can be substituted, alternatives can be found. But when all the birds have gone what in God's name can we ever put in their place?" Gently, handing the feather back to Feiffer, Chao said, "It's from a frogmouth. *Podargus strigoides*, a mopoke, sometimes called a nighthawk— vaguely related to the family of owlet-nightjars." Chao said, "Not from here. From Australia. It's a wing feather from an Australian tawny frogmouth."

He smiled his odd, secret smile.

He had nothing. The room in which he lived, except for the birds, was nothing. He had only, for his own reasons, the one thing in his life that made his life livable.

Detective Senior Inspector Chao, looking suddenly bright and excited, said, "Wait. Wait here. In the next room I've got a book with a picture of a real one in flight! Wait! Wait here! Wait and I'll show you!"

He touched it with his fingers. While he waited for Chao, he reached out without thinking and touched the falcon on the wing. It was soft, downy. He found himself, gently, tenderly, with the lightest of touches, stroking it.

Without warning the redness turned into pressure. The cupola, the cocoon contracted, grew tight, shrank. There was a pain, a buzzing.

Inside the redness, on the street, there was a whisper, a rasp, "—*Jakob!*"

On the street no one heard or noticed anything.

"—*Jakob!*"

It released. It stopped.

"—*JAKOB!!*"

It was imprisoned. All the thoughts, the name, the pressure was like something loose and maddened inside the cupola, turning the redness into blood, tearing the cupola, the cocoon to shreds, never breaking through it—birds maddened in a cage.

"JA—KOB!"

It wouldn't go away. Nothing would go away. It was expanding, gaining pressure, finding no way out, imploding on itself.
"JA . . . KOB!!!"
It was getting worse. The birds, loose and screeching inside the cocoon, smashing against it as they fought to get out, were falling, spinning, sailing down in torrents of redness, then, reviving, coming back, smashing at it again, screeching and calling.
"JAKOB!!"
From inside the cocoon, from inside Jakob's cupola, nothing, nothing at all could get out.

There was an elderly man at the Russo Harbin Hong Kong Trading Bank autobank machine with money in his hand.
There was an elderly man at the Russo Harbin Hong Kong Trading Bank autobank machine with no money in his hand.
There was Auden ready.
There was Auden running.
There was a crowd with feet like Frisbees.
The crowd with feet like Frisbees was going, "Aiiyaa . . . !" Their Frisbees, hitting the ground seconds after the Tibetan Tornado's hands hit the money, Auden's hamburgers hit the street, and Auden, waving them back, threatening to hit someone, were going flap! flap! flap! There were feet everywhere. Feet were coming down on the ground in a variety of noises.
They were after the money. Auden, a second and a half behind the Tibetan, still on Old Himalaya Street, yelled in Cantonese, "Hayp, hayp, hayp!" It wasn't Cantonese. It didn't mean, "You are interfering in a police pursuit." It meant, "Hayp, hayp, hayp!" His feet were connected to his lungs. He heard his feet say, "Hack, hack!" and, not turning, not giving a legal order to anyone, Auden, looking down at his feet, ordered them, "Run!"
Where the hell was Spencer?
The Tibetan made the base of Sagarmatha Hill. He stopped. He looked up. He had the money in his hand. No one shot him. He turned to look back. He heard a steam train somewhere off in the distance, or a tea kettle. He looked around to see what it was.
It was Auden. Obviously, there were holes in Auden's lungs somewhere: that was what was making the funny whistling noise. Auden, getting angry at his feet, said, "Run!" Auden said, "Natasha!" That part of his anatomy that would have drawn new strength from a contemplation of Natasha wasn't in the feet area.

The Tibetan began up the hill. He didn't begin up it: he took to the air, he took the steps two at a time—his feet weren't running, they were dancing across the steps. He went up like Nureyev, the steps disappearing under his feet like an escalator.

Where the hell was Spencer? Auden, getting to the first step and making a superhuman effort to mount it, wondering why the escalator seemed to have stopped running the moment he got onto it, put it into his mind to say, "Halt in the name of the Law!" No one had ever tried that. Maybe they had. Auden's lungs, speaking in tongues, said, "Ha—nim—ah—!"

Halt in the name of the Law!

Ha . . . herr—ha . . .

"On!"

Halt in the name of the Law!

"Halt—" He got it! He got the first word! He was on step twenty-three and he got it. Auden, pounding, his lungs falling to pieces, a funny sort of darkness appearing at the top of the hill as evidently night came in four hours early this time of year, yelled, "—in—" Behind him, the crowd was flapping hard on their Frisbee feet. The Frisbees were evidently in the air: there were slapping sounds as someone missed catching one and fell down the hill. He turned around. There were lots of red faces behind him. He saw someone raise his eyes up to heaven and then, receiving a blessing, fall down dead, rolling down the stairs like the baby carriage in *The Battleship Potemkin*.

Auden said, "—the—" It got the Tibetan's attention. You could tell he was wearing the Tibetan down. He stopped to look back and scratched his nose.

They didn't have the staying power, the yellow hordes.

They didn't. Behind Auden, the yellow hordes were falling by the wayside like shot soldiers. They were only after the money anyway. Auden, still pounding, not making any ground, hearing that funny sound from his lungs, yelled, "—name—" He had left out "in." He went back on his lungs a few inches on the tape: "—in—" It didn't make sense. Auden, with a supreme effort, yelled, "—stop! Stop in—stop!" He had plenty of air in his lungs: he could feel it coming back. The reason why was that he was sitting down. Auden, sitting, looking up as the Tibetan watched him, yelled, "Stop—*stop—stop!*"

"I CAN'T!"

It wasn't the Tibetan. It was Spencer. Spencer was at the top of the hill, coming down. Spencer, out of control, flailing his arms to set up an air brake to his body, yelled as the Tibetan ducked as he went by, "I thought I'd head him off! I'll aim at the people behind you!" He couldn't. They had all fallen down. Spencer, going like a hang glidist about to take off, yelled in a fast-receding voice as he went down the hill, "I wasn't going to catch him for you—I was just going to slow him do . . . wn . . . !"

The Tibetan was above him. He had hard, black eyes and a set face. He wasn't even puffing. Auden, squirming as the Tibetan's hands reached out for his throat, said, "Help! Help!"

He was falling, going backward down the stairs.

Auden, gasping, not getting any words out at all, short of breath, about to be throttled in record time, squirming on the steps, said in a whisper, "Natasha—oh, Natasha . . ." and then the Tibetan grabbed him.

The Tibetan, looking concerned, lifted him back from the abyss and setting him on his feet asked him in a soft melodious voice, "I hope you don't mind my asking . . ."

Auden, about to die, said obligingly, "No."

"—but how's P.C. Wang?"

At the bottom of the hill, as Spencer crashed like a shot-down aircraft forty thousand feet away, there was a gentle . . .

. . . *boom* . . .

The bird was from the greatest aviary in the world, Australia. On the cover of the book Chao brought there was a photograph of a pair of great white sulphur crested cockatoos. Feiffer had read about them in his books at the library.

On the open market in America and Asia, smuggled out, live, they brought thirty thousand dollars the pair and, if their reproductive organs had survived being trapped, kept in tiny cages and then stuffed and drugged into smugglers' suitcases or cut-off lengths of galvanized iron pipe wired shut and shipped in with machine parts or enclosed in five-gallon drums purporting to hold corrosive or dangerous urgent chemicals, thirty thousand dollars each.

In Australia, they were considered to be a pest and they were shot.

It was, nevertheless, illegal to export them.

Chao, turning the pages of the book slowly, his eyes on the photographs and drawings of the wonderful birds he would never see and which might not survive into the next century, said softly, "Well, Harry, yes or no? Will you watch the roads for me, or not?"

* * *

Auden said, "Fine." His voice was very soft. There wasn't much of him left.

The Tibetan said, "Good."

Auden said, "I'm doing this for him. It's nothing personal."

"Sure." The Tibetan nodded. The Tibetan said, "Me too. I'm doing it for my family." He had the wad of money in his hand. "I'm not really a thief."

"I'm not really a runner."

"I can tell."

Auden said in a whisper, "Stop in the name of the Law." You had to make it menacing. You didn't have to actually mean it, but at least it had to sound as if you meant it. Auden, falling back into a sort of half-crouching limpness on the step, patting the Tibetan on the hand to terrify him, said, "You damned Tibetan you."

The Tibetan said, "Nepalese."

"What?"

"Nepalese. I'm not from Tibet, I'm from Nepal. It's a small country above India—"

"I know where it is—" Auden said, "You're a Gurkha!" That explained it. The Gurkhas were the toughest people in the world. When the Gurkhas went to war, their opponents went to peace. No wonder he couldn't catch him. Auden said, "You're a Gurkha!"

"No. A Sherpa." The Tibetan—well, whatever he was—said, "A Sherpa is a Nepalese who climbs mountains and—"

Auden, aghast, said, "Awk!"

The Tibetan, stopping to have a chat, said, nodding, a little concerned that Auden had got it all wrong, "You know, Old Himalaya Street. The Himalayas are in Nepal. Sagarmatha Hill—" He smiled. He sighed. "It reminds me of where I used to play as a boy." He seemed to have tears in his eyes. "I have to get home and I've got no money and Sagarmatha Hill . . . well, you know, you're obviously a man of the world . . ." No, he wasn't. The Tibetan, patting him on the hand where Auden patted him, said to lead him, "You know: Nepal, Sherpas, Himalayas . . . Sagarmatha—"

Curse this urge for recognition. The Tibetan said, "Sagarmatha! It's the Nepalese word for where I learned to run!" The Tibetan said, "Everest!" He looked at Auden's eyes. They were goggling.

The Tibetan said with a sigh, "It's the name of a mountain there."

"Oh." That seemed fair enough.

Auden said to the Tibetan, "Okay."

He wondered why, a moment later, someone shot him.

As the Tibetan, clutching his backside and making yipping noises, began to run again with money falling around him in the air like confetti, Auden thought he should shout—

Auden said softly, "No."

Down at the bottom of the hill in the fields of Western France there was the wreckage of what looked like a shot-down three-winged Spad fighter plane with little bits and pieces still falling off as it smoked. It was Spencer.

On the step, just for the pure, calming pleasure of it, Auden thought he might stay just where he was and watch it for a while . . .

He stretched up a little to catch some of the money as it fell down around him.

Someone shot him.

It was a medium-sized grayish-looking bird with a large head that resembled nothing so much as some sort of Japanese samurai helmet, with a yellow cavernous beak that in some subspecies was used as a trawl as the bird flew openmouthed through the air.

The color of dark, burned wood, the bird hid by day, becoming invisible, and only at night became fully alive and animated to hunt.

When it hunted, it fell upon a small creature in the light with its great, sharp beak and, catching it surprised, skewered it to the ground, returning to its branch in the darkness with its prey often still alive.

There, if it had not delivered a death blow, methodically like a kingfisher, it beat its prey to a pulp and then, at once, silently, unseen in the night, devoured it whole.

It came down in the night and killed without mercy, while the hours of darkness lasted, without ceasing.

It was an Australian tawny frogmouth. It was from somewhere far away.

In Chao's, Feiffer said quietly, "Thank you very much."

He had not answered Chao's question. Briefly, he had forgotten it.

He was thinking, instead, of the night.

8

From the Lost Secret Journal of the Reverend Baron O'Yee Concerning the Awful Happenings in Salem-on-Yellowthread Street in the Year of Our Lord 16——

. . . Quasimodo, my loyal Chinese servant, and I at last resolved to seek a solution in the dark cellars of the old building, the true depths of which had not been plumbed for centuries . . .

On the stairs, Lim said helpfully, "I could ring the Japanese Embassy and ask them if what Mr. Hurley said—"

Hurley, the old doddering clerk and historian, I dismissed from my mind—

Lim said, "I could ask them how many English-speaking people they killed down there." Lim said, "They wouldn't mind. The Japanese can be very helpful when it comes to law and order."

I silenced Quasimodo's babblings with a look. Though of vastly different stations in life, the loyal fellow told me with his deferential voice and his entire demeanor how he would, if needs must, follow me through any vicissitudes and brave any danger that Providence might thrust upon us.

Lim said, "I don't mind waiting upstairs until the phones start working again."

O'Yee said, "Shut up." At the bottom of the stone stairs to the basement below the cells, he flicked on the lights.

The lights didn't work.

Trusting to my old bull's-eye pocket lantern which I had thought to

*bring along for just such a situation, together, resolved in heart, we went
bravely on.*

*We paused outside the door to the Crypt. I heard a faint gasp from my
trusty companion.*

Lim said in an undertone, "Oh, shit . . ."

*Science and Reason have failed us. The terrible Affliction that seems to
have befallen us, Gentle Reader, is beyond the powers of mortal men. The
great door to the Crypt, to the last secret, was before us. Dare I rap
mightily on its plywood? For the sake of my companion, I dared not.*

O'Yee ordered Lim, "Come back here!"

*. . . Slipping the old brass-plated tin bolt made by some ancient
Taiwanese boltsmith or his children, I drew open the portal.*

The portal went *creak . . .* The wood was warped in the
doorjamb. O'Yee gave it a kick.

Darkness.

Darkness.

Darkness, the terror of all creatures who live in the light.

Lim said, "There's something in here! I heard it move!"

*It behooved me to settle his fears though I must confess my own stout
heart was pounding. I laid my calming strong hand upon his—*

Lim said, "Something touched me!"

O'Yee said, "That was me!"

*Poor superstitious dolt. Illuminating my own familiar face for the
simple clod in the yellow beam of the lantern I—*

Lim said, "Oh, Christ!"

O'Yee said, "It's me you stupid oaf!" O'Yee said, "I thought you
said you were a Buddhist."

Lim, who would have said anything, said, "Yes." Lim said,
"There's nothing in here. There isn't even dripping slime on the
walls. The walls are just brick and the floor is just cement and
there isn't anything else in here." Lim said, "You touched me. I
thought it was something else, but it was you, sir, and the sound I
heard was just you—just your shoes scraping on the cement
which hasn't got anything on it because the cellars are empty and
no one's used them for years and there isn't anything in here—the
place is very empty—and can we go now?"

O'Yee said, "I heard something."

Lim said, "No, you didn't. I did, but it wasn't anything. I heard
your shoes on the cement or maybe it was your pocket flashlight
making electrical noises and if you heard anything it was
probably me thinking the noises you were making—" Lim said,
"Oh—!"

"Steel yourself!"

Poor chap. A good fellow, but like all his class prone to—

Lim said, "I want to go upstairs now."

O'Yee swung the light to the far corner of the cellar. There was nothing in the far corner of the cellar but the far corner of the cellar. O'Yee asked, "Can you hear anything?"

Lim said, "No." He turned to go.

O'Yee said, "Listen!"

Was there the faintest of murmurs?

O'Yee, waxing eloquent, said, "Hark—"

Lim said, "What?"

I suddenly heard, in the distance, the mournful murmurs of something in torment . . .

He flicked the light onto Lim's face and decided to go back to his journal.

. . . a distant disturbance, perhaps a crack in the fabric that curtains the other world of the passed-over from the gaslit world we know in which it is forever 1898 . . .

Lim said, "It's a rat!" It moved in the far corner as a dark blur.

Ah, yes, our old friend, the rat. Perhaps, from my knowledge of its breed, Rattus norvegicus, the ships' rat, or—

It was big, beady-eyed and scuttly.

. . . or Rattus exulans, the far-traveled Polynesian rat, or—

It was a roof rat.

Rattus rattus, the Bringer of the Black Death . . .

Lim said, "It's listening to something! It's got its ear near the wall and it's listening to something!"

A scientific fact, recently unearthed in my biological studies—done in an amateur way—came back to mind. Rats, as we all know, have powers of hearing far different from—

It moved.

Lim said, "*Shoot it!*" He wasn't wearing his revolver. His hand made slapping noises against his belt as he tried to manifest it from thin air. Lim, hopping back and forth as the rat, in the beam of light, stopped, sniffed, scurried, stopped again and then stood in the center of the room quivering, said, "*Shoot it!*"

O'Yee said, "It's only a rat."

"What's it doing down here? There isn't anything down here!"

"Rats get into the strangest places."

"They don't get in where there isn't any food!"

I started. Perhaps in his own foolish, unscientific way, in his terror he had stumbled on some truth, the import of which, naturally, was lost upon his simple gabbling mind, but which I, trained, might—

Lim said, "It's listening! That's what it's doing! It's standing around down here without any food just listening!" He took a step forward to frighten it. It worked. The rat, scurrying back to the corner, fell forward onto its front legs and, half squatting, began breathing rapidly in terror. Lim said, "Listen! It can hear something!" There was only a faint insistent bubbling whisper too distant to make out. Lim said, "Okay, that's it. I don't care about being a cop. There are plenty of other jobs. My brother has been begging me to go into the furniture business with him for years and I've decided to accept." Lim said, "Thank you for everything, Mr. O'Yee, but I'm resigning now."

"*Aaaa—ra—ggg . . .*"

Lim said, "Yes. Thank you. Good-bye."

"That came from upstairs."

"The rat heard it!" Lim said, "Look at the rat!" The rat was starting to go around in little circles, falling and tipping over onto its front legs.

"*Haasst—*"

That awful sound haunted me . . .

O'Yee said, "What the hell's that whispering sound? It isn't coming from here, it's coming from upstairs through the walls—"

Lim said, "It's The Thing!"

"It isn't The Thing! It's something ordinary and explainable and scientific!"

"No, it isn't!"

The rat was listening. Panting, trying to catch its breath, the rat was getting bigger and bigger.

Lim said, "It's a giant rat! It's expanding! It's—" Lim said, "I don't have to put up with this. I didn't join up for this. I came down to this cellar and I thought that because the cellar was empty and that all there was in the cellar was emptiness, I thought that—"

O'Yee said, "It's just a rat!" O'Yee, holding the poor, harmless creature in the beam of his flashlight, said, "Look, it's frightened of me. I'm not frightened of it, it's frightened of me!" He went forward making cooing noises. O'Yee said, "See? Look!"

It was nought but one of God's tiny creatures, in its own way but a tiny perfect reflection of the genius of the directing force of the Great Mechanic Who, in His wisdom, had—

O'Yee said, "It's sick, poor mite."

The rat, its ears twitching, fell over.

O'Yee said, "Very sick. As a matter of fact, it's dead." O'Yee turning to Lim, said curiously, "If I were by myself down here . . ."

He was.

O'Yee said, "Lim? Lim?"

He had deserted me. It was all too much for him. Sadly, slowly, I began to retrace my steps from that strange place back out to the light, no further advanced in my knowledge of—

"Twenty-eight."

O'Yee said, "What?"

The wall, far above the cellars, said in a shriek, "Twenty-eight! Twen-ty-eight! *TWENTY-EIGHT!*"

The flashlight beam went full on the rat. Its fur was bloody. It had no eyes. Under the fur it looked like it had been torn to pieces.

O'Yee's Lost Secret Journal, as he went out the cellar door and up the stairs two at a time, had only on its last unfinished page, as its final cryptic entry for generations of the curious who would study it, merely an exhortation to that comfort and strength of the fearful, the name of the Son of God. O'Yee, running, panting, shrieking, gone white in sheer, rampant dead rat mournful whisper terror, only seconds behind Lim, falling about on the stairs trying to make progress as his legs gave up, yelled to anyone who might listen, "Oh Christ! Oh Christ! OH CHRIST—!"

There were events taking place. Inside the cocoon, inside the redness, there was a progression of events taking place. There were whispers, rasps, the incoherent patterns of voices, the movement of time.

There were no memories, no dreams. The dreams were memories and the memories dreams within a dream. There were colors, intimations from the outside world like blurs through smoked glass: there was a series of events beginning.

". . . *Jakob* . . ."

It was a tiny old man with washed-out pale eyes: that was what existed inside the cocoon, hidden behind the smoked glass.

It was nothing like that at all.

It was a dream, a shadow play, it was—

—whatever it was turned on the corner of Canton Street and began to move northwest and nobody, nobody at all on the other side of that smoked glass, seeing it, thought to notice it at all.

". . . *Jakob*—"

Inside the cocoon, inside the redness, visions of death and blood and killing were forming as events, and there was nothing, nothing that could be done to stop them.

". . . Jakob . . ."

Outside the cocoon, on the street, there was no sound at all and no one passing by the person moving through all the events in the cocoon, dreaming the dream, heard anything at all.

In the bank, Natasha, dabbing at Spencer's wounds, grazes, abrasions and assorted contusions with a Kleenex dipped in alcohol from a bottle marked IBM MACHINE ROLL CLEANING FLUID, said with concern, "Won't we come in for help?" Outside in the street Auden was standing in a public phone booth going through his pockets for change. From the way he kept trying to put his hand in his pocket and then pulling it out and looking at it, even the muscle against his trousers pocket hurt. Natasha, her eyes glistening in sympathy, said softly, walking behind Spencer's chair and working at the back of his neck to try to set his head back on straight, "You are both so brave."

At the counter Ivan was counting out money for the elderly man who had been at the autobank. Ivan, glancing across through the glass doors to the fragile telephonist in the street, said in English, "Three thousand dollars short." He turned back to the elderly man, one of Mr. Nyet's best customers, and changed to Cantonese, "But the Russo Harbin Hong Kong Trading Bank is glad to replace your lost money." The portrait of Mr. Nyet, looking like Beria, looked down at him. Ivan gave it a snarl. Ivan, finishing counting the money and smiling to the elderly man as he in turn began counting the money, said across to Spencer, "It's three-thirty. The bank is closing."

Out in the street Auden got his hand into his pocket without touching any part of his anatomy and touched the coins in his pocket. They must have jingled. Auden, bending in the middle and taking his hand out again like a claw, mouthed, "Ow . . ."

His neck went back into place. Natasha had wonderful hands. They ached for Auden. Spencer, feeling guilty, said as Natasha's gaze went toward the Man Who Knew No Fear trying to get his hand back into his pocket, "He'll be all right." He nodded to the elderly man as he went by on his way out with nary a word, "The people chasing us got the rest of your money."

The elderly man, pausing, took out a little notebook and wrote something down. He looked at the portrait of Mr. Nyet. He turned to Ivan. He was writing Ivan's name down. The elderly man shaking his head, sighed.

"We're closing now!" It was Ivan. He was groveling. Ivan, coming around and opening the glass doors for the elderly man, said in desperation, "We're closing the doors now. We're closing the autobank! We're doing the best we can!" He looked to Natasha to say something winning. Natasha's eyes were on Auden. Ivan, bowing as the man paused at the doors, said fervently, "We're not keeping the autobank open because there wouldn't be anyone in the bank to replace any stolen money which might be stolen because—" He turned and near-genuflected to the portrait, "No one is going to work any overtime to replace money taken from the autobank so we'll close the autobank down!"

The elderly man said, "Huh."

Ivan said, "They're going home now: the police. They'll be back in the morning when the staff is here on normal hours, but nobody is going to sneak in a bit of overtime to—" Ivan, whining, said, still bowing and holding the door, "Please don't tell Mr. Nyet!"

The poor fellow was obviously in danger of losing his job. Spencer, unloosing himself from Natasha's hands, rising, said to console him, "That's all right." The elderly man was quite a pleasant-looking old Chinese gentleman with watery eyes. Spencer, patting him on the shoulder and at the same time with the other hand getting Ivan up from his bowing and scraping, said to encourage him, "The Royal Hong Kong Police always get their man." Spencer, giving the man one of his best grins, said to charm him, "We are only human. We all make mistakes. At first, like the world of finance, we stumble a little in the dark jungle of the unknown, but then, after we have found our way, we—" He made a chuckling sound and grinned wider, "We find our way. We'll be back here tomorrow with a plan." He looked across to Natasha for a sympathetic smile, but she was looking out at Auden trying to solve the problem of getting into the telephone box without actually touching anything and looked sad. Spencer said, "Trust us!" He saw the man's face. To get through to people like him you had to use psychology, human interaction, relationship motivation and a deep knowledge of the human psyche. You had to use tact, diplomacy, understanding and the authority of the law meted out in careful doses. They were all watching him, even Natasha. Bruised, abrased, beaten, contused and here and there through his filthy shirt and trousers still bleeding, Spencer grinning winningly, said, "It's a bet! We're doing it this way for a *bet!*"

The elderly man said, "Huh!"

The elderly man took out his notebook to write that down too.

Out to sea, the typhoon, blowing itself out, creating a vacuum in its wake, brought in following clouds and turned them north toward Hong Kong.

Billowing and then falling, the clouds passing over the ocean approached, and, taking the sea's chill, met with rising air from the land and pressed down on it, darkened and became fog.

Beyond the typhoon shelter in Hop Pei Cove briefly the fog turned back toward the sea as it met a crosscurrent blown in from China to the west and then, passing through it, cutting it with a sharp edge, darkened again and came in swiftly across the land.

Far above the fog there was lightning. Through the fog it flashed like something boiling inside the darkness of the fog itself. The fog was thick and cold. It settled on the land a building, a street at a time and covered it, muffling sounds and life and movement.

It moved toward Hong Bay and Yellowthread Street and, piece by piece, building by building, blotted them out.

He felt it.

In the Detectives' Room, O'Yee, sitting at his desk with his head in his hands, felt something cold pass by the window.

". . . twen-ty-eight . . . twenty-eight . . ."

Outside, the fog was at the window, rising against it, turning it cold and gray, running with condensation.

Outside, the person inside the red cupola, dreaming the dreams, passed by the station traveling north.

It was *Assault on Precinct 13.* All they had left inside the deactivated, cut-off police station to defend it as outside the psychos and killers gathered, was a half-caste, over-the-top detective senior inspector and a quivering P.C. The quivering P.C. was somewhere out in the charge room making quivering sounds and trying to ring someone on the telephones that kept making jingling noises and didn't work.

The walls were running with wetness. The window was graying with fog.

". . . twenty-eight . . ."

Outside, in the street, he felt as a cold, deadly shiver, something awful pass by.

". . . twenty . . ."

The wall felt it too. It fell suddenly silent.

All was stillness. Even the phone stopped jingling . . .

On the phone, Auden, holding the receiver carefully between two fingers away from his head, trying to find a way of standing where nothing hurt, said in Cantonese, "I just want to know how P.C. Wang is doing following his unfortunate heart attack."

The Sister on the other end of the line said, "Are you a relative?"

Auden said, "No."

"A friend?"

Auden said, "How is he?"

"We can't give out information over the phone. Perhaps if you—"

Auden said, "I just want to know how he is!" He touched the side of his leg against the phone box. Auden said, "Oh . . . !"

"Please don't upset yourself." The Sister, obviously a nice person, said, "I realize how hard it can be for people to understand hospital rules sometimes, but if we gave out information on the condition of our patients every time someone rang up, what we'd have in the end would be—"

He touched an elbow. He didn't think his elbows hurt. Auden said, "Ahh . . . !"

"But we—"

A shoulder. Auden said, "Mmm . . . !"

"But in some cases—"

"Oh—ah . . ." (the knuckle on his left hand on the glass of the booth).

"We—"

"Nggghhh."

"But I can tell you in this case—" She sounded upset. She was an Angel of Mercy. "That in this case, P.C. Wang—"

Auden said, "Will he die soon or not?"

The Sister said happily, "No, I can promise you: he isn't going to die." She said in the silence, "Hullo? Hullo?" She waited for the sound of relieved weeping and a long drawn-out sigh of heartfelt joy.

Auden, heartfelt, said, *"Damn!"*

* * *

. . . In the Detectives' Room, as the coldness outside passed by, the wall began, slowly, cautiously, to make soft throbbing noises. There was nothing beyond the wall, nothing underneath it but nothing.

It had been the rat.

It hadn't been the rat. The rat was dead.

The rat was dead.

In the lightning, in the fog, all the lights flickered.

"AAA—Raaa—gah!" It sounded as if it was coming closer.

". . . twenty-eight . . ."

There was slime running down from the wall.

The phones were jingling with the lightning and there was moisture forming under his hands on the top of his desk.

His hands did not move. The moisture was forming around them and making pools and puddles and streaking the surface of the top, but his hands stayed where he was.

He stayed where he was.

It didn't bother him. He wasn't there anymore. He was somewhere else.

". . . twenty-eight . . . Arr-raaa-*gah!*" He was in a field of waving wheat and bluebells running through the forest under a warm sun with naked nymphs and shepherds singing and laughing all around him. He was happy.

He was glazed.

He had blinked out.

Scotty, at last, had beamed him up.

4:05 P.M.

In his own little world, listening to the jingling, smiling at the shepherds, swimming his little happy hands in the soft limpid pools of condensation and sweat as the fog and horror closed in all around him, O'Yee waited the minutes through until 5:00 P.M., when, smiling all the way, he could go home to his wife and children and womb somewhere.

He waited, singing his little songs.

5:00 P.M.

He stood up and, at that moment, at that instant, with full fogged-in darkness outside—of course—all the sounds in the station and in the wall stopped and all the telephones stopped jingling and all the walls stopped running with moisture.

It had been the rat.

The rat was dead.

O'Yee, smiling, said to one of the shepherds or one of the nymphs or whatever it was, "That figures, doesn't it?"

O'Yee said, "Twenty-eight! Twenty-eight!"

The wall said nothing.

O'Yee said, "Great. Wonderful." O'Yee said, "Thank you very much."

Tomorrow was another day.

O'Yee, rising, his hands dripping water like the Beast from Forty Thousand Fathoms, wanted to say like Marlon Brando in *Apocalypse Now*, "The horror! The horror!"

He didn't. He was past that, gone deeper.

O'Yee, on his way out, seeing Lim also on his way out, said only, shaking like a leaf, "Twenty-eight! Twenty-eight! *Twenty-eight!*"

The wall through the open door of the Detectives' Room behind him said only softly—maybe it wasn't even the wall, it could have been the fog or a breeze in the fog—or anything—"Haaaa . . ."

"*Haaa* . . ." In the fog, in the darkness, in the night, it was a soft, a mysterious sound from a dream. In the darkness it silenced all the birds and things that lived and turned them into parts of a mute, silent dream.

Inside the cocoon, it turned them into redness.

It hid Jakob as he whispered and rasped in the settling fog.

It was not darkness or fog or the night.

It was a blackness.

It was getting worse.

At night, inside the kaleidoscope, the dreamer thought only, suddenly, upstoppably of death and killing.

The dreamer thought of knives.

9

"I don't care about conservation or goddamned wildlife protection just so long as when I retire someone's left me a forest or two with a few wildflowers and animals in them." It was his little joke. It fell flat. On the phone to Feiffer in his fourth-floor apartment at 11:00 P.M., the commander said, "I don't like this one, Harry. I don't like the sort of things people are saying about it at Headquarters—I don't like the way people are confused about it." He ran the Division. There was very little he didn't hear about most things. The commander said, "I'm confused about it." He became for some reason suddenly angry, "And you—the chief cop in charge of the Confusion Squad—you tell me your main, your only piece of major—or minor—evidence is a goddamned feather!" Outside, to make it worse, there was the fog. The commander said, "No one's been killed, no one's even been bashed over the head, no one's even been lightly *nudged*—so tell me why I can't sleep over it! I slept through riots, chainsaw massacres, mass murders, and half the goddamned Korean War!" The commander said, "I've represented the Department at seven hangings! Why the hell does this bother me so much?" He asked, "What have you found out? Why the hell does any of this even *matter*?"

In the bedrooms his wife and son were asleep. Feiffer, at the phone in the darkness, watching the fog rising against the big picture window facing the harbor, said quietly, "It matters."

"Why? Has anyone even been threatened? It was just one

isolated incident! For all anyone knows it could have been kids!"
There was a pause. The commander said suddenly, "Birds and
animals get slaughtered all the time! Even bloody crocodiles end
up as somebody's handbag! If the world didn't go around
slaughtering animals on a regular basis we'd all be walking
around like starving survivors from Auschwitz! People need to
kill animals! They kill them for food, for protection—they kill
them for sport!" The commander said, "So a pile of animals in
some third-rate zoo has been knocked off—what's the essential
difference between that and knocking off a line of bullocks in a
goddamned abattoir for your breakfast steak? The difference is
nil! And don't tell me it's different because I don't see the bullocks
getting knocked off—I didn't see any of this and it still worries
me! I don't even like bloody birds! They shit on people. *So why
does this bother me?*"

"They all look the same." He had been alone in the dark before
the commander rang, thinking about it. Feiffer said cautiously,
"Maybe, because people all look different to one another the
death of one is just the death of one. Maybe, because, at least to
the ordinary eye, birds and animals of the same species all look
the same maybe it's not the death of an irreplaceable individual,
but somehow part of the demise of a finite and limited species. I
don't know." Scientifically, maybe it made sense. It didn't explain
the feeling he had about it. Feiffer said, "What surprises me is
that no one has asked if whoever did it is going to move on to
people." He touched at his face. Feiffer said, "It doesn't seem to
matter. Moving on to people—after this—doesn't seem a step up,
a progression at all—"

"If it were people at least we have the mechanism to deal with
it! It'd be understandable! People kill people for a reason! This—"
The commander said again, "This confuses me."

"Maybe if you kill one animal, in a funny way you kill them
all."

"This isn't even us! We shouldn't even be doing this!" The
commander, spluttering, said, "This isn't police work, it's—it's
somebody else's! Even if you get whoever did it, what the hell are
you going to charge them with? Breaking and entering? Theft?
Destruction of property? Poultry slaughtering without a license?
Making old men of sixty-one who think they know everything,
who think they've got the world pretty well taped by now, stop to
wonder? *Murder?* Reading the papers and listening to people at
Headquarters, it isn't a murder, it's something worse. With a

murder you get an anger, a feeling of indignation." The commander said, "Harry, people are talking about this in whispers as if it's something else—something just . . . *wrong*! I can't sleep over it. I'm sorry to ring you so late and at home, but I just can't file it away in my mind and let it go. It doesn't worry me that a few pretty birds and animals have been killed, it doesn't even worry me that someone attacked and killed them in the night for no reason, what worries me is the way it was done!"

"Maybe if it had been a gun it would have been better."

"It would have been! Birds and animals are shot every day. I've shot them myself. You just stand there with a highly sophisticated product of some five hundred years of mechanical progress, pull the trigger, release a sear and a lump of lead designed expressly to do the job does the job and whatever it is you're shooting drops and—"

Feiffer said tightly, "Whoever did this got up close. And while they did it they carried an umbrella so they wouldn't get wet from the rain."

"There are probably people in this world who could explain it to me, but by the time I finished listening to them—" The commander said tightly, "Maybe what it is, Harry, is that I don't like feeling ignorant!" He asked abruptly, "I ran across that lunatic Chao out at Lo Wu Station once—" He said quickly, "Oh, yes, I know all about him and his bloody dead birds—and he tried to tell me some theory of his that once all the birds and animals had been moved out to oblivion by high rises and land development the bloody sky would darken over or turn green or—"

"He probably wanted you to collect birds for him."

"What he's doing, collecting his birds, by the way, is totally illegal!"

"Yes."

"They're all bloody nuts, these bird people!" The commander said, "What the hell's happened to the Chinese lately? They've become as stupid as everyone else! In Shanghai, before the war, when a Chinese became rich enough to own a dog he didn't bloody moon over it and pat it the way we do—what he did was hire a man to walk it on the Bund for him so everyone could see he was also rich enough to hire a man to walk his dog! According to, at least the popular Western press, the Chinese haul dogs off the street and eat them!"

"That's a particular breed of dog bred for—"

"I know what it is!" The commander, getting angry at everyone, said in disgust, "Now the bloody Chinese have picked up the Walt Disney syndrome and they think that every little deer and doggie flits through a Technicolor forest having conversations with the bloody songbirds in high, female kindergarten California accents!" The commander said, "This goddamned feather you've got—what sort of bird is it anyway?"

"It's an Australian frogmouth. It's a horrible-looking thing with a beak evidently a little like a trawling net with a spear on the end. It's the color of burned wood. It kills things and then takes them back to its tree to eat them." Feiffer said, "I've got a call in to the Australian Federal Police in Canberra. I'm waiting for it now."

"If it had been some sort of bird or animal that had done the killing—"

"Birds and animals don't carry iron bars and machetes."

"What the hell's the point of killing a bloody crocodile?" The commander said, "According to the newspapers the bloody thing even had a name. It was called Daisy! And the Wishing Chair? Why smash that up and nothing else?"

"I don't know." Feiffer said, "I thought I'd put the Canberra call on the departmental account if that's all right."

"Why does it bother me?!" The commander said abruptly, thinking it through, "It bothers me for the same reason that it bothers you. It bothers me because something's gone wrong in the world and there isn't any explanation for it, *isn't that right?*"

There was a silence.

The commander said abruptly, "It's a psycho, that's all it is. The thing is that it's a psycho using psycho logic and anyone who tries to make sense of it using reasonable sane thought processes—" The commander said self-assuringly, "We've had psychos before. You've had them. All cops have had them. I'm getting dotty and senile and past it and I've got too much on my hands and I'm forgetting the first, simple rule of psychos: that you don't try to understand them, that all you do is just grab them, cart them off to a loony bin somewhere in a straitjacket and then bloody forget about them!" The commander said, "Yes, that's what it is: it's a psycho." The commander said, "It's that and the bloody lightning and the fog and all the rest of it: it puts you slightly off stride and turns the whole event into some sort of dark Shakespearean drama, but it isn't a dark Shakespearean drama, what it is is just some fucking loony with a knife and an iron bar who's killed a few animals and birds in a bloody zoo somewhere!" The commander said, "It's people like George Su and D.S. Chao and all those bloody madmen with their rimless glasses and their binoculars and their bird-spotting books, it's—" The commander said, "It's—" He was sixty-one years old and there was very little he had not seen at one time or another in one place or another. The commander said suddenly, "There's something all wrong about it and it bothers me and I don't know what it is and, maybe, above all, that's what bothers me." The commander said, "I can't sleep." He asked in a voice so low Feiffer had to strain to hear it, "What if it doesn't happen again? What if we never hear anything more about it? What if it was just the one, isolated case? What then?" The commander said softly, "George Su and Chao, I know what they think. What the hell does the person who did this think? *What does he think?*"

The commander said, "Harry, sometimes I sit in my car near the harbor and watch the birds. I hate birds. They shit on you. They—" He had already said that. "They—"

There was a silence.

Feiffer said gently, "Neal, are you still there?"

The silence continued. It was a little after 11:10 P.M. on a dark, still night.

Feiffer said, "Neal, are you still there?"

He had to have something. What he had was his job. It was what he did and what he was. It was very little. Sometimes, at night, getting old with his wife dead three years, it was nothing at all. He clung to it. The commander said briskly, "Yes, put the call to Canberra on the departmental bill if it's official business." The commander, at the other end of the line, clenching his fist hard to hold in something inside him that did not exist anymore, said tightly, "Yeah." The commander said, making his little joke, for the third time, "Birds. They shit on you. Christ, who the hell needs that at my age?"

It was the wall. It wasn't *the* wall, it was his wall. It was the wall of his apartment. It was him. He had seen those movies where the pubescent girl was the one doing all the things and it was him. The pubescent girl was him. O'Yee, creeping along the wall in his darkened apartment, listening, said satisfied, "Good."

He listened. He heard.

In the wall, he heard noises, shufflings, sounds, movement. He heard . . . was it? Yes, it was! He heard words. O'Yee said in triumph, "Ha, ha." It was the lightning. He had looked up lightning in one of his children's encyclopedias after everyone had gone to bed and it was there.

Lightning is the sky falling down. It makes you feel funny. But it isn't something you should be afraid of . . .

Right. He wasn't afraid.

He heard words in the wall. He crept along the wall, tapping and putting his ear to it.

O'Yee said coaxingly to the wall, "Twenty-eight . . . twenty-eight . . ." He listened.

Two words. He heard them. They were there. It was him. They were there. O'Yee, grinning, creeping, listening, pounding on the wall with his fist, cried in his joy, "Twenty-eight! TWENTY-EIGHT!" He pounded on the wall.

He heard the words. He heard the wall hear him speak. He heard as logic decreed he would, two words.

Those words were, "SHUT UP!"

It wasn't a pubescent girl, it was his neighbor, Mr. Wong. Mr. Wong worked for a living. For a living he broke rocks in the Aberdeen Street quarry. Mr. Wong screamed out through the wall in Cantonese, "GO TO BED, YOU FILTHY, WALL-LISTENING PERVERT OR I'LL COME IN THERE AND BREAK EVERY BONE IN YOUR BODY!"

". . . twenty-eight . . . ?"

Mr. Wong screamed, "FILTHY MASTURBATOR!" He had someone in there with him. Maybe it was a pubescent girl. Mr. Wong yelled, "DO I MAKE MYSELF CLEAR?"

He did.

Twenty-eight . . .

It was the lightning.

It was the fog.

It was twenty-eight.

O'Yee wondered, tiptoeing his way to bed in utter, absolute, thoughtful silence, what the hell the number *meant.*

In the cocoon, Jakob's eyes were pale, unblinking. They were dead. Moving, traveling, passing through the events, there was only a whisper, a rasp.

"Twenty-eight."

The pupils of the eyes were white, like alabaster. They were not human.

"Twenty-eight."

He was traveling north.

It was night.

He was traveling unseen in the fog like a shadow in a dream. The knives were there. Inside the cocoon their edges glittered silver against the redness.

"Twenty-eight . . ."

Then the sound was still and, as the buzzing began, there was nothing left of it at all.

The events were unstoppable.

The events had begun.

The person inside the cocoon drew a long, soft sigh.

". . . twenty-eight . . ."

It sounded, with the sigh, like some sort of secret, something hidden.

—It sounded, the way it was said, like a prayer.

On the phone to the Federal Police in Australia, Feiffer said to make it clear from the outset, "I've got a single wing feather from a tawny frogmouth, *Podargus strigoides*—"

"Well, good for you." Senior Sergeant Beth Durning, with one of those Australian accents you could use to cut butter, said with what could either have been a very late night sense of humor or a very late night sense of annoyance, "Now give it back. It's illegal."

"Is it?"

"Yes, it is. The Wildlife Preservation and Protection Act states among other things that it is an offense to take, possess, keep or otherwise remove a protected bird or animal from the wild or any part of such a bird or animal or any eggs, young, pelt, claws, feathers or any other—" She faltered, "—bit therefrom. Or words to that effect."

"I see."

"Unless the taker, keeper or person requesting such a bird, animal or part thereof is an agent of a recognized museum in which the object may be kept for scientific study, a licensed zoo or person authorized by the Minister to engage in bird or animal keeping or breeding or has special dispensation for some other reason as stipulated by the Minister or his agent of the Crown." Senior Sergeant Durning said, "Thank you for the confession, Mr. Feiffer. The whizzing sound you can hear in the background is me rushing to get a request form to take three long weeks in Hong Kong to extradite you for this heinous crime." Senior Sergeant

Durning said, "The various Australian state police forces usually deal with this sort of thing. The Federal Police get interested when this sort of thing crosses state borders in the gunnysacks of smugglers or go out on jumbo jets to America stuffed in suitcases." In the background there wasn't the sound of whizzing. There wasn't any sound at all. In the Records and Information Section of the big, gray building in Canberra she was alone. Senior Sergeant Durning said, "Presently, the Federal Police have got over five hundred and sixty drug-smuggling cases we haven't even started, two hundred and six we can't get the overtime authorization or money to proceed with, and a growing cocaine and heroin problem that's beginning to reach epidemic proportions." She said lightly, "So you can probably keep the feather." She asked, "You do realize it's two A.M. here?"

"Yes." Feiffer said evenly, "We've had something awful happen here—"

"In the zoo. Yes, it made the papers here too." There was a silence. "I thought that was what it was about."

"We found a single frogmouth feather on the scene. Nothing else. Just that. I've been told it's an Australian bird—"

"The tawny frogmouth, yes." There was a brief silence. "I've got the federal copper's *Guide to Protected Birds* here in front of me and the only bird anything like it is from New Guinea—who told you it was the Australian variety? The natural history museum there?"

"Someone reliable. There isn't a natural history museum here in Hong Kong." It was worth seeing how much he could get. Feiffer asked, "Like to start one up?"

"Yes, please!"

"Tell me how many frogmouths a year get smuggled out of Australia and I'll put in a good word for you."

"None."

Feiffer said, "What?"

"None. Zero. Zilch. Numero nothingo. None at all. They're not considered smuggleable birds."

"Why not?"

There was a silence. "They're not pretty enough." The silence had been to think of another way of putting it. There was no other way of putting it. Senior Sergeant Durning said, "That's it. That's always it in the end, I suppose, but in the case of the frogmouth, that's it." There was a sound on the line as if she made a clucking noise. "It's a fairly nondescript-looking bird during the day—it hides in trees and camouflages itself so you don't even know it's there—at least, you don't notice—and at night, when it comes out, it lives in the dark and moves around on the edge of the light. And it walks funny."

He listened.

Senior Sergeant Durning said, again amused or irritated, "And in case you think I'm being metaphorical, let me tell you that even though I sit out the lonely hours here in a deserted bloody great stone building looking out at the lights of other deserted bloody great stone buildings, I'm shatteringly beautiful, the object of much unrequited love and when I walk on my four-inch stiletto high heels in my silk stockings and long-wearing serge uniform dress cars crash into plate glass windows." She said suddenly, "I've never been to Hong Kong. What's it like?"

Feiffer said, "Full of plate glass windows." He asked, "If it's so ugly and not worth taking, how would it have gotten here to Hong Kong?"

"It sure as hell didn't swim."

"On a boat?"

"Maybe. As more and more of the outlying areas around our towns and cities get cleared for development more and more birds and animals seem to be coming into the suburbs and along the coast." Senior Sergeant Durning said, "I've got a room in one of the monoliths the government here in Canberra calls apartment blocks and we've started to get crested pigeons feeding on the verandas." She said quickly, "It's a sort of bush pigeon. A few years ago you never saw one. It's possible frogmouths could be moving closer to the coast—maybe even to the docks to pick up things on the wharves: small mice or grasshoppers or whatever they eat. It's possible it could have got on board a ship and been trapped."

"And then what?"

"And then, out of its natural habitat, say on a ship, it would have died."

"And then?"

"And then it would have been in bloody Hong Kong and that's your department!"

"Sorry."

"You don't believe I'm ravishingly beautiful. If you did you wouldn't talk to me as if I was bloody thick!"

"I do believe you're ravishingly beautiful." Feiffer said, "Since I happen to be heart-stoppingly handsome I'm used to being

surrounded constantly by beautiful women. Consequently, I have
no respect for them at all."

"In Australia, Customs and Quarantine go over any ship that
docks. Anything like a dead bird would be automatic bell-ringing
time. It'd go straight into a plastic bag and then in a sealed box to
the government vet and then, if it didn't have rabies or tsetse fly
or ten thousand other diseases birds can take from one country to
another, it'd be unceremoniously burned in an incinerator."
Senior Sergeant Durning said, "Also, by the time it reached Hong
Kong in the hold of a ship it would have been dead for days. It
would have stank." Senior Sergeant Durning said, "Take my
word for it, any bird that high anywhere in the world—Hong
Kong, Australia or bloody Timbuktu: the moment that bird was
even vaguely noticed by someone from Quarantine it would have
been straight into a sterile plastic bag, straight to a vet for
examination, straight back into the bag and then—psst . . .
straight into the nearest convenient vaporizer, feathers and all."

"Then what the hell have I got?"

"What you've got is the feather from a tawny frogmouth." She
paused briefly. Maybe she was ravishingly beautiful. She was
certainly efficient. "And if I were you, I think I'd hotfoot it down
to beautiful downtown Hong Kong Quarantine and I'd ask them
in no uncertain terms if they've been doing their job properly why
the hell did I have it!"

She asked, "Okay?" She asked, "And your government vet—
what's his name?"

"Hoosier."

"And I think, if I were you, I might have a little word to friend
Dr. Hoosier too." She waited to see what he was really like.

Feiffer said, "Thank you very much indeed."

"Okay." Senior Sergeant Durning said, "Fine." She wasn't
beautiful or ravishing at all. What she was, was good.

Without another word, in the deserted stone building at night
that housed the Australian Federal Police Records and Information Section, she hung up.

In the fog, through the cocoon's redness, there were water and
trees. There was a bubbling sound, like a fountain.

There were faint noises and movements. The trees, through the
grayness of the fog, were like bars.

"Daisy . . ."

That event was finished. They were all, merely, events,

happenings with no chain, no progress, no causality; they were merely unstoppable events.

In the cocoon, the knives glittered.

In the cocoon, there was a buzzing.

Fog and night and all the sounds and rustlings.

The cocoon was opening, cracking, breaking. There was a whisper, a rasp, white-pupiled, dead, unblinking eyes: the person inside the cocoon.

"Jakob . . . !"

He escaped the body, the cocoon.

He went forward into the fog.

10

"'**A**nd God said, Let the waters bring forth abundantly the moving creature that hath life, and the fowl that may fly above the earth in the open firmament of heaven. And it was so.'" Standing on the edge of the fog-shrouded artificial lagoon in the Hong Bay Botanical Gardens off Beach Road, the commander, at 6:00 A.M., said softly, "The Bible. Genesis." The fog was lying low on the ground, blue and swirling above the water. The commander said, "I was here first. After the radio room took the call I came straight here and I was here first." Gazing out across the lagoon toward the stands of bamboo and banyan trees rising out of the mist like fingers, in his overcoat he looked old and impermanent. He looked ill. He hadn't slept. The commander said, "Someone, probably scavenging in the park, called it in about five. One of the cars from North Point caught it." He looked across the expanse of thinning fog past the trees toward the harbor. "I sent them to call for help and to close off the gates." He was alone. He had been alone there for over twenty minutes. The commander said, "They were here first, birds, animals—it's in the Bible. It's why we—" He asked suddenly, "I've given up smoking. Do you have a cigarette on you, Harry?"

"Yes." Feiffer offered him his pack and took out his lighter.

The commander said, "Okay: the layout of the area is this. Dead center there in the fog which should clear in the next half hour or so there's a little artificial island. The lagoon is also artificial, full of saltwater pumped in from a pipe in the harbor.

The area is part of the park and the park is left open all night so anyone could have come in. Surrounding the lagoon is a circular walkway and"—he nodded to his right—"over there is a bamboo forest and, beyond that, clumps of oak and elm, alder and birch. The lagoon is full of reeds and water lilies and the bottom supports various crustaceans, small frogs and tadpoles—"

He could see nothing. Feiffer said, "What happened, Neal?"

"The fog should clear quite soon. I heard the weather forecast on my car radio on the way over and according to them—ninety-percent correct in their forecasts like weather forecasters all over the world about ten percent of the time—the fog is giving way. By about now it should all be gone and just be a light mist which will give way in turn to a warm, slightly humid day with occasional flashes of harmless heat lightning from the disturbance caused by the typhoon." The commander said, "I've had North Point call in Hoosier and Forensic, your uniformed people from their beds, and if you need it, because I believe it's quite deep out there in the center of the lagoon, you can have divers from the Water Police or uniformed men with grappling hooks, whichever you like."

"All right."

The commander, not hearing him, asked, "Is that all right?"

"That's fine, Neal."

"I think I've thought of everything."

"That's more than enough." Feiffer, standing to one side of the man, not wanting to move in front of him and see his eyes, asked gently, "Do you know what's happened?"

"The fog comes and goes. When I was here first it was clear." He shrugged. The commander said, "The Weather Bureau says it'll clear soon."

"Do you want to go home, Neal?"

"*No, I don't want to go home!*"

In the lagoon, hidden beneath the fog, there was absolutely no sound at all. The fog was not moving. It was still. It hung there motionless, hiding something. There was no wind, no sound. Whatever it was— Feiffer, touching the man gently on the shoulder, said earnestly, "Look, you haven't slept—"

"I'm still in charge here!"

"I know that."

"You may be in charge of the investigation, but I'm still in charge of you!" The commander said suddenly, "Christ in heaven, whatever happened to bloody discipline? There was a time when people who believed in God and read the Bible weren't treated like senile lunatics! There was a time when a man like that was looked up to and considered to be bloody moral!" The fog was swirling around him. The commander, brushing it away, said, "Christ in heaven, there was a time when people didn't do things like this! When people knew how to behave! When the world was regulated!" It cleared. Out in the center of the saline lagoon, the fog cleared and the top of the little island became visible, like the cone of a volcano. The commander said tightly, "It's clearing. They said it would and it is." The commander, looking away as if it was something he could not bear to see, something offensive, said, "There it is—now you can see." The commander, looking back, his mouth twisted, some vise tightening at the sides of his mouth, said in a rasp, "And God saw it and He saw that it was good." The commander shouted suddenly, "Look at it! *Look at what someone's done!*"

The commander, taking his hands out of his pockets and holding Feiffer's eyes, said in a strange, soft, low voice, "Look at it, Harry, because I can't. I can't."

The commander said, shaking his head, "I can't. I don't know why. I don't understand it, but I can't." The commander said, "It's wrong. It's all too wrong. I'm too old. It's too wrong for me and I just—"

It was the end. He was finished.

The commander said softly, still shaking his head, turning to go, "I'm sixty-one years old. I'm in command and I don't have to look at anything anymore if I don't choose to . . ."

The fog was lifting. Section by section, the saline lagoon and all the dead creatures in it were appearing.

They were flamingos. There were altogether twenty-two of them, males and females, nesting pairs, five feet long, pinkish white and cream with their distinctive down-bent beaks, all floating on the water in twos and threes or in colonies by their cone-shaped nesting mounds.

They were all dead.

They were all, during the night, while they slept, gutted. In the growing light their intestines floated around them like snakes, their wings broken and useless, half submerged on the surface of the lagoon like fans.

". . . *Oh, Christ* . . ."

The commander, nodding, said softly, "Yeah." He had turned back. He was looking at the lagoon.

The commander said, "Yeah." He touched at his face. He was

sixty-one years old and he, in his time, had officiated at seven legal hangings and so many deaths and murders that they had all turned into a single, ghastly blur.

The fog lifted and on the lagoon there were only the slow, dead, floating birds.

The commander said in a whisper, looking at him for the first time, "God in heaven, Harry . . . God in heaven!" The commander said in total, awful desperation, "God in heaven, Harry, *who the hell is doing this?*"

The buzzing hadn't stopped. It continued. The whispers, the rasps, the dreams—they never stopped. They grew worse. They increased.

"JAKOB! *JAKOB!!*"

The creature inside the cocoon, exploding, in pain, caught, locked in, imprisoned, shrieked one final time, *"No!"*

The pain went. There was only the pale, white-pupiled eyes in the cocoon. There was only a whisper.

"Twenty-eight . . ."

"Twenty-eight . . ."

In the cocoon, there was neither day nor night, there were only, merely events.

The events continued.

By God, he was going to put a stop to it.

In the Detectives' Room, O'Yee, book in hand, said to the wall so it would know just where it stood, "By God, if I have to knock you down plasterboard by plasterboard, lath by lath, interior brick by brick, cavity by cavity and then external brick by brick, I'm going to do it!"

He could do it. He spoke the wall's language. He had a book on wall demolishing. It was Mr. Wong's book. After he had explained he was quite probably under some awful Satanic influence he had had no trouble borrowing it from Mr. Wong at 5:15 A.M. at all. O'Yee said, warning the wall fair and square, *"Right?"*

The wall—typical—just stood there.

O'Yee said, *"Right?"*

O'Yee yelled, "Lim!"

Lim, far below in the basement with the dead rat, called up faintly, "Here, sir!"

O'Yee, squatting down, said as he had said to Mr. Wong, that most obliging of neighbors, *"Haarragh!"*

Lim called up, "Haaa!"

In the Detectives' Room O'Yee placed the chisel and mallet in position on the wall. O'Yee said, "AAARAAA—GAHH!"

There was no more.

One more.

"One more." It was a whisper, a rasp. It was in English. The creature inside the cocoon said softly, "Yes."

One . . . more and then everyone, all of them, all the animals, all the people—everything, finally, at last—

All of them would be dead.

"There's no profit motive, Phil." At the garbage skip in Annapura Lane a little after 7:30 A.M. Spencer, shaking his head, peering up and down the street, said, puzzled, "I've been thinking about it all night and there's just no profit motive to it." He could tell Auden was listening. Auden had a glazed stare on his face. He was looking straight at him. "Take it one by one—" Spencer, scratching his nose and then bringing his hand out with the fingers outstretched, began counting them off: "One, the Tibetan doesn't make a profit because he drops the money—"

He waited for Auden to nod.

Auden didn't nod. Auden said, "Hmm."

Near enough. "Two, the person who's robbed doesn't make a profit. He doesn't make a loss either because the bank refunds his money, and three, the air gun shooter doesn't make a profit because he doesn't pick up any of the money that the Tibetan drops after he's been shot, and four, the people who pick up the money after you've dropped it after the Tibetan's dropped it, what little profit they make—" He was standing in the middle of the pavement thinking deeply. He had a rapt audience. Through it all, Auden's face didn't change. "—well their profit is so small and spread among so many people—"

Auden said, "I couldn't sleep last night because of the pain."

"—That any profit they did make wouldn't be worth the trouble hiring an air gun shooter and a Tibetan and risking two cops catching them." Spencer said, "Yes, that's right." He put his hand back to his nose and, thinking about it, did a sort of duck-diving air-holding grip on it. Spencer said, "Yeahrbz."

"I read a book." Auden said, "It was a book about guns."

"—so why do it?" Spencer, letting go his nose said, "No, I can't see it. There's nothing in it for anybody at all." Spencer, shaking his head, said, "No."

"Everyone has been treating me as if I'm a .17-caliber 30-grain bullet with a muzzle velocity in excess of four thousand feet a minute." Auden said, "I thought maybe I might be something like a .221 50-grain Jet at maybe twenty-four hundred feet per second because I keep myself fit, but I'm not even that." He looked sad. Auden said, "No, I have to accept that I'm getting older and I'm putting on weight. What I am is not even anymore a 5.7mm Johnson Spitfire. What I am is something bigger, something slower—"

"Then why do it?" Spencer, getting angry or short of air, said, gasping, "Someone's making a profit, but whoever it is, it's someone we can't see!" He demanded, "Who is it?"

"—what I am is a .577-500 Number 2 Holland and Holland 360-grain Express!"

Spencer said, "What?"

Auden said, "What I am."

Spencer, smiling, patting him on the shoulder, said, "You're a pistol."

"No." Auden, looking hard down the road and then up toward the cloudy peak of Sagarmatha Hill, dreaming his own dreams, said softly, "No, what I am is a *bullet*!" He saw Spencer put his thumb and fingers to his nose to go down for air for the third time. He had a strange, faraway, dreamy look about him that came with no sleep, reading a lot, and having a very sore arse. Auden, putting his face closer to Spencer's, dropping his voice to a whisper, said, letting him in on the terrible secret, "Bill, guess what? When I looked up the .577-500 Number 2 Holland and Holland 360-grain Express bullet in my book, guess what it said? I'd never looked it up before, I promise! It said—" He was whispering. His eyes were two inches from Spencer's. "It said . . . it said . . ." Auden, goggling, glazed, happy, giggling, said ecstatically, "It said it was a round designed exclusively for Himalayan game!" Auden, his eyes wide, said encouragingly, "Well, what do you think about that?" He demanded, "Aye?"

He was happy. He was ready for the new day. He smiled at the garbage skip.

Auden, mad as a hatter, said joyously, "Heh, heh, heh!" He looked up at Sagarmatha Hill, at Everest. Auden, fiercely triumphant, said to a question he thought he heard Spencer ask as he recoiled, "Why? Why? *Because it's there!*"

* * *

He paused, stopped by something. In the bamboo forest, halfway down the packed-earth path that led to a dogleg of the lagoon, he stopped.

He had seen something. He was not afraid. In the forest of planted forty-foot-high closely laid-out thick bamboo, he stopped, listening.

He had seen something. In the forest there was still a light gray mist between the thick yellow trunks and about the earth. There was the smell of wet earth and old, rotting vegetation.

He heard sounds. It was bamboo touching bamboo. In the absence of wind it was only a faint tapping. Looking across the lagoon as the commander had gone to meet Forensic coming through the park in their truck, he had seen something at the edge of the lagoon move. It was at the edge of the forest, where the reeds met the lagoon. It was a backwater of the lagoon. He had seen a grayness there, a change—he had seen something move.

Stopped on the path, listening, Feiffer touched at his gun.

It had been a shadow.

He listened.

Far off, he heard a siren coming and then, through the tapping, someone call out and give an order. It was Forensic. He heard a splashing sound and then another shout as someone began wading into the water for the birds and called for more people to follow. He could see to the end of the path where it met the water: the path turned to the left and there was only the darkness of the bamboo.

Whatever it was that had been there at the edge of the forest, it had moved the moment the commander did.

"Bring over evidence bags to the right!" It was the commander speaking in Cantonese to P.C. Lee. An engine started. The commander called, "You won't need that. Sergeant, get those men to the far side and form a search pattern along the shore!"

The government vet, Hoosier, called out in English, "Leave that one—"

Lee shouted back, "Yes, sir!"

In the forest, on the path, he heard the tapping.

"Mr. Hoosier—!"

The voices were becoming fainter. There was another sound behind the tapping. Feiffer strained to hear it. He touched his gun in its holster. It was a buzzing.

". . . we'll take you three with your wading gear . . . and we . . . to the edge describing a . . . pattern and . . ."

Hoosier said, ". . . those people with glassine bags . . . from the Quarantine truck . . . larger . . . and I can . . ."

They faded. The voices were gone. In the forest, he had begun to walk and above the buzzing there was only the sound of his shoes crunching on the packed earth.

What it had been had been nothing. It had been a shadow. It had been a presence.

He heard the buzzing.

The voices came back.

". . . Mr. Feiffer gone . . . ?"

Lee called back, ". . . sir . . . and I . . ."

He felt a coldness. He heard something move. He was not afraid. It was not that. It was something else. In Shanghai, the Chinese had hired coolies to walk their dogs for them. In the West, birds and animals and little creatures were drawn in Technicolor and had human characteristics and the kindergarten voices of blonde-maned Californian actresses. It was something else. What was happening was something else.

The path turned off to the left on its dogleg down to a dark, overgrown path to the lagoon. On the earth there were no footprints. Whatever had come down here before him, whatever was still there if there was anything still there did not leave signs as it passed.

All he had seen had been a shadow.

He reached the end of the path. At the end of the path there was only a broken half-submerged bench in the waters.

". . . bring it around and . . ." He heard the commander say in a whisper, "Oh, my God . . ." He heard it clearly. It came not from across the lagoon, but in it. It came from the edge of the forest where, overgrown and in darkness there was something lying on its side in the reeds.

". . . bring . . . to . . ."

The buzzing dropped in intensity. It was a humming. He was standing a little behind the bench with his hand still on the butt of his holstered revolver and there was nothing there at all.

He had thought he would be able to see the lagoon. There was nothing. It was a backwater, a stagnant pool choked with crushed and fetid reeds. The bench lay partly submerged in it, rotting.

He could not see anyone in the lagoon and all their voices were gone.

Touching the back of the bench, he looked along the reeds, following the line of the shore and the bamboo forest's edge. It was all old, disused, let run wild. Where the water met the land there was still a faint gray mist. He heard tapping, the buzzing turning into a soft, insistent humming.

It stopped.

There was silence.

Looking along the fetid weeds into the forest itself, following its twisted and curving line, Feiffer said softly, "Oh, my God!"

He saw, twenty yards away in the reeds, a second bench.

He saw, next to it, by it, to one side of it, a grayness.

The grayness was moving, forming, becoming real.

Feiffer said softly, "Oh, my God . . ."

He saw, for the first time in his life, something he knew did not exist.

He saw forming, becoming real, creating itself out of the mist and the grayness, a shadow.

He saw an old man with his hand on the back of the bench looking over, directly at him.

It rooted him to the spot. It was a shadow. It was forming, wavering, coming and going as if it hung on only tenuously to whatever combination of fog and sound, water and reeds had brought it there. It was by the bench. The bench was real. The bench, in sharp focus, was old and splintered, disused, left there when the lagoon had been remodeled. The shadow beside it was only a shadow.

It formed. It had shape. It had the line and shape of an arm and then an upper chest and then, wavering, losing touch, it went again and dissolved, then came back. It had a face, eyes. The eyes were blurs. It was something—

It was a dream, something from—

Feiffer said in a whisper, "Oh my—" and it firmed, and the face was there and then as a chill ran through him and he thought to look away, it began to go and become only mist.

It was him. He was doing it himself.

He tensed, staring at it and the mist became real again and began forming.

It was him. He was doing it himself.

He tried to look away, but could not, and the blur began to melt. In the forest he heard the tapping of the bamboo. There was a buzzing. It was getting louder and louder.

It was an old man. It was not real. It was an invention. It was the tapping and the mist and the water and all the dead things and all the places in his soul he could not explain and all the questions about the birds sailing alone in the sky and he was doing it himself.

Feiffer said suddenly, "*No!*"

It faded. Locked into some awful, minute niche in the world, not part of it—locked into some awful part of Feiffer's mind—it seemed to turn back into mist and had never been.

It was not real. It had no face. It was across the reeds and the water and however close you came to it you would never come close to it. It was something from a dream, a shadow.

It was a memory.

It was, fading and coming, sharpening and then blurring away again, a bent, old man with no face holding a rolled-up umbrella.

He saw the eyes. They turned on him and he saw them stare at him.

They were pale. In a dark Asian face, the eyes of something nightmarish. The pupils were pale, blind. They stared. They stared at him.

The blur was sharpening. It was a memory. It was something drawn back and made real and held there. Whatever it was, it stared.

It looked. It looked directly at him.

There was a hissing sound, a whisper, a rasp, a sadness. He had invented it himself. It was not real. It was a lie. It was only the mist and the feeling he had and he had made it up, hallucinated it and it was not real. He had not seen it with the commander, he had sensed it, felt it, brought it up from somewhere inside him that did not exist. It was the soul. It was that part of him that he did not believe in.

They had been there first, the birds. Then, in that time, in that long dawn, they had—

The figure was shimmering, turning away, becoming lost.

"Commander—!" It was Hoosier. There were sounds, commotion. There were sounds of people doing things.

It was an old, tired man. It was an old, tired man with staring white pupils. It seemed, once, to shake its head, and then—

"Harry! Harry!" The commander, giving an order, called to someone, "Find Chief Inspector Feiffer! I think he's over there! You and you, get Mr. Feiffer over here *now!*"

—and then, suddenly, instantly, as if it had never been, whatever it was, wherever it had come from—whatever it meant—it was gone.

In the cocoon, without warning, there was a terrible knife of coldness.

It was an agony, something wrenched free and then, turning the cocoon boiling and alive, coming back again.

The person inside the cocoon, in the street, audibly, cried out, "*No!*"

The person inside the cocoon, in the street, audibly, cried, "Help! *Help me!*"

The person inside the cocoon killed things. In that instant, suddenly, the person inside the cocoon, for the first time, was afraid.

11

"**I** can't break through!"

"Get the screwdriver in between the bricks and twist!"

From the basement, Lim yelled, "I can't break through *the paint!*" Obviously the builders must have built the basement and then gone immediately on strike or caught typhoid fever and died. There were no fewer then forty-seven coats of green, puce and a color as yet undiscovered on the spectrum on the basement wall. So far. In the Detectives' Room there had only been thirty. Lim yelled up, "And I've got nothing to hit the screwdriver with!"

Mr. Wong's book hadn't mentioned paint. O'Yee, squatting down at his wall in a layer of masonry dust, cement rendering and something on the bricks that looked like penicillin culture, yelled down, "Hit it with the butt of Mr. Auden's spare gun!" When you wanted a blunt instrument you could always be sure of finding something in Auden's bottom desk drawer.

"It's got ammunition in it!"

"Then unload it!"

"It's got some sort of funny ammunition in it! I've opened the cylinder and the base of the cartridges say .357 Magnum and the side of the barrel where it says Ruger Speed 6 says that it's a .357 Magnum, but the cartridges won't come out!"

"Try the screwdriver with the cartridges still in the gun! They won't go off!"

"They're dripping something and there's a percussion cap on the tip of each of the bullets! I think they're explosive homemade bullets!"

111

No, they weren't. Explosive homemade bullets were illegal. They were Auden's bullets. They were explosive homemade bullets. "Hit it with the butt of your own gun!"

"My own gun is brand-new!"

"Well, hit it with something!" O'Yee, setting the chisel against the wall and whacking it with the mallet, yelled, "I've got the book to read! You work it out!"

. . . cement rendering, followed by a layer of bricks set from the cement footing of the foundation and keyed in on the external wall with two . . . O'Yee turned the page *. . . and caps on galvanized iron where the footing and the floor joists intersect and an RSJ . . .* He recognized that. An RSJ was the thing builders you asked about the possibility of knocking down a flimsy dividing wall between your dining room and your kitchen said was the only thing stopping you. O'Yee, wiping his hands and sending a shower of masonry dust onto the book, turned to the index under RSJ. There was nothing under RSJ. There was a suspicion, held by all home handymen planning nonprofessional alterations to their homes, that an RSJ was merely a figment of professional builders' imaginations. He was sure the wall didn't have one. The wall only had bricks. He put the chisel in and gave some of them a whack.

". . . I can't work it out! The only thing hard enough down here to hit the screwdriver with is—"

"Use a brick!"

"I can't get a brick!"

O'Yee yelled, "What the hell's an RSJ?"

"What is it in Cantonese?"

"How the hell do I know what it is in Cantonese if I don't know what it is in English?"

Lim called up with sudden, brilliant inspiration, "I could shoot the wall with Mr. Auden's bullets!"

"No." It was some sort of steel girder. He scratched his head and turned his hair white. It was over doorways or lintels—what the hell was a lintel?—or something. Wasn't it? It was. He hit the bricks with the chisel and the bricks shuddered. They were good solid nineteenth-century bricks. In the nineteenth century they had never heard of RSJ and lintels or ant caps or keyed-in joists or —No, in those days they built things to last. O'Yee yelled down, "This is a combined operation! When I break through the wall up here you should have broken through the wall down there and we can see if there's any connection or a secret passage or—" The wall, even to a man who knew nothing about RSJs, was nine inches thick with, according to the book, a four-inch cavity between the inner and outer layers of bricks that made the cavity. If there was a secret passage in there they didn't have a lot to fear from a four-inch-thick man. O'Yee yelled, "Use your initiative! Find something down there! Improvise! Put the blade of the screwdriver in against the wall and, if you have to, use brute force!"

There was a silence from the basement.

Lim said, "The screwdriver hasn't got a blade. It's a Phillips head screwdriver. What it's got is a sort of blunt spiral." Lim yelled up, "I've looked at the bullets in the gun and they're hollow points drilled out and filled with something wet like nitroglycerine and then topped off with a pistol-size percussion cap."

"They're illegal to shoot!"

"Not at walls!" Lim shouted up, "It's either that or trying to bash my way through the paint with the dead rat!" He added, "Sir." There was a pause. It was a critical pause. Lim, feeling left out, yelled, "I should have had a chisel and a mallet too!" He called up, "It's only eight A.M., maybe your friend Mr. Wong has another set you could borrow!"

O'Yee hit the wall. Through the last of the paint and the cement rendering, at last, he saw a brick. It was a red brick. Leaning forward, he put his ear to it and listened hard.

Lim's voice yelled through the pores of the material, "I'll buy a set out of my own money if that's what you want—"

The brick was cold, a little wet. There was a fungus on it. He wiped the fungus from the brick and his ear and listened hard.

"—but the shops are closed around here until nine."

The wall was silent, waiting.

Lim said, "I'm only an underling—"

O'Yee tapped the brick with the point of the chisel and it powdered and came loose. O'Yee yelled down, "The bricks are easy."

"The paint isn't."

"Once you get to them they're all old and powdery and they haven't got any support—!"

Lim yelled emotionally, *"Neither have I!"* Lim, his eyes filling with tears at the humiliation of it all, yelled up, "Mr. O'Yee, I went around to my girlfriend's house last night. She's studying psychology and she says that occult manifestations aren't always

caused by sixteen-year-old girls in puberty! Often, they can
be caused by the male menopause and waning sexual powers
and—"

"I'm forty-four! I'm not in the male menopause!"

Lim yelled up, "I'm twenty-three! It isn't me!" Lim, smarting,
shouted, "Down here there's just me and the dead rat! I never get
any of the glamour jobs! I just get shoved away to the menial
tasks because I'm the youngest and everyone thinks they can—"

He was right. O'Yee said softly, "Shoot the wall."

"What?"

He had been a good and true and loyal companion for all his
faults. O'Yee, flipping quickly through the book in case there was
a drawing of an RSJ tucked away on one of the pages, called
down, "You're right!"

"I always liked you, Mr. O'Yee!"

"Shoot the wall." The wall, like the sea, at the last trump, was
about to give up its secrets. O'Yee, placing his chisel point hard
into the powdered brick and readying his mallet for the great
blow, yelled down, "Shoot the wall!" He waited for his old friend
to mutter in his harumphing, embarrassed way, "Oh, hem, thank
you, Holmes, hem . . . ha . . . well, thank you very
much . . ."

He didn't. He yelled, "Haiii-ya!"

He was happy.

Down in the basement, with a detonation that shook every
atom, not in the wall, but probably in the entire street, Lim, from
the hip, with a wild look in his eye, shot the wall.

He was shooting. Leaning against the garbage skip with his
eyes closed Auden, with his head cocked to one side, was quietly
shooting his .17 caliber Remingtons and his .577-500s on the rifle
range of his mind.

Only the corner of his mouth moved. The corner of his mouth
said softly, "Kra—rack . . ." That was a .17. ". . . Boom . . ."
A .577-500 Express. ". . . Click . . ." The reloading.

The corner of his mouth said, "Hmm . . ." He nodded. It was
all to do with trajectories, muzzle velocities, bullet drops at mid
range, footpounds of energy, terminal tumble, wound tracks and
hydrostatic knockdown. Very technical. All in the book. All there
if you knew where to find it. He knew. Eureka: he had found it.
Q.E.D. Thus it is proven. Auden, still leaning, making burbling
noises, opening his eyes a fraction, said softly, "I'm right. This

time I'm right." He looked hard at Spencer standing there with him.

Spencer wasn't standing there with him. He was gone. It didn't matter.

Auden, a strange, twisted, determined smile on his face, said, "And Bill, I am prepared to be shot to pieces to prove it."

8:14 A.M. precisely.

Auden said as the timelock advanced another click, "Time to go."

He closed his eyes and went.

He said softly, "Boom . . . Kra-ack!"

He put the .17 Remington aside.

He said softly, precisely, over and over, "Boom . . . bam . . . *Boom!*"

It was all quite straightforward: the Tibetan wasn't a Tibetan at all, Ivan, Sergei, Igor, Nicholas and Natasha all looked the same, the air gun shooter shot only at the Tibetan and Auden, people chased Auden and the Tibetan and scooped up the money when the air gun shooter shot them, they weren't always the same people who scooped up the money—and because there were so many of them what money they got was negligible—and the customers who had their money stolen got their money back from the bank. It would have been easy if the customers who got their money stolen could have claimed they had taken out more money than they actually had, but there was a computer record of what they took because they took it from an autobank.

It all made sense if you believed that, philosophically, the world was a place of utter chaos and noncausality. Spencer had been to an English public school as a boarder. If the world had really been noncausal and chaotic the food would have been better. Spencer said softly to himself, "No."

He didn't believe that. Standing in front of the closed autobank he glanced at his watch. His watch, as it always did, went around. It didn't go backward. The numbers on the autobank keyboard read 1,2,3,4,5,6,7,8,9,0—they didn't read 6,8,2,1,0,9, 3,7, and 7 again. The world was discoverable by logic.

He looked across the street at Auden by the garbage skip and felt a glow of reassurance. He was a brick. In a world gone mad, he was a rock, a beacon. He saw the corner of Auden's mouth moving. Poor fellow, he probably wanted a cigarette. For P.C. Wang he would forgo that pleasure. No, somewhere, somehow, someone was making a profit.

For Auden, for order, for his own satisfaction, Spencer, scratching his nose and staring down hard at the numbers on the autobank keyboard—the pure, unvarying shining truth of mathematics—concentrated all his powers of logic and deduction in one last, great effort of will to work it out.

Mr. Nyet. Mr. . . . *NYET!* Spencer, his mouth suddenly falling open with the pure, simple, wonderful shining logic of it, said, rooted to the spot, "Mr. . . . *Nyet!*"

He looked at his watch.

8:23.

He looked at the autobank opening time.

8:24.

He looked in through the glass doors into the bank. Ivan, Sergei, Igor, Nicholas, Natasha—they had come in through the staff entrance at the back.

He looked at Auden. He heard, across the street, Auden go Click! There was no time. There was no time now for logic. Spencer, steeling himself, going quickly across the road and disappearing down a side street, catching Auden's half-open eye, *knew.* He knew how it was done.

He decided. He was prepared to be shot to pieces to prove it.

8:24 and a half. Spencer, getting down on his haunches, said softly to Annapura Lane, glaring across to the autobank, said softly to himself as the first of the day's customers began to turn into Old Himalaya Street to trustingly go about their business, "Boom."

It was not a .577-500. It was the Big Bang theory.

It was like the universe. It was, after all, once you mastered a few things like the theory of relativity, the death and birth of supernovas, black holes, time travel and infinity, all perfectly simple.

He was ready.

He was prepared, like all original thinkers, to be martyred to prove it.

8:26.

Scrunching down lower in the land, until, like simple, uncluttered intelligence, he was almost invisible in the world, Spencer waited for the proof.

He only had six rounds.

No, he didn't. He had a boxful. Lim, on the eighth round,

blasting at the wall so hard the floor under O'Yee's legs jumped and masonry powder and fungus miasma went up and down, down and then up again like a secret panel out of control, yelled, "Hit the bricks up there now!" Give a man a gun with explosive bullets and he thought he was in charge. "Don't wait around for me to bring the bricks down here—hit the bricks up there!"

He was. O'Yee shrieked, "I am!" He wasn't. Every time he got the chisel against the bricks, the entire station shook and the chisel jumped off.

There was a blast. Lim yelled, "I got the paint!" And another. Lim yelled, "I got the cement rendering and I'm onto the bricks! I'm where you are!" He must have had ears made of stainless steel. Lim yelled, "I can't hear you tapping! You're falling behind!" Lim shrieked, "I can't hear anything from the wall now! We've got The Thing on the run!"

Well, at least the male menopause theory had gone. O'Yee, ducking as the dead fly took flight with a blast from below, yelled, "Will you wait a minute! I can't get the chisel to stay still! Will you—"

"You've got five seconds!"

"I need—"

"Yaa!" He let fly twice. The room shook. The chisel jumped. The fly went up again. At the wall, the last of the chipped rendering flew off in a cloud of shrapnel and O'Yee got the chisel back in and whacked. The brick broke in half. It powdered. There was another blast and it turned to steam and vaporized. Downstairs, Lim yelled, "I'm through!"

"Get the screwdriver in!"

He ignored that one. There was another blast.

"Get the screwdriver in and give it a—"

He gave it an explosive .357 Magnum right where it hurt. There was a sound like a train wheel losing traction on a steel rail and in the Detectives' Room the wall moved.

"The wall moved!"

"Yeah, down here too!"

"No, I mean the wall *moved*!" There were cracks forming from the floor to the ceiling. There was a ripping sound. O'Yee, swimming his way through the falling cataract of masonry dust and dead flying fly, yelled, "Something's happening!"

There was no sound from the basement.

"What's happening down there in the basement?"

Silence.

"Lim! What the hell's—"

Lim yelled, "The bricks are falling out!" Things must have been in flight down there too. Lim said, "Ya!" He must have ducked the dead rat as it reached apogee and then declined in orbit and missed him by an inch.

The bricks went, "Slish!" They disappeared in a line to the ceiling two-bricks wide straight down into the floor like a stage magician's guillotine knife disappearing down in a single slash into the magic box where the lady in the sequined swimsuit was. Behind the bricks there were wooden laths and the cavity. The laths, caught in the fall of the bricks, turned to splinters. The cavity in the wall was full of old, rusted gas pipes.

O'Yee said, "Pipes! I can see gas pipes!" The place had been part of the original building of 1872. Jack the Ripper time. O'Yee, slapping his hands onto the top of his head and raising talc from what looked like his peruke, yelled in triumph, "We've solved it! It's nothing! It's just fungus slime amd gas pipes!" He even knew about the fly. O'Yee said, "We never even thought of it! But the fly—it does happen, you know—*the fly probably died of natural causes!*" O'Yee yelled down in the silence of comprehension, "Don't shoot anymore."

Gas pipes. So simple. Old abandoned gas pipes behind the wall. Child's play. With some movement of the earth—probably the pressure from the typhoon—the bricks had simply moved and exposed a hole in one of the old gas pipes and air had got in and—and, and the fly, poor bastard, like O'Yee himself, just wasn't feeling in top form and the pressure and the noise . . . well, he probably had a weak heart and—O'Yee shrieked, "We've solved it! We've solved it! The movement of the bricks sealed the hole where the rat got into the basement and he couldn't get back and he starved to death down there!"

The rat had also been torn to pieces.

O'Yee said, "What about the rat?"

What about twenty-eight?

What about Aaaragg-gah?

What about—

Lim had the gun. O'Yee shrieked down, "Well? Contribute a theory!"

"Shut up!"

O'Yee said, *"What did you say?"*

"No, shut up, listen!" From below, Lim yelled in a tight, strained voice, "Listen! *Listen!*"

There was nothing.

"Nothing!"

"*Listen!*"

"I am listening! All I can hear is—" He heard it. It was air in the ancient gas pipes. It was a single mournful organ note. It was an F flat. It came from the wall, from the pipes with perfect pitch.

Lim, in a ghastly voice from the basement, hearing something a second before O'Yee did, said, "Listen . . . !"

O'Yee listened. He was sitting in a sand hill of powdered rendering and brick dust. He listened as a child listens in its sand pit for the voice of its mother calling it home.

The wall, softly, gently, said, "Elephant . . ."

It was a woman's voice. It was low, sad, coaxing, lost.

The voice said softly, slowly, in English, "Elephant . . . Elephant . . . !"

"*Elephant!*"

In his car parked by Hoosier's van in the botanical gardens, Feiffer watched as the last of the dead birds in their glassine sterile envelopes were loaded into the back and Hoosier closed the doors on them. He watched as Hoosier paused for a moment before getting into the van to drive away.

He watched Hoosier's face.

He tried to read what was written there.

He had said nothing to him about the call in the middle of the night to the Federal Police in Australia. He waited only to follow him to the Quarantine Station.

He had said nothing to anyone about the figure of the old man by the bench.

He merely waited for Hoosier, tapping with his fingers on the steering wheel of his car with no expression on his face.

In his car, in the park, with no expression on his face, Feiffer waited.

The woman's voice through the wall said sadly in English, "There, there . . ." The voice said softly, sadly, "Elephant . . ." The voice cried out in sudden terror, "*Don't leave me!*" The voice cried out, "No! *No!*"

"Twen-ty-eight! *Twenty-eight!*"

The voice shrieked, "Someone! Someone!" The voice shrieked, "*I can't get out!*" The voice cried, "Someone—! Someone—! Is there anyone—*is there someone there?*"

In the Detectives' Room, it chilled him to the bone.

He put out his hand and touched the wall.

O'Yee said in a whisper, "Lim—"

He was there behind him. Lim said in a gasp, "Yes." He had heard it. O'Yee saw his face.

It was nothing but bricks and cement rendering and laths and old abandoned gas pipes from 1872. The voice was coming from there.

The voice said in an awful, appalling soulless whisper, "No!" There was no one there.

She was alone.

The voice said or perhaps they just imagined it, "Elephant . . ." It sounded as if, briefly, she wept.

The wall, against his hand, was as cold as death.

". . . Elephant . . ." It was the voice, not of a woman, but of a little girl.

They waited.

They waited.

The wall fell suddenly, abruptly . . . silent.

12

"**I**t came in on a yacht!" In his office in the wired-off Quarantine Station on Aberdeen Road, Hoosier said with surprise, "I remember it! I actually remember it! It came in on a tiny little five-point-three meter yacht called the *Where Away* from Brisbane, Australia, and it was found by Customs when the boat anchored at the clearing buoy in Hop Pei Cove! *Podargus strigoides*: tawny frogmouth—I looked it up. I remember because the boat was crewed by some seventeen-year-old kid sailing around the world on the maddest route Customs had ever heard of and at the maddest time of the year—in the typhoon season—and we prosecuted him because we thought it might keep him in port until after the typhoons were over." He had his *British Museum Identification Guide to Every Bird in the World* open on his desk with his finger on the picture of the frogmouth. "But it didn't. He paid his fine and he left for God knows where the next day." Hoosier, shaking his head, said, "It was a pet. He claimed he found it wounded on the boat when he was out to sea. He claimed it wasn't well enough to fly back to the coast. I had to look it up for Customs, for the court case." Hoosier, excited, said, "He fed it on fish. According to the *Museum Handbook*, frogmouths don't eat fish, but this one did." He said, for some private reason, elated, "I remember it!" He stabbed at the picture. "It was like the boy skippering: it was the scruffiest, hardiest, most beady-eyed and determined thing you'd ever seen in your life." He said suddenly, "He looked after it. He fed it up and it got strong. If it hadn't, if it

121

had been just staggering around the boat maybe we would have kept it for him until he left, but it wasn't, it was getting stronger—it could have flown in."

Feiffer said, "So?"

Hoosier said evenly, "So we killed it." He looked down at the feather in the glassine envelope on the book. "No one could recognize a bird from one feather—well, I couldn't anyway. Customs took it from the boat in a cage—it just hopped in and stood there glaring at them—and it was transported here to Quarantine in a sealed van where it was identified, the necessary paperwork done, it was entered up in the Quarantine Book and a Destruction Order issued under the Health Act." There was something private going on in his head. He looked up from the book and, not to Feiffer, but out through his sliding aluminum window across the flat compound of the station to a line of low gray buildings, said, "The Destruction Order was signed by me and the bird was painlessly put down by the inhalation of lethal gas." He answered Feiffer's question before he could ask it. "About two weeks ago. The boy paid his fine the same week and sailed out."

"Is there any possibility that the feather—"

"The bird came in here intact. It died in here intact and then the remains were incinerated intact. Its droppings came in here. They were scraped off the boat and then the boat disinfected before the boy was even allowed to land. Customs even took his shoes and had them sterilized in an autoclave." Hoosier said abruptly, "We're without pity here. We're the Civil Service. Everything is written down, notarized, checked, dotted and crossed and what comes out at the other end is carcasses all humanely, quickly, efficiently and lawfully slaughtered with no room for discussion, exceptions or humanity." Hoosier said, "It has to be done. If it wasn't done—" Hoosier said to the window, "Here we kill anything without papers. Anything that says Unclean on its brow, anything that tries to get in or get away, anything that people try to smuggle or hide or sneak in, we kill. It has to be done. It's easy when what you've got is something like some drooling, filthy cur from India with incipient rabies and you're so frightened of it you shoot it in its cage, but with the others—with things like the bird—it's harder, but it still has to be done." Hoosier said violently, "The worst offenders aren't bird smugglers making a fortune with their suffocated and dying birds packed into briefcases for sale in America or Europe or wherever they're going—the worst offenders are ordinary, sad lonely people with no children who can't face the prospect of leaving their little doggie-woggies at home and who give them names and birthday cards and talk to them." He had a strange look in his eyes. It looked like shame or embarrassment. "Sometimes they even come out here and beg me. Sometimes, even if we offer them ninety days quarantine they'd rather we put their dog down. Sometimes—" Hoosier said, "I'm a vet. I love animals. But I don't use them for my own purposes and I don't risk infecting the Colony with them!" Hoosier, shaking his head, hardening his resolution as he must have done day after day, time after time, occasion after occasion, said, "Anything that comes in here without proper Quarantine clearance is destroyed!" He turned his eyes to Feiffer and the look was gone. Hoosier, trying to smile, said lightly, "If I was going into this business again, I'd go into botany. The Plant and Fruit Section across the compound, all they do is put their stuff in little plastic bags like greengrocers and toss it into an incinerator." He was still trying to force a grin, "Sometimes here when they have their burns it smells like Mom's apple pie baking time." Hoosier said, "That would be easier, wouldn't it? It'd certainly be easier to justify to people at cocktail parties."

"Between the time the bird was caged by Customs and its destruction—"

Hoosier said quietly, tightly, "I've been around animals all my life. My parents had a farm. When I see a bird up in the sky, something soaring not for food or prey or purpose, but for the joy of simply soaring, I still . . ." He looked down to the book, "Between the time the bird was caged by Customs and its destruction it was kept here in a bonded holding area. It was caged and the cage sealed with an official lead seal."

"Who had access to it?"

"No one."

"What about the yachtsman or his friends?"

"Like the frogmouth, he had no friends. No, he wasn't allowed in. Any dealings he had with Quarantine he had with me by phone." Hoosier, shaking his head, running through the routine line by line, said without room for argument, "At night the bonded holding area is locked and patrolled by armed officers of the Prevention Section of Customs, and during the day, as you saw when you came in, you have to be admitted by another armed guard on the main gate from the road." Hoosier said,

"Once or twice we've had to kill apes. When you shoot them they fall over like men."

His face at the botanical gardens had not been for the flamingos, but for the unnecessariness of it. His face had been for the way it had been done.

Hoosier asked quietly, "Do you ever do that? Do policemen ever stop to watch a bird soaring in the air?"

"Who does the killing?"

He was gazing out the window. Hoosier said softly, not to Feiffer but to someone else, maybe himself, "I read Shakespeare. What I like most about him is his humanity, his view of the world not as a series of isolated happenings, but as part of a great scheme, a great wheel of things." He came back, "The killing is done by contract. It's done by a trusted man with a love of animals who knows how to kill cleanly and quickly and whose greatest qualification—" Hoosier said, "It's all crazy! —whose greatest qualification is that he doesn't like doing it so that when he does it we'll all sleep better knowing that he didn't enjoy it!" He pointed stiffly with his index finger out through the aluminum window to one of the low, windowless buildings, "It's done in there. It's a gas chamber and a shooting room and behind it, out of sight, are the incinerators and the pits. It's Auschwitz, I'm Eichmann: what we do we do because it's right and the law and we're following orders. If we let one tainted creature by it would contaminate the entire Colony, so we don't. We do all the paperwork and the prosecutions and we make all the reports in lines and columns and, in the end, all you come to do is have no pity and set your face to people's pleas. You console yourself that the people pleading with you are the ones responsible anyway and it's not your fault, until all, all you have in the end, is just a highly organized, efficient, clean production line dealing in death and incineration and—and *everything*, everything I thought I was going to do in my life—" Hoosier said, touching his face, seeing his own reflection in the window as if Feiffer was no longer there, "'I am not yet of Percy's mind, the Hotspur of the north; he that kills me some six or seven dozen of Scots at a breakfast, washes his hands, and says to his wife, "Fie upon this quiet life! I want work."' I'm a vet! I'm a goddamned vet! I'm a goddamned civil servant!" He was caught, caged as surely as anything in his bonded holding areas. Hoosier said softly, "*Henry the Fourth, Part One*. I can't do anything these days except take refuge in other men's thoughts." He said softly, "All the killing is done by a man called Idris, a Malay. His office is over there near the killing block. You'll find him." He was still staring out the window thinking his own thoughts.

Hoosier said, "We use him to kill because he hates killing. God only knows what he'll make of the flamingos from the Gardens when he has to burn them. He used to go there all the time, I'm told. There and Yat's. He told me once, funnily enough, that what he liked most about Yat's was, of all things, the Wishing Chair." Hoosier said, "We all make wishes."

Hoosier said softly, "He's a little old man with pale eyes from cataracts. You can't miss him. He's got bad skin cancer of the face. On hot days he carries an umbrella everywhere to shade himself." He tried to concentrate, but it was impossible.

He advised Feiffer curtly, "Go ask Idris. He was the one who, with his lethal chambers, put an end to everyone's doubts about the frogmouth." He said with sudden anger, "Go and ask him about your bloody feather!"

From the gas pipes, there was only the faintest whistling sound of air or wind. O'Yee ordered Lim, "Get Hurley on the phone! I want to know where the old gas pipes lead." He answered his own question. "They lead away under the streets!" O'Yee ordered Lim, "Get a metal detector!"

Dialing the numbers quickly and without mistake, Lim got Hurley. Lim said in a whisper as O'Yee took the phone from him to talk, "I'll be back in ten minutes."

It was 8:28 A.M. An hour ago he hadn't been able to get a screwdriver. An hour ago, he hadn't heard the wall scream. As O'Yee began talking quickly on the phone to Hurley, Lim paused. He looked at the wall one last time. He touched hard at the butt of his gun in his holster.

He went to get a metal detector.

They were coming. At 8:29 A.M. as the Russo Harbin Hong Kong Trading Bank got ready to open its doors and its autobank for the day's business, the thieves with feet like dinner plates were coming.

Somewhere someone was pushing the first .177 air pellet into his air gun and breaking the barrel down to cock it.

In the gunsmoke drifting range of Auden's mind, all the shooting stopped and there was silence.

8:30 A.M.

There was a click from his time lock. There was a shiver from his feet. In one of the synapses of his brain there was a single spark. It was the spark that told him he was a .577-500 Number 2 Express bullet. It was all the information he needed from the synapses.

He was ready.

He quivered.

He had decided.

He *knew*.

"*We were strolling along . . . On moonlight bay . . .*"

Wrong synaptic spark.

Auden, all bone and muscle, cutting out his brain and turning solely to the only friend he had, his central nervous system, said in a low snarl, "Grrrr . . ."

Down on his haunches in Annapura Lane, Spencer, staring hard across to the glass doors of the bank, watched as Ivan and Sergei, Natasha and Igor and all the rest of them went about their business setting up the day's transactions.

He watched, his eyes glued to their every movement.

Spencer said softly, "Hmm . . ."

He watched, and waited, and wondered.

8:30 A.M. exactly.

He saw the smoked glass window on the keyboard of the autobank against the wall of the bank open for the first customer of the day.

He watched as the first customer of the day, a tall Northern Chinese carrying a briefcase, came down the street unsuspectingly to use it.

In the Detectives' Room, O'Yee shouted down the line to Hurley, "What do you mean you don't know where it goes? You're writing a history of the Hong Kong Police—this is Hong Kong Police gas pipe! *Where the hell does it go?*"

It went north. He heard Lim coming in. He heard Lim banging something metal on the edge of the Charge Room desk as he dragged it. O'Yee, slamming down the phone on Hurley, demanded, "Yes? Yes? Have you got it?"

He had it. God only knew where, but he had it in his hand. It was in a long cardboard box marked TREASURE FOR PLEASURE— DETECT YOUR WAY TO UNTOLD RICHES. O'Yee shouted, "Right! Good!"

From the wall there was only a soft whistling sound.

All thumbs, O'Yee, wrenching the box from Lim's hands, got it up on his desk to tear it open and assemble the thing.

He heard—

He thought he heard—

The whistling stopped. The wall said softly, ". . . twenty . . . twenty-eight."

He had the box open. It was 8:31. It had no batteries. O'Yee shouted, "Get batteries!"

Good old Lim. You could always rely on him.

At top speed, running out of the room again without a word of complaint, Lim went to get batteries.

At the door to the killing chamber, Hoosier said in a gasp, "My God!" He had wanted to stay in his office after Feiffer had gone. He could not. At the door to the killing chamber, Hoosier, rooted to the spot, said, "Feiffer—Chief Inspector? *Are you here?*"

Everything was smashed. On the little narrow-gauge tram track they used to push the cages down along the line of side-mounted forty-four-gallon oil drums converted to gas chambers there were cages, boxes, bits and pieces of mechanism. The shooting trough at the far end of the room by the furnaces had been twisted: the bars had been bent and smashed down with a sledgehammer. The hammer had been used on the killing drums themselves. Three of the row of five lay on their sides with their hinged metal doors hanging off their hinges—they had been hit over and over and mangled like aluminum beer cans. He saw the line of poison gas cylinders behind the drums. They were on their sides. He sniffed. They were intact. He could not see Feiffer anywhere. He saw the open steel door of the furnace. It was scarred, marked as if someone, again and again, had beaten it with something hard and then, failing to break it, had turned to the masonry around it. There was dust from masonry everywhere: it was like a carpet. The walls had been holed. They had been smashed to their bricks and rendering. Hoosier called urgently, "Feiffer!" There was a trolley for one of the gas cylinders upside down in the center of the shooting trough where the drain was. There were cages in the killing trough and cardboard boxes for the transport of smaller animals. The transport dolly was bent and broken with one of its wheels hanging off. Hoosier said, "Feiffer! Are you there?" He heard a noise, a click, then a humming and then another click. Hoosier, going forward into the room, watching the poison gas cylinders in case they rolled or fractured, called, *"Feiffer—!"*

It was hot. In the room, the air-conditioning unit had been smashed. It had been a plastic box on the wall. Its sides had been stoved in. Its fan unit lay near the open furnace with the beaten-in wire and cardboard cages. He heard the hum. It was coming from Idris's office to one side of the furnace. Hoosier, his shoes crunching on masonry and wooden laths from the wall as he walked, went toward the office.

He saw Feiffer in there by a Xerox machine. The machine was the only thing left standing in the office. Hoosier, looking at the turned-over desks and filing cabinets and, again, the smashed-in walls, demanded, "What the hell's happened?" He sniffed. He could not smell gas. He saw the open arms locker on the wall behind the overturned and splintered desk. He counted the rifles and humane killers. Hoosier said with his civil servant's mind, "There's a pistol missing, a Webley .455 Mark Six revolver." The humming was the Xerox machine. Feiffer had turned it on. Hoosier shouted, "Did you hear me?" Hoosier, looking around, still sniffing, demanded, "What the hell happened?"

"You tell me."

"I haven't been here for a week. We haven't had to kill anything for—" There was a faint smell. Hoosier said in terror, "Gas!"

"It's the machine." It was on, humming, a faint smell of ammonia and warm treated paper about it. Feiffer said tightly, "It was still on when I got here. It was printing. All the paper had run through and it was still printing." Feiffer, looking up from the machine, asked with a strange look on his face, "Is there a way Idris could have gotten in and out of the compound without anyone seeing him?"

"There's a back gate."

"And, like executioners all over the world, the prison prefers him to come and go unnoticed through it. Am I right?"

He was going to say— Hoosier said tightly, "Yes."

"When was the last time there was a killing in this place?"

"The last time was the frogmouth—"

He had smelled the carbolic on the floor the moment he had come in. The smell of ammonia from the Xerox machine overlaid it. Feiffer said savagely, "Then why the hell do the furnaces have dust in them? Why the hell are the poison gas cylinders all jammed tight and rusted? Why the hell—" Feiffer shouted in the ruined, wrecked room, "Why the hell didn't anyone ever come in here and check? Where the hell's your unbreachable Civil Service order and conveyor belt system?" Feiffer said, "The trough was the only thing that looked clean! The only thing that's been going on in here for months is the shooting of dogs and cats! Nothing's been gassed in your goddamned bird-gassing chambers for weeks, maybe months!" He had put paper in the loading cartridge of the Xerox machine. It began to print. Feiffer, yanking the first copy out and shoving it toward Hoosier, ordered the man, "Here! You know so much about what goes on in here! You have all the morality of it all worked out to your own satisfaction! You know what sort of kind, thoughtful, gentle, merciful man Idris is—*read this*!" He had killed too. In the course of the last five years he had killed four times. He knew what killing cost. He knew what people thought about you. Feiffer, his face contorted, yelled, yanking more of the papers out of the storage bin and throwing them in a cascade into Hoosier's face, "There are plenty of copies! Read this!"

NORTH POINT WOMAN IN DEATH FALL
Wrote Last Letter To Husband

It was a tiny clipping from a newspaper, from something minor, unimportant: judging by the little line box it had been printed in, something hidden away on page 18 or 20.

> *Police are treating as suicide the death last night of Mrs. Mata Idris, 51, who fell from the balcony of her eighth floor apartment in the New China Housing Estate block in Pottinger Street, North Point.*
>
> *A police spokesman at North Point Station said that Mrs. Idris had been under a doctor's care for some time and had been treated for depression for several months prior to her death.*
>
> *The spokesman said that the police were not seeking any other person in connection with the death and that no suspicious circumstances were involved.*
>
> *The spokesman confirmed that police had taken possession of a letter left in the apartment block by Mrs. Idris for her husband, but declined to reveal its contents.*

The clipping had been pasted onto a sheet of foolscap paper and placed in the machine to print.

It had printed. During all the destruction and the blows from the sledgehammer it had printed. It had gone on printing until the entire ream of 500 sheets of paper in its loading cartridge had been exhausted.

With the new paper in the cartridge it went on printing now.

It was merely a few lines of an unimportant story centered on a thirteen-by-eight-inch sheet of blank foolscap Xerox paper.

In the office, Feiffer, for some reason unable to control himself, yelled, *"Read it! Read it!"* He had seen him. He had seen him standing there at the edge of the lagoon. He had seen his pain. He had seen him.

The machine, humming, was printing, printing. It was printing the story over and over again.

He had seen him. He had seen the small, old man with pale eyes who loved animals and killed them, who thought of wishing chairs and who, like Hoosier—not like Hoosier at all—wished, and who, all his days in this awful place was alone. Feiffer shrieked, *"Read it!"*

It had happened at the New China Housing Estate in Pottinger Street: it had happened outside his department too. It had happened in North Point, two streets away from Hong Bay, his precinct, his files, his papers, his Civil Service mentality—but it had happened.

It had happened to someone. Like the killing in the killing chamber, even though no one saw it or wanted to see it, or pretended they had nothing to do with it, it happened.

There was no smell of poison gas in the room. There had not been the smell of poison gas in there for a very long time. In the room there was only the warm, electric smell of the Xerox machine and the carbolic from the cages.

It printed. Not knowing what it printed, not knowing what it meant, obediently—a machine—it went on printing, clicking, over and over.

NORTH POINT WOMAN IN DEATH FALL
Wrote Last Letter To Husband

Over and over . . .

Over, and over.

In the awful, still, ruined room, over and over, until the pages spilled out of the collection trough, over and over, the machine, humming, printed the little, unimportant story in the color it had been set to: a bright—on the white foolscap page—full tonally adjusted bright Civil Service red.

It printed.

It clicked.

Somewhere, somewhere else inside a red cupola, it *hummed*.

8:33 A.M.

In the Detectives' Room, to no one but itself, the wall said in a whisper, weakening, in distress, "Twenty-eight . . . *Twenty-Eight!"*

13

Choofa, choofa, choofa, choofa . . .

Auden opened one eye. He saw the Tibetan at the far end of the street, coming. He was coming choofa, choofa, choofa—he was a train. He was gathering speed, pacing himself, flexing his hand for the mail pickup at the autobank.

Choofa-choofa—he was speeding up, his legs starting to get traction on the pavement, his shoulders moving, tightening. At the autobank the tall Northern Chinese with his briefcase was counting his money . . . One hundred, two hundred, three hundred . . . Choofa-choofa . . . choof. Choof. Choof. Auden opened his other eye. There was a crowd forming around him. They were looking down the street and then the Northern Chinese and then to Auden.

Five hundred . . . six hundred . . .

Choof, choof, choof! *Choof!*

Auden said, "Back!"

The crowd got back. They were a crowd of toothless unemployed Chinese in shorts and singlets. They had feet like meat dishes.

He was a .577-500. Auden said again, "Back!"

"Seven hundred . . ."

Choofachoofachoofa—*choofa!*

He had always wanted to be a sniper. He was a sniper's bullet. He closed his eyes again and then opened one a fraction and got a warm, tunnel womb vision. Auden said, "Click." He cocked the

131

hammer. Choofa, choofa, choofa . . . He began to . . . squeeze his trigger . . .

The crowd, moving, seeing the Tibetan come, seeing the Northern Chinese reach one thousand with his banknotes, said in a hiss, "Weee . . . !"

He was moving. His legs began to piston, his arms began to stiffen. Choofa, choofa, *choofa*! He was gathering speed, getting traction. The Tibetan, pushing, pistoning, his eyes set on the Northern Chinese, his feet disappearing into blurs, was coming. Auden yelled to the crowd in Cantonese, "Back! Stand clear!"

The crowd cheered. They were running on the spot. The Northern Chinese with the briefcase and the money looked up.

CHOOFCHOOFCHOOFCHOOF! The Tibetan's whistle at full speed shrieked, "Tooo-wee!"

"Back!"

The crowd yelled, "Waaeee!"

"Tooowee!" ChoofchoofCHOOF—*roar*!

Auden yelled— He was ready to yell, as he fired, *"Boom!"*

The tall Northern Chinese yelled as he saw a blur coming at him with its arm outstretched and a wild look in its eyes, "Aaii-ya!"

Auden, firing, yelled, "BOO—"

Looking across, pointing to him, waving his hand as it became in an instant filled with the Northern Chinese's money, the Tibetan yelled, "Ready! Set! *Go!*"

"—OOM!" He tripped, he fell, he crashed into the crowd as, as one man, it began to run. Auden, scrabbling, getting up, his bullet all bent and off target, all his powder wet, shrieked, *"That wasn't fair!"*

CHOOFACHOOFACHOOFACHOOFA—the train was going, speeding away, becoming an express, the mail arm with the money retracting for streamlining, a single sharp contrail of steam and breath coming out from behind it as it went for the record. The pavement was a railway line, nonstop, express. The road was the station. Barefooted people were running after the train shouting and waving their arms trying to catch it. He wasn't a bullet, he was a goddamned war bride standing there with tears in his eyes as the train roared away into the night without him on it. Nobody in the whole goddamned world was on his side. Auden, hopping up and down and about to punch the garbage skip, yelled in Cantonese, "No one's on my side anywhere!"

Someone was. It was the Tibetan. The Tibetan, turning at full speed, waving the money, catching his eye for a moment as—so help him his feet rose six inches above the pavement—yelled, "You! Cop!" The Tibetan, calling to him, beseeching him, needing him, yelled, "Run! Please! For God's sake, *RUN!*"

He couldn't see anything. In the street the crowd had gone toward the hill after the Tibetan like a wave of attacking Korean suicide troops. At the end of Annapura Lane they missed running him down by inches.

Spencer, jumping up and down, trying to see over them, still spinning in the wake of their acceleration, tried to see Auden. Auden was at the garbage skip, hopping up and down. He stopped hopping. He was half hopping, trying to get his legs into order. Spencer, running toward him, looking up at the flat roofs along the street behind cars, back to the garbage skip where the sniper might be, yelled out, "Phil! I can't see anyone! Can you see the shooter?" He looked across to the Russo Harbin Hong Kong Trading Bank. The glass doors were dark at that angle. He saw a blur inside moving past the doors and then disappear. He heard a disappearing dot somewhere through the seething, running crowd, yell, "Where the hell are you?" and Spencer, thinking it was Auden, yelled back, "I'm here! The profit motive is—" It was the Tibetan. Spencer yelled, "Phil! Phil, he's got an accomplice!"

"All right!"
Addressing the garbage skip, Auden, on the boil, reaching vapor point, snarled, "All right!" For two days people had been trying to kill him. He had watched his health. For two days people had been trying to— He had tried to be a bullet. It hadn't worked. People hadn't let it work. *All right then*—all right then— He was moving, all the nerves and muscles and sinews in his legs and lungs were coiling, filling with air. Sometimes a man had to do what a man had to do. Bullets didn't count. Men counted. Men who were bullets were men who weren't men. All right then. He had been found out. Fuck Wang—Wang didn't count. The Tibetan and the crowd were fifty yards away. Fifty yards didn't count. Auden shrieked to the heavens at the top of his voice, "All right then! I'm here! My name is Phillip John Auden and I'm ready!" He saw the tall Northern Chinese at the autobank looking at him with his mouth open. Maybe he didn't speak English. Auden, shouting in Cantonese for him, cried bootless to

the heavens, "I'm here! I'm ready! I'm me! This time, *I am prepared to die!*"

The tall Northern Chinese, cringing, said, "Oh, my God!"

He did speak English. Good. Auden, his legs beginning to work, his legs turning to blurs, Auden, able to leap buildings in a single bound, yelled from the bottom, the depths of his soul, "For England! For the Empire! For me!" He heard the Tibetan seventy-five, eighty yards away, being pursued by the black storm of running bums, yell, "Run!" and he, at last, for the final time—for the great, ultimate act of his life—girding his loins, coiling his essence, exploding like a .577-500 Number 2 Express and a .17 caliber Remington both at once—he *ran.*

In the New China Apartments in Pottinger Street, Feiffer, outside the door to apartment number 816, commanded the caretaker, "Key." There was no sound from inside the apartment—nothing. The caretaker was a worried middle-aged Southern Chinese with slicked-down hair and a good job. He had his ring of keys in his hand. He slid them quickly to find the right one in the bunch. He looked up to Feiffer's face trying to find the right key.

Feiffer said tightly, "Hurry. Please hurry." He had his hand on the butt of his gun under his coat. He listened, holding the caretaker's eyes as the man fumbled at the keys.

Inside the apartment there was no sound at all.

He fumbled.

In the corridor, beginning to sweat, the caretaker fumbled, panicking at the keys.

"Nijāmba!" It was Spencer. It meant Stop! in an obscure Sherpa dialect that he had found in a book on yetis. It was too obscure. The Tibetan—the Sherpa—was going toward the hill like an express train, his legs invisible blurs with the crowd behind him slapping their bare feet down.

"Nijāmba!"

The tall Northern Chinese at the autobank, cowering, said, "Aaah!" He saw the blond lunatic in the street—as opposed to the dark lunatic blasting off from the garbage skip—as opposed to the street full of lunatics everywhere—shout at him, "It must be too obscure!" and the tall Northern Chinese yelled back, "Anything! Anything you say!"

"It's the profit motive! I can't work out who has the profit motive!"

"It isn't me!"

"I am prepared to DIE!" It was the garbage skip. By it, something had taken wings. It looked like a tank. The tank, as it went out of control and disappeared into the seething mass of meat dish runners, yelled residually, "Boom—no good . . . boom . . ."

The tall Northern Chinese yelled to Spencer—

"Nijāmba!" One last try.

The tall Northern Chinese yelled, "Oh!" He looked everywhere in the street. The entire street was going toward Sagarmatha Hill, going east. They were running.

"RUN!" It was the leader of the loonies, the one almost at the base of the steps. He looked like some sort of obscure Sherpa. "NIJĀMBA!"

He wasn't.

The tall Northern Chinese yelled in desperation—

The blond one yelling Nijāmba! yelled, "The money—"

The Northern Chinese yelled back, "Keep it!"

Why not? Everyone else was doing it. He ran. They were all running east. The tall Northern Chinese, making the best decision of the morning, decided to do the same.

He ran.

He ran, as fast as hell, *west.*

In Yellowthread Street, O'Yee, with the earphones clamped against his head, turned on the metal detector.

Hurley had said the old gas lines ran north.

North was to the left.

The detector, finding it immediately under the pavement, the depth meter registering exactly three foot six below the surface, went strongly, loudly, *"Ping!"*

Following it, tracking it, sticking to it like glue, the detector as O'Yee walked went firmly, unshakably, "Ping, ping, ping, ping . . ."

He passed through the crowd. The crowd were peasants, also-rans. He passed through them as if they were nothing. They broke and gave him room as he sped by on winged feet, as a god passed through mortal men. He was Zen. He was running itself. Everything was working. He knew he was doing it—his brain was working. His brain knew he was doing it. His brain, like a kind wife, had given his legs and his lungs permission to do it and she was there beside him urging him on. Someone loved him. His brain loved him. His brain, as he slipped through the seething mass of poor, second-rate humanity going slapaslappa-slappa on their bare feet while his gilded extremities went swish, cried in exhortation and love, "Ahh . . . !" He heard someone say in Cantonese, "Look at him!" and his brain looked and saw that it was good. He was at the base of the steps, Sagarmatha—Everest. He said merrily, "Ha, ha." He flicked his head. He wished he had had a pencil-thin mustache and pirate clothes. His brain could have arranged it. His brain was on his side. Auden said, "No, it's all right." Good old brain. Kind old brain. He saw the Tibetan laugh with a careless laugh. Auden said carelessly, "Ha, ha!" He was on Sagarmatha Hill. Sagarmatha Hill was as nought. He was going up the stairs, higher and higher. He counted. Step number twenty-one, twenty-two, twenty-three, twenty-five—he bounded two steps at a time—twenty-seven, twenty-nine—he was going where no man had gone before. He cried at full throat, his battle cry, "A Wang!" Fuck Wang. He cried, "Auden! I'm Phil Auden!"

"Ranjit! Ranjit Gopol!" The Tibetan had the money in his hand.

"I can do it! I can do it!"

"You can! I knew you could!" The Tibetan, grinning, his eyes bright and shining and admiring, yelled, "You're a noble fellow—I could tell from the first!"

"I am!" Auden, drawing level, yelled, "I keep myself fit!"

"Me too! I climb Mount Everest when I'm at home!"

"I go to the gym Wednesdays and Fridays!"

"I rang up about P.C. Wang this morning—he's been discharged! It wasn't a coronary at all—it was indigestion!" The Tibetan, turning his head, catching Auden's eye as they ran shoulder to shoulder, said, "Phil—is it?"

"Yes!"

"I think it's very unfair that someone else has gotten into all this!"

Auden shouted back, "I've been shot too!"

"You took it bravely!"

"So did you!"

The Tibetan, grinning, showing off, yelled, "Three steps at a time!" The steps weren't even there anymore. They were pebbles.

Auden yelled, "Three at a time!" He went up three at a time—Auden yelled, "Four at a time!"

"Sherpas are short! Our legs aren't as long as yours!"

"Stay on three then!"

The Sherpa yelled, "Lope!"

They loped.

The Sherpa yelled, "I love this! I live for this!" The Sherpa yelled, "Phil, watch this!" He turned in midair, pirouetted, spun. The Sherpa yelled, "Want to try it?"

What a fine fellow was Ranjit. Auden, grinning, yelled, "Sherpas have better balance than people with long legs!"

"You noble fellow!" The Tibetan yelled, "Someone's going to shoot me any second because I've got the money!"

"If they shoot you they shoot me too!" Auden, not noble, but positively illustrious, yelled, "Give me half the money!" He reached out. He felt the warmth of comradeship. He touched at the Sherpa's hand. It wasn't even perspiring. Neither was his own. (Auden said, "Ha, ha.") He took half the money. Auden dared the world, "Shoot him and you shoot me!" Auden at one with the world, yelled, "Ha!" Auden, suddenly shot in the arse, yelled, "OH!"

He saw Auden stagger. He had some of the money. He saw the Tibetan reach over and take the money back. Someone shot him too. He saw the Tibetan stagger. He saw Auden grab for him, hold him, set him upright.

Spencer, running back and forth in the street, reaching the garbage skip and leaping up to see inside it, yelled to no one, maybe to the mass of barefooted runners collapsing one by one on the steps with exhaustion as nothing—nothing—stopped the Tibetan and Auden, shrieked, "I can't find him! I can't work out who gets the profit because it all gets repaid by the bank after they've counted it and I—"

The bank. In the bank, Ivan and Natasha and Sergei and the rest of them counted the money.

The bank!

No one else checked their count because Mr. Nyet wasn't there! The Pan Asia Games. What the hell did people play in the Pan Asia Bank Officers' Games? What were bank tellers good at?

On the hill, the Tibetan, shot again, said clearly, "Ugh!" His friend Auden reached for him.

Pistol shooting! They played pistol shooting! He looked up to the roof of the bank. It was flat. He looked through the glass doors into the bank. It was empty. He looked for the tall Northern Chinese who had been robbed. He was gone.

Spencer, cracking it, solving it, feeling pleased with himself, yelled out to encourage him, "Phil! I worked out who's doing it! It's the bank staff! They're claiming more of the money was stolen than was stolen and they're paying out the full amount from the bank's money as restitution!" It was all so neat once you knew. "They're claiming only probably half as much was recovered as we recovered—each time—and they're putting the difference aside—stealing it—to send themselves to the Pan Asia Bank Officers' Games because they're the best bank air pistol shooting team in the Colony!"

They were. On the roof, aiming carefully, the bank pistol shooting team, shooting up the hill, began shooting both Auden and the Tibetan simultaneously.

The caretaker got the door open. He recoiled. He had never smelled it before, but in the room, as Feiffer moved him to one side and went in with his gun drawn, he smelled death.

They were gone. The last of the barefooted hordes had fallen down crimson-faced and gasping for air on the steps like fish and they were alone. They were three steps from the top of the hill. Shot, Auden yelled, "Urk!"

Two steps away. The Tibetan, staggering, blood running from a pellet wound on his lower back, said pitifully, "Ark!"

One step away. Auden, taking a pellet in the leg, said, "Oh—" He slowed. He began to stop. The last, the final step, the summit seemed to be moving away, his little flag destined never to fly there, his—

"Mmm!" It was the Sherpa. It was Ranjit. He was his truest and best friend. If he would not be there on the top with him then the top was no good and he did not want it. Auden, at the last foothill, the last piton, the last giant step for mankind before the summit, stopped. In *The Red Badge of Courage*, the dying man had passed on the flag to The Boy. The Sherpa was going, falling, collapsing, sinking to his knees. He looked up to the top of the hill—to the last step—and there he saw his home and his family so near, so far . . . going away, failing in the light that burned. The Sherpa said, "Here . . ." He raised up his hand with the money in it, "See that it gets . . ."

He was up the stairs inside the bank to the roof. On the roof the shooters were running down the fire escape into the street.

Spencer, ten yards behind them, yelled, "Nijāmba!" They took no notice. Even Natasha. Still carrying her Feinwerkbrau .177 caliber target air pistol in her hand, she went over the wall and into the street like a mountain goat. Spencer yelled, *"STOP!"*

Say not that the struggle naught availeth. The Light was failing. The Torch was being handed from one passing runner to another. On the step at the summit of the hill, the Sherpa, blood running from his flesh wounds, out of step, hope, family and puff, said in a strangled voice, "Phil, what a day we had . . . What a—"

It was the finest moment of his life. Auden said with nobility and illustriousness dripping from every pore, every atom in his body, "Ranjit, to conquer without you the World would say was a great victory for the endurance of man. To me, it would be but dried grass blowing in the wind."

"Thank you, Phil." His eyes shone with devotion for his Captain.

"Here. The honor is yours." Sir Gawain, he lifteth his good trusty Squire up.

"Nijāmba!"
They ran.
Spencer yelled, "STOP!"
They ran.
Spencer, drawing his Detective Special and letting go in a blast all six shots at once into the air, yelled, "Stop, please."
They stopped.

Even Natasha. Spencer shook his head in disappointment looking at her. Natasha said, dropping her air pistol with the rest in the middle of the road, "Don't shoot—"

It wasn't Natasha. It was Sergei. He had the deeper voice.

"Phil! I've got them all down here and you've got the Tibetan!"
Auden said in a quiet voice, "He's a Sherpa. He climbs mountains." One step away. He helped Ranjit to his feet. In all his life no one had ever called him noble before. Auden said, "He's going home." He helped him take the step. He stood on the summit.

From the street Spencer yelled, "What?" Spencer yelled, *"He's got the money!"*

"He needs the money." Auden, holding Ranjit by the wrist,

pushing him up, wiping away with his free hand the blood from the wounds of his battle, said firmly, "Go."

"Thank you, Phil."

Auden said softly, "Go."

"How the hell are we going to get the money back if you let him go?"

Ranjit, nodding, had no words.

Auden said curiously, calling down from the mountain, "I don't know really, Bill. Do you think you'd be up to running after him and catching him?"

He sat down as Ranjit, looking back, went around the corner of the hill and disappeared.

He kept himself fit.

He kept himself noble.

It was the greatest moment of his life. Sitting down, he put his fingers in his ears so Spencer, hopping up and down and shouting far below on the flatlands, could say nothing, nothing at all, to spoil it . . .

14

He was still traveling north, turning into Singapore Road toward North Point. In his ears the metal detector was pinging a strong, unbroken signal at the three-foot-six level. On the controls on the handle O'Yee, moving the squelch button, tightened the sound until it was a continuous whine. He had his eyes fixed firmly on the pavement watching the detector dish as it swept for sounds. Really, people were very good. As they saw him coming and realized something was afoot they got quickly and without demur completely out of his way.

Behind him, tracing the course on a street map, Lim was also very good.

A lot of Chinese cops in full uniform following a Eurasian with a metal detector through the streets they had grown up in would have been embarrassed.

Not good old Lim. He was made of sterner stuff. He didn't know the meaning of the word embarrassed.

Behind him, at the top of his voice, Lim yelled over and over, "Bomb squad! Communist bombs planted in the street!" He kept tapping at his nameplate as he shouted, "P.C. Lim—local boy! No risk too great to keep you all safe!"

Really, the way people ran to give you room to work was very good. It gave you hope for the future of civilization.

The deafening whine changed pitch and O'Yee, stopping in the street, swept the pavement carefully to bring it back to strength.

* * *

NORTH POINT WOMAN IN DEATH FALL
Wrote Last Letter To Husband

Police are treating as suicide the death last night of Mrs. Mata Idris, 51, who fell from the balcony of her eighth-floor apartment in New China Housing Estate block in Pottinger Street, North Point.

It was the redness. It was the redness on the paper, over and over and over as the machine spilled out the words.

It hummed. In the death chamber where he had worked it hummed.

A police spokesman at North Point Station said that Mrs. Idris—

It hummed without cease. In the cocoon, in the redness, in the blood there was no end to the hum, to its loudness, to its insistence, to its increase—to all the papers, red on white, spilling out into the little holder and onto the floor while the machine hummed and hummed.

Redness. Red on white.

—The spokesman said the police were not seeking any other person in connection with the death and that—

It could not be turned off. It grew. It lived. It was her, reaching out.

From the grave—through the machine—she reached out. *The spokesman confirmed that police had taken possession of a letter left in the apartment block by Mrs. Idris—*

He thought he saw an elephant.

That practiced on a fife:

—but declined to reveal its contents.

He looked again.

"Daisy . . ." In Yat's, from the cocoon, from the humming machine, from inside, the voice said softly coaxingly, "Daisy . . ."

Blood. Everywhere inside the cocoon, flowing down the sides and filling it, drowning everything inside, there was the blood and the cries of the birds as the glittering machete cut them to pieces. Heads, wings: the birds had broken up in midair and they were falling like pebbles inside the cocoon.

Falling.

Falling . . .

"Jakob!"

"At length I realize," he said, "the bitterness of life."

NORTH POINT WOMAN IN DEATH FALL
Wrote Last Letter To Husband

Over and over in the cocoon, it hummed. It . . . hummed.

It—
It *consumed*.

"Nei toh-so kei-shi hai uk-k'ei?"
The smell in the apartment was awful. At the door to the bedroom, the caretaker, trying to swallow, said, "I speak English!" His hands were fists in front of him. He was clenching them, gripping hard, holding something back. Behind him the main room of the apartment was dark and curtained. It had not been lived in for some time. He looked down to his polished leather shoes and saw dust under them. The caretaker said, "I'm home most of the day. I'm a lay preacher at the North Point Chinese Baptist Church. I counsel people. They come here. I see what happens in the apartments—" His eyes were starting out of their sockets as he stared up from the floor to the closed bedroom door. "I see people come in who shouldn't be here and I—" The caretaker said, "My name is Shek Pak Kin—Peter Shek—I—I—"

Feiffer said gently, "Harry Feiffer." He had his hand on the doorknob wrapped in a handkerchief. He had holstered his gun. Feiffer said gently, "You don't have to stay."

"I have a duty to stay!"

"No."

"I have a duty to the owners!" He saw Feiffer's face. The eyes were blue, flicking back and forth watching him. He felt small. Standing next to the tall man he felt small, like a child. Peter Shek, brushing back his slicked-down hair, said almost as an excuse, "I knew her: Mrs. Idris. She was a Malay Catholic and she—" He asked suddenly, "Do you even know what she looked like?"

"No."

"She was a middle-aged woman with bad varicose veins! She was dumpy and she wore housecoats and—" The smell was from the bedroom. It was a smell he had never smelled before. It was death. Shek, his hands coming loose from themselves in front of him and starting to fly outward, said suddenly angrily, "Why are you in here if you don't even know what she looked like? This is her house!" He looked back into the room. It was clean, polished. "She wasn't a criminal! She was a respectable tenant!" He was losing control. He wanted to go. There was nowhere to go. He tried to look away from the blue eyes watching him. He tried to read what was in them. Shek, shaking his head, trying to pull away, being held by something invisible—something awful—said on the edge of hysteria, "You're not even the cop who came to see me after she died! You're from somewhere else! You don't even know what she looked like!" Shek said, "She was a good woman! She was lonely! Sometimes—she was a Catholic, not of my religion—sometimes—" He wanted to run. He was anchored to the floor. Everywhere was the awful, thick cloying smell. It was the smell of decaying meat and—somehow—in it, coldness. "—sometimes, on my rounds I heard her door open. I knew she was there. She wanted to talk. She wanted to accidentally run into me and talk—" He waved his hand, "No, not because she was anything to me—she was a respectable woman—but because she was so—because she was lonely." He looked up into the man's face. "Have you any idea how humiliating that must have been for her? Have you ever in your life waited for someone just so you could—" Shek said, "In God's name, what could we have talked about? The *plumbing*?"

"Mr. Shek—"

Shek said suddenly quietly, "Thank you." Beside the tall man he felt small, like a child. He saw Feiffer draw a breath.

"What about her husband?"

"I never saw him." Shek said, "No, I saw him once on the stairs. A small, old man with pale eyes—"

"Cataracts."

"And—" He looked back into the room. It was neat, orderly. There were two chairs. Shek said, "I don't think he came here much. I—" The chairs were waiting for someone to come in to talk. Maybe, time after time, as she opened the door a fraction— Shek said, "I counsel people who can't talk to each other anymore. I—I saw him on the stairs once and I called out to him in English that it was nice outside and he wouldn't need his umbrella and I saw him turn, but he didn't say anything." He said suddenly, distantly, "They don't. Sometimes, people don't. They have it in them, but there's something that stops it and they—" He was talking to a policeman. He said abruptly, efficiently, "I don't know. It's only speculation. I'm only the caretaker."

"Do you believe that someone's spirit can come back?" There was something else in the eyes, something troubled. Shek could not read what it was.

"I believe the soul survives. I believe that the spirit of God moves in people and—"

"Yes." Feiffer said softly, "Have you ever seen anyone dead before?"

"I believe that love and gentleness and time—"

"You don't have to stay."

"—and that understanding and the comfort of fellow children of God, fellow worshippers and communicants—"

"Mr. Shek—Peter—"

He was shaking. His hands were trembling and he could not control them. He felt his mouth start to go. He felt a muscle there, twitching. He felt his bladder begin to ache in a long, terrible pain. Everywhere, everywhere there was the smell. Shek, trying to close his eyes, said softly, "Our Father who art in heaven . . ."

He had no idea how bad it was going to be when he opened the door.

It could not have been worse.

At the doorway, collapsing from the knees so suddenly that Feiffer had to catch him to stop him falling as he saw it, Shek cried out at the top of his voice, "Oh!" He was no longer praying, he was shrieking.

Shek, at the door, looking in, shrieked over and over, "Oh, Jesus! Oh, Jesus! OH, JESUS!"

He lost it.

On the corner of Singapore Road O'Yee, sweeping the pavement with the dish of the metal detector, said abruptly, "I've lost it."

There was only a heavy humming in the earphones. Behind him he saw Lim look at the open street map in his hand and shake his head.

O'Yee said, "I've lost it! It's gone." There was a public telephone box across the street, unoccupied. O'Yee, shaking his head, sweeping the pavement wider and faster, ordered Lim urgently, "Quick! Ring Hurley and ask him where the hell it goes from here!" They had come across a full half mile from the station. O'Yee said with his head full of the humming, "Now! Do it now! Ring Hurley and find out where the hell it goes!"

Whatever it had been on the bed, it had been cut to pieces. Everywhere there was blood. Whatever it had been on the bed had been dead for a week.

It had been Idris. It had been a man with pale, cataracted eyes. The first blow with the machete had almost severed his head from his neck and, after that, as he writhed, the machete had fallen across him at least another twenty times. Once, the sheet he had been lying on wearing only his pajama pants had been white—it was black and crusted with blood.

The smell was the flies. They had begun to breed.

Feiffer said quickly, "Ring Yellowthread Street Station and get me some backup." He was still holding the man across the chest. He felt his chest heave. He felt him start to retch. It was out, loose, the smell—it was like a fog. Shek, shaking, heard the flies start to rise up. Feiffer, helping the man, nodding to him, said firmly, "Not here. Don't ring from here. Go down to your own apartment and ring from there." He saw the man's eyes. They were not seeing anything. Feiffer, taking him by the shoulder and forcing him around to look at him, said clearly, not in English but in Cantonese, "Is there a toilet on this floor?"

"What?"

"Is there a toilet on this floor you can use?"

"Yes."

"Then use it. Don't run. Go to the toilet first and if you want to throw up, throw up. Don't hurry. And then go to your apartment and ring the station." He saw the man nod. "Yellowthread Street Station in Hong Bay, not North Point, and then stay in your apartment and wait."

"Yes." He tried to speak English, but he had forgotten all the words. Peter Shek—Shek Pak Kin—said, "Hai. Hai. *Yes!*" He tried to be someone he thought he was. Shek, shaking his head, not knowing why he asked, putting his hand to his hair to try to think, asked, "Will you be all right?" In the bedroom, one of the hands had almost been completely severed from the arm. It hung down on a bloody sinew, swarming with small black flies as if it had been a ribbon. Whatever it was in the bed had shrunk. It had receded into the bed, become small in death, like a child. His hands were shaking. He could not control them. He wanted— He wanted as he had always wanted to be kind.

It was not, this time, his turn.

"Thank you. Thank you very much." He forced himself— because he might have to some other time in the future at some other place—to look.

He stopped shaking. He became who he had always hoped he might be.

Shek said quickly, "I'll ring your station. Yellowthread Street Station, Hong Bay. Rely on me." He nodded. Shek, still nodding, turning to go, remembering what it was he had been told to do, said to the room, "Rely on me."

It passed. He had seen it and it had passed. He was a lay preacher at the North Point Chinese Baptist Church. Doing what he did best, he went quickly and without detouring to the toilets to call for help.

* * *

At his desk in the Detectives' Room, Auden looked at the wall. It had a large hole knocked in it.

He shrugged. Such things happened. So what? In the cells downstairs he heard Spencer call up, "There's a hole down here off the cells in the basement!"

"Hmm." Auden, yawning, said without interest, "Really?"

He yawned again.

He shrugged.

He sniffed.

He bathed in nobility.

The phone on his desk rang and, always at the service of the poor downtrodden peasantry, his chivalry gleaming like a grail, craning a little forward on his chair to stop his arse hurting, Auden the First, lending his ear, asked kindly—majestically— "Yes . . . ?"

Coming back from the phone box out of breath, Lim said, "Singapore Lane. It turns off left into Singapore Lane." He pointed down at the pavement. "Setts. The bricks set in the pavement and on the road are handmade nineteenth-century bricks—it's the only street in the entire area that hasn't been ripped up or redeveloped or bombed. Hurley says the old gas pipes come down here and they start to divide down the end here." He looked at the end of the lane. The end of the lane marked the beginning of the new Japanese shopping town development. "He says you've probably got your depth on the detector at three foot six or two feet—the gas pipe here is only twelve inches below the surface! The old part of the station and Singapore Lane—they're the only two intact nineteenth-century features left in the entire area!" He was shouting at O'Yee to make himself heard above the traffic and the earphones. "Set your depth at twelve inches!"

"Okay." It came back, the pinging. The hum died, became thinner, turned into a whine and, at exactly twelve inches, the pinging came back.

It was louder, tighter. It sounded close. O'Yee, sweeping the pavement and finding the sound everywhere as it echoed and bounced off the detector dish, said, pointing, "That way! It goes straight down that way on the left-hand side of the pavement." It was the nineteenth century. It was twelve inches below his feet. Starting to break into a run, O'Yee going forward, followed it.

* * *

Whoever had done it had had a key or been staying there. There was nothing in the apartment that displayed any sign of a forced entry. The apartment was as Mrs. Idris had probably left it ten days ago: clean, polished, orderly. Only the flies had come in secretly and they rose up as he moved in the bedroom in swarms. They were breeding, infesting the corpse. He touched at Idris's shoulder, trying to move it to one side with his handkerchief clamped over his nose, and the flies rose up around him in swarms.

The smell was awful. It was everywhere in the room, moving out into the rest of the apartment like a fog. It moved out with the flies. It was the sickly, thick rancid smell of decay and bad meat and it turned his stomach.

Whoever had done it had been in the apartment for some time. He had known who it was, felt comfortable enough with them to stay in his pajamas or close his door as they stayed in the main room. They had not been staying over: there was no divan or couch in the main room, nothing in the bathroom cabinet that should not have been there or had not been purchased some time ago and, when the first blow had caught him in the neck, Idris had been lying alone in the center of the bed. All the pillows had been piled up into one stack: he had been lying there alone thinking or reading or calling to someone. Then, after it had been over, they had gone into the bathroom, washed the blood off, cleaned up the bathroom again and, changing the clothes they had come in or discarding something they had put on over their clothes, they had gone again, silently, unseen, out through the main door.

In the cupboards in the bedroom there were women's clothes. They were housecoats and slippers and underwear—they were the clothes of a dumpy housebound woman who listened at doorways for someone to talk to. She had been dead ten days. The thing on the bed had been dead for a week. In that time, no one had come. In all her life, waiting at the door, no one had come for Mrs. Idris either. The smell of decay was not only coming from the bed and the dead man and the flies—it had been in there a long time as, little by little, day by day, hiding, waiting, hoping, she also had decayed. He went back to the bed and looked down hard and carefully at the corpse.

The second blow had caught him on the side of the chest as he had writhed as his neck pumped blood. The second blow had opened his chest. It was a home for the flies. Then he had twisted back and the third blow had hit his hip as he doubled it up, the fourth and fifth the severed arm and then, after he was dead— after he had stopped moving—the blows had come at spaced, timed intervals up and down his body and striped him like a flaying. Feiffer tried to put his hand under the shoulder to move the body a fraction, but the smell was too bad and he recoiled. In the room, through the handkerchief, Feiffer said, "God Jesus—" He wanted to throw up. He tried again and got his hand flat under the shoulder and felt something wet and viscous where the blood had soaked through the mattress and puddled on the bed support.

The eyes stared up at him. They were pale, milky with cataracts, dried out. There were fly eggs everywhere on the face. The face was no longer a face but a flat picture of a face. He pushed a little harder under the shoulder and felt something hard. It was a cheap ballpoint pen covered in blood.

All he wanted to do was get out of the room and throw up. The smell was everywhere in the apartment. All the windows were closed. Reaching under farther, feeling his hand touch something soft and wet, he retrieved the notebook Idris had been writing in when he had been killed.

He read only the word NOTES printed in gold on the leatherette cover before the smell finally got to him and, gagging and dry retching, he had to run to a window in the main room and smash the lock open with the butt of his gun to get it open to breathe.

At the open door to the caretaker's apartment on the first floor, Spencer, banging hard to attract someone's attention, called out in Cantonese, "Hullo! Is anyone there?" There was no one. The apartment was empty, deserted. He asked Auden in English, urgently, "Phil, this is North Point. It isn't our precinct. Did the caller say it was Harry or not?"

"Yes!" Auden, glancing up and down the corridor, banging on other doors, said, "Yes!"

"What apartment is he in?"

"I didn't ask!"

"Why not?"

"Because I didn't, that's all!" He was at the apartment door three numbers away, pounding on the knocker. Like all the other apartments on the floor, there was no one there. Auden, going down the line banging at first one door and then the next without waiting for a response, yelled, "He said he'd meet us here!" He saw someone turn into the corridor eight doors away and he snapped at him in Cantonese. "You! Where the hell's the caretaker?" He saw the man's face. Auden going toward him said, "Shek? Are you Shek the caretaker?" He saw traces of vomit on the man's shirt where he had thrown up. Auden, dreading what they were going to have to see, said as the man, nodding, came quickly toward him, "Oh Christ . . . Oh Christ, not *today*!"

In his little office on the third floor of Police Headquarters on Artillery Road, Hurley had all the old maps spread across his table. He had a clear line drawn through Singapore Lane. He followed it with his finger until it slipped off the edge and joined Map 567A on the 1899 Authorized Street Map of the southern parishes of Hong Kong. There was no Map 567A. There were, these days, no more parishes. He had an old map done by the Japanese that almost joined the section, but all the streets seemed to have been changed or bulldozed through to make military supply lines or holding areas or perimeters and even if he could have made sense of the Japanese characters, all the names of the roads and streets and perimeters were in code.

He found one street on the map for some reason marked in English. The name of the street was All Conquering Victorious Army Street. He had absolutely no idea what street on the 1899 map it had represented or, now, forty years later, what street—if any, if it was even still there—in the midst of nonstop development what street it represented now. It was hopeless. In Singapore Lane O'Yee was on his own. After that, like the old maritime maps of the unknown world there were only dragons.

He looked again. He could find nothing.

Hurley, useless at even that simple, small task for a historian, said in disgust, "Damn it! God bloody *damn it*!"

"*Twenty-eight!*"

It was a cry of pain, of terror.

"AARAGG—RAAG!"

In the cocoon, it penetrated.

"Twenty-eight! Twenty-*eight*!"

In the cocoon, where all the movement had stopped and there was only waiting, there was a whisper, a rasp. There was the glitter of something blue-black and then something silver.

The silver thing was a machete.

The cocoon waited, the redness glowing.

There was a whisper, a rasp.

"*Twenty-eight!*"

It was a scream of approaching terror.

". . . Jakob . . ."

Over and over, in the bedroom where he lay on the bed making his notes, over and over he heard the woman in the housecoat call to him.

He had heard her.

He had not come.

"*Twenty-eight!*"

In the cocoon, the machete's edge glittered like ice.

"Apartment number eight one six!" In the corridor Shek, trying to wipe his mouth, said urgently, "He told me to wait here. It's apartment eight one six!"

He saw Auden and Spencer begin to run for the elevators. He saw the big one, the one who limped, touch at the butt of his gun under his coat.

The door to his apartment was still open. From it as they found an open elevator, Shek yelled, "He told me to wait here!" He had even used the toilet on the corridor rather than his own as he had been told.

He could not face it again.

He did not have to.

Shek called out, "He told me to wait here!" He only wanted to get inside to be alone to pray. Shek called as the elevator doors closed behind them, "It's different for you—you're used to it!" All he wanted to do was pray. "You're used to it!"

Shek, at his open door, afraid to go in, not knowing what to say to God, said softly, sadly in his native Cantonese, "It's different . . . It's different for people like you."

It was a new notebook and he had only just begun on the first page when it had happened.

On the page there were only five words.

They were *Podargus strigoides*
            Frogmouth
            Sick

In the bedroom Feiffer looked down at it. On the bed there was what was left of a tiny old man who had carried an umbrella

against sunspots and who—part-time, trusted, working alone—
had legally, efficiently and humanely slaughtered anything Quarantine had taken.

Podargus strigoides
Frogmouth
Sick

They were four words. They were what it was, what it had
been and— And the fifth word what had happened to it.

Podargus strigoides . . .

Frogmouth . . .

Sick . . .

—*Cured.*

In the awful room with the flies swarming over the thing on the
bed, with the caked blood and viscera all over his hand and the
notebook, Feiffer, his eyes unable to move away from the single
word, wondered with no hope in the world of knowing, where—
where in hell—the strange, alien, ragged, fierce, hidden little bird
was now . . .

In the cocoon, in the redness, the machete glittered like ice. The
blue-black thing was the Webley .455 revolver from Quarantine.
NORTH POINT WOMAN IN DEATH FALL

It was heavy, crude. Like the machete, it was for killing.

Stillness and silence.

In the cocoon, there was only the whispering.

15

On the phone in the bedroom Feiffer said formally and clearly to Detective Chief Inspector Osgood at North Point Station, "It's a male Malay in his late sixties with cataracts on both eyes who's been dead about a week in a sealed room. The body appears to have about twenty to thirty deep machete or sword-type wounds from the larynx area of the neck continuing in an irregular pattern from the right to the left side of the body and across to the right hand and arm." He was looking down at Idris trying not to see him. "The right hand is almost severed from the body and there are numerous areas of arterial and venous blood on the bed he's lying on, the walls and the floor." He heard Osgood suck in his breath. "Flies have begun to breed in the wounds." Feiffer, properly, almost primly, said officially, "It's your district, not mine. If you want it regulations say you should have it. Do you want it?" In the main room and kitchen, Auden and Spencer were searching. He heard Spencer in the kitchen opening drawers and pulling their contents out. Feiffer said tightly, "On a scale of one to ten it's ten." Feiffer said, "You're the first call I've put in. If you want it it's up to you to call Scientific and Medical. I'll take my people and hand over the notes and—"

Osgood said, "Keep it." Osgood said, clearing his throat, "Thanks for telling me." Osgood said, "Keep it."

"We haven't disturbed anything and the caretaker let me in with a key. If you want to take it over all you have to do is just

153

come over here and we'll pass it over to you and you can have it—"

Osgood said, "Keep it!"

"If you handled the suicide—"

Osgood said, "His name is Idris, wife Mata Idris—"

"What happened to her?"

"She went out a window." Osgood said abruptly, "She went out a window about ten days ago while he was out at work, during the day. He worked part-time at—"

"At the Quarantine Station."

"When we got there she was plastered all over the pavement from eight stories up, a neighbor or the caretaker had rung him and he was just arriving on a bus." There was a silence. Osgood said, "Yeah, on a bus. Maybe his van was on the blink. I don't know. He had one. I checked with a Customs guy I know at Quarantine." He said quickly, getting rid of it, "It was exactly what it seemed to be: there were no signs of a struggle in the apartment, she had been treated lately by her local doctor for depression, she was wearing a housecoat that looked like it had been worn day and night for the last six months, the autopsy showed she hadn't eaten a meal for a day or so, so she wasn't living the high life—" Osgood said abruptly, "No joke intended— and there weren't the usual exotic little clues Sherlock Holmes would have found to prove she wasn't planning it like theater tickets for tomorrow night, air tickets for Timbuktu or CIA poison pellets or bullet wounds in her left ear and, therefore, she was, nice and simple, easy and straightforward, usual, run-of-the-mill, common or garden-variety suicide." Osgood said, "And her husband arrived by bus. By the sound of it if I had been her I would have jumped long ago."

"What was he like?"

"Idris?" There was a silence. There was some other reason Osgood didn't want the case. Osgood said, "I don't know. I hardly spoke to him."

In the kitchen, Spencer said loudly, "Phil, look at this!"

Osgood said, "Are you searching the place?"

"My people are here."

"Then it's definitely yours. Once you've started on the scene—"

"You must have spoken to him!"

"I said about two hundred words to him and he said about two to me!" Osgood said, "It was a suicide plain and simple!" He was getting angry. Osgood said, "Harry, I didn't like him, she obviously didn't like him and, for all I know, nobody in the entire world liked him, but that didn't mean he killed his wife because he didn't, and, because he didn't, he wasn't obliged to say any more than two words to me! He called me sir, he was polite, he wasn't there when it happened and when I asked him if his wife had been under a doctor's care he said yes, gave me the man's name and volunteered nothing." Osgood said, "He worked at the killing grounds out at Quarantine. He had pale, cataracted eyes and he talked in a rasping voice that I had to strain to hear and forced me to lean close to him and that—that I didn't care for!"

"Was there a lover involved?"

Osgood said, "No."

"What about his side?"

"Does it matter?"

"It matters!"

"I don't think so."

"Was there or wasn't there?"

"I don't know! It was a suicide! It doesn't matter why it happened! My job was just to make sure that it did happen and that it was what it appeared to be!" Osgood said tersely, "It was. It was the suicide of a desperately unhappy, probably neurotic middle-aged housewife in a block of apartments who didn't know or didn't care that if she threw herself out from eight stories up it was going to take her a long time to get down and when she did get down her head would go like a watermelon hit with a sledgehammer!" Osgood, losing control, said, "All right? Are you happy now? She looked like nothing on earth—she looked bloody awful—probably almost as bad as what you're looking at now— and what you're looking at now got off a bus, walked over to her and me, looked down as if he saw death every day of his life— which he did, slaughtering poor, bloody dumb animals—and just stood there like a good little boy with those eyes of his waiting for me to ask him questions—which he answered politely and courteously and in order, one at a time!" Osgood said, "He had something wrong with his voice. He had to work to make himself heard. I leaned down to hear him and all the time I did his eyes didn't blink once!" Osgood said, "If he had been speaking Cantonese I could have got one of my Chinese officers to talk to him, but he wasn't: he was Malay, he spoke English, so he talked to me!"

"Why has it unnerved you, Charlie?"

"It hasn't unnerved me! If you say the case is ours I'll do it!"

"I don't mean that, I mean him."

"He didn't unnerve me! People don't unnerve me!" Osgood said, "Harry, I'm six foot two and two hundred pounds and I've been a cop for twenty years and I've killed two men in firefights and I've—" There was a silence. In the bedroom, the smell was beginning to dissipate through the smashed window. The flies had settled. They were breeding. Osgood said, "I just—"

"Was there any mention of birds?"

"Of what? Of *birds*?"

"Yes."

"You mean, as in flap-flap?"

"As in flap-flap."

"No. Why?"

There was a silence.

It was a silence Osgood did not care for. Osgood, his voice still low, said tightly, "It was weird, Harry: the whole thing. I've seen a lot of reactions to death and there he was just standing there about five foot nothing looking as if the first breeze would blow him away, but he—" Osgood said curiously, "I'm six foot two, Harry and I could have . . ." Osgood said, "He was weird, frightening." It seemed to surprise him to say it: "He just stood there, an old, half-blind old man saying yes sir, no sir and—" Osgood said, "And he frightened the living hell out of all my Chinese officers and he frightened the living hell out of me!"

"*Why?*"

"The silence. He was talking to me, answering my questions, but he—" Osgood said, "You know when you talk to people the silences are—the silences are—the silences aren't part of what—" Osgood said, "I don't know. I can't work it out! You're the third or fourth person I've said I'm six foot two and two hundred pounds to and that I've—" Osgood said, "You know when people talk they say things to hide what they're really thinking in the silences. That was him! That was what he was! He—" Osgood said, "All the time he talked to me, all the time I leaned down to hear him, all the yes sirs and no sirs, all the answers and questions, I heard it! For the first time in my life I heard it in someone—I heard all the silences!" Osgood said, "And . . . and it frightened the shit out of me!"

"What was in the letter? The newspapers said the text wasn't released. It must have been released at the inquest."

"It was. It was in an envelope addressed to him by his wife. It was left, not in the bedroom or on a table or a desk, but on the veranda." Osgood said, "She must have stood there with it in her hand for a long time and then just dropped it onto the ground before she jumped." Osgood said, "You keep this case, Harry. You do what you want with it. You tear that place to pieces because nothing on earth would get me back in there again!"

"What did the letter say?"

"Nothing." Osgood said tightly, "Nothing at all. The envelope was addressed to her husband and sealed, and when we opened it there was a single sheet of paper in it." He fell silent for a moment. "It was blank, Harry. It was the sum total of their lives together, everything she wanted to say to him before she died, all the recriminations and explanations and—" Osgood said, "And it was totally, utterly, one hundred percent *blank*! That was their life together. That was what it all came down to. Even at the last, even when she could have said whatever she liked and because she was going to be dead when he read it it would have been listened to as something important, even then it was totally, completely *blank*!" Osgood said, "And he arrived on a bus to look at what the fall had done to her and he was extremely polite and he tried to speak up so I could hear him without straining." He sounded, at the other end of the line, smaller. Osgood said in an awful, strangled voice, "God, Harry, isn't that the most ghastly thing you've ever heard of in your life?"

Osgood said, "God . . . God only knows what their life together must have been like—God only knows!"

He had found it in an old 1898 copy of Stringer's *History of Hong Kong*. He had found the date the gas lights had been turned on in the city. January the first, 1865. He had also found a dog-eared, hand-drawn little booklet from North Point Division from 1866, a constable's beat book giving all the beats through the streets and the names of all the buildings of importance that had to be checked.

In his office in Headquarters on Artillery Road, Hurley began going through the pages one by one. The booklet was on rice paper to be carried in the tight uniform of the day and he had to be careful turning the pages. In those days the constables had carried .450 caliber single shot Martini rifles painted with a layer of protective grease against the humidity. On page eighteen— Beat Number Eleven—where the names of the streets were carefully written out in English and Chinese there was a stain from the grease where, at some time, for some reason, the constable who had carried the book had got it out quickly with his rifle in his other hand to find something. The page, like the grease, was old, ancient, from another century.

He went through the pages, following the streets: Jordan, Watchman's, Ice House, Battery, Kan Su—he found the boundary Yellowthread Street made into Hong Bay—Waterloo, Yuet Loi, Phoenix, Kwong Wah Street, Singapore Road, Singapore Lane. The booklet had everything important listed: shops, private homes, the warehouses and banks, money lenders, public works. He found a single mark on Map 21 as Singapore Lane went north into Hanford Hill Road and then twisted away toward Central in the middle of the island. It looked like an additional mark put in by the man who had carried the rifle.

It was a single character scribbled in pencil.

It was the character for *Gas*. It was to one side of Hanford Hill with an arrow pointing east into Temple Street.

The booklet had been owned by someone called Constable Chee. He had done it. It was the direction of the gasworks in case of an emergency or a leak.

In his office, turning the pages two at a time, following the direction of the arrow through all the streets and lanes, Hurley tried to follow the little hand-drawn arrow to its source.

He lost it. At the end of Singapore Lane, all the sound in the detector stopped and he lost it.

In front of him where Singapore Lane branched out into Hanford Hill and right into Temple Street, the road had been ripped up to make way for new development. The development was going into the old warehouse area bounded by Wylie Street and the old public square to the east. The area had been condemned. It was an area of old, prewar warehouses and godowns for the spice and silk trade. It was closed off by Department of Main Roads cordons and cement pylons in the middle of the roads to stop traffic.

The signal had stopped.

He listened.

He heard only a humming.

O'Yee, looking first one way and then the other, into Hanford Hill, Temple Street—down into the empty, rubbish-blowing canyons between the blackened wooden and brick buildings from a century ago—said desperately to Lim at the street map, "Lim?"

He didn't know. He guessed. Lim said, "Straight ahead into

Temple Street!" He listened. He heard the humming. Following O'Yee as he went into the closed-off street, past the gray pylons, into the blowing rubbish and the sudden silence of all the dead buildings, gripping the street map hard in his hand, he heard only the humming.

It pinged. In the silence, he heard it.

It pinged. It picked up the metal pipe under the street and it pinged. O'Yee said in triumph, "Got it!" He looked back at Lim.

He was running, trying to keep pace with O'Yee as he moved faster and faster, following the sound, hearing it get louder and louder.

Lim shouted above the sound, "Straight ahead! Straight down toward Godown Street!" He had found something on his map. It was not part of the modern map at all, but because it was about to be torn down anyway, an insert from an old original map printed directly onto the modern streets. It showed arrows, lines, symbols. It showed a single faded word in type almost too small to read and a Chinese character overlayed on it from what, surprisingly, looked like an old constable's beat book of the type he himself still used.

The character read *Gas*.

Lim, running, hearing the pinging through the earphones as O'Yee followed it, yelled, "Yes! Straight on!"

The pinging turned into a single screaming high-pitched note. Lim, running with it, yelled, "Go! *Go!*"

It was a photograph. It had been hidden in the cutlery drawer, held there by a single tiny square of plastic tape upside down under the paper lining so nobody would find it. In the kitchen, Spencer, holding it out for Auden to see, said curiously, "What is it? It looks like some sort of white rock or cement cut out to make a seat." There was what appeared to be some sort of clinker-built boat behind it. There was a sign on the clinker-built boat in English and Chinese and Urdu and some other language that had come out blurred.

The sign read, NOAH'S ARK.

It was a chair.

It was a family photograph.

It was a little out of focus, blurred.

The person sitting in the chair, looking straight into the camera lens, was smiling.

* * *

He found it. It had been on the corner of Shanghai Street and Market Lane. *Hong Bay Gas and Light, Station Two.*

It was the substation. It was not the main gas-generating plant at all, but a storage substation that had been built later, probably when the constable had made the arrow. The arrow was to show that there was some possible danger and the direction it might come, or to show that—

Hong Bay Gas and Light, Station Two.

It was there.

It was at the corner of Shanghai Street and Market Lane. It was intact. It had survived the nineteenth century and half of the twentieth and more, it had survived the bombing and the war. Hurley, correlating it with a modern map, said, *"Christ!"*

It was there. It was on the modern map. It was listed on his modern police map as warehouses and light engineering businesses due for demolition and redevelopment. It was there.

He had no way of getting in touch with O'Yee unless he or Lim rang back.

The phone on his desk was silent.

Hurley, the maps in his hands, ready, staring hard at the phone, willing it, said as a command, "Ring! *Ring!*"

There was something else in the photograph. It was a dog, a Labrador. Curled up to one side of the chair, gazing up at the person in the chair, it seemed to be contentedly sleeping.

> *He thought he saw an Elephant*
> *That practiced on a fife:*
> *He looked again, and found it was*
> *A letter from his wife.*
> *"At length I realize," he said,*
> *"The bitterness of life."*

It was in English. It was from Lewis Carroll's *Sylvie and Bruno*. It was written in a woman's hand. It was a poem on the back of a photograph that had been hidden.

It was a photograph of someone sitting in a wishing chair and smiling.

It was a photograph taken in the Wishing Chair at Yat's.

Feiffer said suddenly, "When he came by bus, was he carrying an umbrella?"

Osgood said, "No. Why?"

Why was because he never went anywhere without it. Why was because she had gone over the edge ten days ago, and, when Osgood or one of his constables had rung him at Quarantine to tell him to come home urgently he had been putting the frogmouth in the van—he had put the umbrella in the van with it ready to drive somewhere—and it had got damaged. Even his damned ghost—if that was what it had been—carried the umbrella. *He had come by bus because the frogmouth was flying free in the van.* It had got caught up, damaged itself, and one of its feathers had been caught in the closed umbrella, the umbrella that had lain unused until—until— Feiffer said urgently, "What else do you know about him? Anything—anything at all!"

"All I know is what a pal at Customs told me plus the usual background. He was a part-time contract worker with the destruction section of Quarantine—a law unto himself because evidently the vet there has a weak stomach—"

Feiffer said, "Hoosier. The vet's name is Hoosier."

"Is it? I didn't talk to him. And that he was sixty-eight years old and, according to my pal, very fucking taciturn, very fucking silent and—" Osgood drew a breath, "—very fucking weird!" There was a silence on the other end of the line. He wanted more. Osgood said, "From what I gather, from what my pal gathered—"

Feiffer said, "Charlie, you had your pal look up his personnel file!"

"That's not legal."

"You did it anyway!"

"Harry, if you'd seen him—"

"I have seen him! I can see him now! He's lying here on the bed like a goddamned squashed cockroach! I'm standing in the middle of his stink!" Feiffer said, "You didn't just ask your pal about him. He worried you. You did a full background on him! Now, who the hell was he?"

"He didn't murder her, she fucking jumped!"

"I know she fucking jumped! She wasn't the only one! You fucking jumped! You took one look at him and your goddamned blood ran cold!" Feiffer said quickly, "I would have done the same! You did a full background check on him and then after you did it, to get flesh on the bones, you rang up everyone you knew who might have run across him!" Feiffer said, shouting, "Charlie, I've got nothing here! *I don't even know his first name!*"

"Jakob. His first name was Jakob." He didn't have to look it up, he knew. Osgood, speaking formally, reciting it line by line from all the times he had thought about it, said, "Jakob Idris, age sixty-eight, Malay origin, resident in Hong Kong thirty-three years, employed as part-time contract specialist labor at Quarantine Station, Hong Bay, original occupation company director, wife Mata, currently deceased, no suspicious circumstances." Osgood said softly, abruptly, "He didn't make my blood run cold, Harry, he frightened me. I don't know why. I don't know how he did it, but he frightened me. I looked at him and I knew that he was something that should have frightened me." Osgood said tightly, "I thought he might have been someone who— I thought—" Osgood said, "But he was as clean as a whistle. All he was, all he was before he was what he was when I met him was a company director of a light engineering works here in North Point. I thought—" Osgood said, "The Idris Garden Implement and Engineering Works—ridiculous. He'd owned the place about twenty-five years and evidently done a fair trade—it wasn't a public company, it wasn't listed on the exchange, but my pal checked with the export section of Customs and it was doing all right until the Americans started doing more and more legal business with China and the Chinese started making the sort of things he made at about one-fifth of the cost." Osgood said simply, "He went broke. One of the guys in the companies squad said that there had been a suggestion that his partner had absconded with the company's funds, but if it was true Idris didn't lay a charge." Osgood said, "He did say something else when I spoke to him. I said something about death—I don't even remember what it was, something bloody saccharine and according to the manual of what to say to distressed relatives—and he said in a whisper, 'like wind, like wings.' " Osgood said, "I was bending down to talk to him. He took a single step back when he said it and smiled at me." Osgood said, "That was when my blood ran cold, that was when—" He said with irritation, embarrassment, "Why the hell am I telling you this? What the hell have I got to do with anything? I'm a cop! I'm supposed to be the opaque bloody repository for bloody bald statements by people I interview. I'm not a participant, I'm a goddamned neutral, unemotional, untouchable observer!"

"What sort of factory was it? Was it big?"

"He made goddamned shovels! It was somewhere up in the redevelopment area. He didn't even have a long lease on it. When the business went bust the lease had about eighteen months to run. Eighteen months ago when the development was in the planning stage the developers were paying millions to buy leases. They didn't have to buy his: they just had to wait and let it run out. It's due to run out in about three weeks." Osgood said, "I don't know—should I feel sorry for him? Maybe he was a man who, all down the line, had had life kick him in the teeth." Osgood, losing control, going too far into it, said, "I don't know! I'm not going to tell you anything else because anything else is just speculation!" Osgood said, "You've got it! You want it! You fucking do it!"

"How big was the factory?"

"It was the old gasworks at the corner of Godown Street and Tung Kun Street! I didn't go there! It was all closed up! He had the whole place for the business! The business failed! He was going to expand into the lawn mower business or the bloody bulldozer business or something so he leased the entire building, but the tide of bloody world politics overtook him and what he had was just a bloody great empty—"

Feiffer said tightly, "*Aviary.*"

Osgood said, "What?"

Feiffer asked almost casually, "Did he make machetes along with his rakes and his shovels, Charlie?"

"I suppose so." Osgood said, "What are you talking about? Has this got something to do with Yat's? *You're not saying he did that?*" Somehow, it would have made everything clear. Somehow, it would almost have been a relief. Osgood, sounding anxious, said with hope, "*Are you saying he did all that at Yat's?*"

"I'm saying—"

It made sense of it. It made sense of it all. It made sense of the way a six-foot-two man had felt when a tiny, pale-eyed old man had said something to him in a whisper. Osgood, seizing it, said quickly, "He wasn't some poor bloody victim of life! He was the one who did the victimizing!" Osgood said, "Even his poor bloody daughter—even her— He put her in the bloody loony bin with the way he was!"

"What daughter?"

Spencer, at the door to the bedroom, holding up the photograph, said urgently, "Harry—"

"*What fucking daughter?*"

"The one in the loony bin in St. Paul de Chartres hospital! I couldn't get to talk to her! I only found out she even bloody existed when I saw the funeral notice in the paper!" Osgood, reaching hard for something to hang on to, looking for a way out, said as a command, "Look around! There isn't even a bed in the bloody apartment for her! He must have put her in, thrown away everything that even reminded him or his wife of her and then, as if she had ceased to exist—"

"Why is she in St. Paul's?"

"Depression. She's not a fucking loony. She's a sort of come-and-go patient who never goes. She—" Osgood said, realizing where it was leading, "No, it wasn't her, no."

He had the photo. Spencer, putting it into Feiffer's hand, said again, "Harry—"

"Harry, she—" Osgood, at the other end of the line, said, "No. No. No!" There was a limit. He had come to it. It wasn't possible. Osgood said over and over, "No! No! No!"

He looked down at the photo. It was of Yat's. It was of the Wishing Chair at Yat's. He saw the dog sleeping by the chair with a blur where, even it its sleep, before it had been gutted in the rain, its tail wagged for anyone who came to it. It was her. Sitting in the chair, half smiling on a day a long, long time ago, it was her.

Osgood said in desperation, too much threatened, too much unsure, unknowing, incapable of dealing with it, with what it all meant if it was true, "Harry, for Christ's sake, *she's only fourteen years old!*"

It was her. She was the one. In the photo, taken years ago, taken when she was about eleven or twelve, sitting on the Wishing Chair, she was smiling. It was her. On the bed, Idris's hand had almost been severed from the wrist. It hung down covered in flies, by a single ribbon of sinew.

On the other end of the line, Osgood, in the terrible hush, said desperately, "Harry! Harry, *are you still there?*"

He found it. There, at the corner of Godown and Tung Kun streets, in the deserted rubbish-blowing, closed-off roads and lanes of the development area, he found it. Now, on a peeling derelict wooden sign above the boarded-up windows and doors, the brick, warehouselike building read IDRIS GARDEN IMPLEMENT AND ENGINEERING WORKS.

In his ears, the pinging reached a crescendo and then stopped.

O'Yee, taking the headphones from his ears, in the faint wind through the deserted, silent street, listened.

He saw Lim's face.

He listened.

He heard no sound at all.

He listened.

* * *

She had killed them. All of them. In the cocoon, with her hand and wrist moving and tensing as she held the machete, she heard her mother call. *"Jakob!"*

She heard her call.

"Jakob—!"

She heard her call.

"JAK-OB!"

She heard her.

She saw her.

She heard her go in silence as she fell: she saw it in her mind.

"JAKOB—!"

He lay on the bed writing something.

He wrote a note.

She wrote a note.

What he was writing was what she had written.

"He thought he saw an Elephant—"

She wrote it. She stood beside her mother as the pencil she used wrote it on the back of the photograph. She saw her mother look up at her. She was not crying. She was writing all the lines of the poem and she was weeping.

"JAKOB!" She heard her call.

"JAKOB! JAKOB!"

She had killed everything. There was more. She had killed everything and still there was more and more and more—

"JAKOB!" She was weeping. Her mother was weeping with tears rolling down her face and in the kitchen where she wrote, she was shaking her head writing the words and weeping.

The machete, in the cocoon—in the room where the machine, over and over printed the single square of paper she had cut out from the newspaper over and over—the machete gleamed like an icicle.

He had looked at her once as he lay on the bed writing down what her mother had written, he had looked with his blind, unseeing eyes at the keys she had gotten from somewhere, and then—

Then she had killed him.

"Daisy . . ."

In the rain, holding the umbrella in the darkness, she had called softly. The iron bar and the machete were on the ground beside her.

"Daisy . . ."

In the cocoon, his rasping soft whisper called, "Daisy . . ." He knew all their names.

"Daisy . . ."

"Daisy . . ."

"*JAKOB!*"

In the cocoon, in the redness, in the factory, she waited.

"*JAKOB—!*"

There was no sound and no one knew she was there.

"Godown Street and Tung Kun Street?"

On the phone, Osgood, knowing now he would have to take what it was that had been left there in that awful apartment, said quickly, "Yes."

"What the hell's her bloody *name*?"

"She's fourteen years old!" Osgood said, "Mata! Her name is Mata—Mata Idris—the same as her poor bloody mother!" Osgood, shrieking, everything he had ever believed in—himself—gone, gone forever, yelled, "What else? What the fucking bloody goddamned hell *else*?"

She touched at the blade and felt its edge. In the redness, in the darkness, it glittered like ice. She touched at the gun and felt its weight.

In a photograph once, in it now, she smiled. The dog beside her by the chair, even though it was asleep, was wagging its tail.

It dreamed its dreams.

In the blackness of the unlit, boarded building, she dreamed hers.

"*Twenty-eight!*"

He heard it.

O'Yee, touching at his gun, put his shoulder a little to the closed corrugated iron door at the main entrance to the place.

The door gave. It was open.

O'Yee said to Lim with his hand wet with perspiration around the butt of his gun in its holster, "Wait here. You wait here."

He listened.

He heard it.

O'Yee, steeling himself, giving an order, said a moment before he pushed in the door and went in, "Wait here. Whatever happens, you—" He saw Lim's face.

O'Yee said with a sudden, inexplicable, urgent anger, "You! *You just wait here!*"

16

"**G**et the shotgun out of your car and ride with me!" Outside the New China Apartments as Auden ran to his car, Feiffer ordered Spencer, "You two ride with me! You drive, Bill!" He saw Auden working the lock on the boot of his car. He saw him limping. Feiffer yelled, "Are you all right?" He saw Auden nod hard. Feiffer ordered him, "Move! Move!"

Spencer still had the photograph in his hand. He looked down at it. At the other car the shortened pump action 12 gauge was coming out. He saw Auden pull it free and cock it in a single motion. Spencer said urgently, "Harry—she's only fourteen years old!"

Feiffer ordered him, "Drive!" He saw Spencer's face. "It's not for her!" He ordered Auden, closing the boot, "Run! *Run!*"

All the windows and doors were boarded up. Only the main entrance seemed opened and it had two sheets of corrugated iron nailed onto it. At the old gasworks, O'Yee, putting his arm against it and pushing, felt it give. He listened. There was nothing, no sound. Through the inch he got the door open he could see only darkness. He had been shouting orders at Lim. He felt his mouth go dry. In the darkness there was nothing. O'Yee said quietly to Lim two feet behind him, "Wait here." There was nothing, no one around but them. He looked back up and down the street and saw only empty canyons and papers and rubbish blowing in eddies in the ground currents. It was not a two-story

167

building, it was a building two stories high without a second-floor level. Inside it was a giant hangar. O'Yee, his arm still on the corrugated iron, kneading his fist, said again, "You wait here."

"Yes, sir."

O'Yee said again, "Wait here."

He heard Lim take a step backward.

O'Yee said—

There was nothing to say.

The door opened another inch as he pushed on it and he moved his fingers along the corrugated iron and got them around the edge of the door. It had resistance. Ten feet high, it balanced on two rusty hinges that made a grinding noise as they moved. He felt resistance. It was spring-loaded. There were two holes in the corrugated iron where there had been a padlock and chain.

The padlock and chain were no longer there.

O'Yee, swallowing, said—

Lim said quietly, "You can rely on me."

He pushed. The door gave a little more, grinding on its hinges.

He touched his free hand, he thought, to his gun in its shoulder holster. His hand only got as far as his shirt and flattened against his chest, rubbing it. His hand was wet. O'Yee said in a whisper, "Can you hear anything?" He could see, as the door opened, only darkness. There was the faint musty smell of ammonia and oil and disuse. O'Yee, feeling for the corner of the door, pushing, hearing the sound as the hinges moved, said so softly Lim had to strain to hear him, "Wait . . . wait here."

"Maybe there's nothing there."

"Yeah." He listened. In the hangar he could see only darkness. As the door opened it let in only a little more light. He saw shapes, shadows, machines. He smelled the smell of oil and ammonia and disuse. He wished he had a cigarette. O'Yee said to a question he thought Lim had asked, "Yes, yes, that'll be all right."

He listened.

He listened for twenty-eight.

He listened for anything.

There was nothing. There was only the darkness. O'Yee, pushing the door, nodding, said in a voice he could get no volume to, "Yes." He heard Lim come closer.

O'Yee, pushing hard on the door and feeling the pressure of it against his hand, getting it open a foot and sliding around it into the warehouse, said for the last time, holding Lim's eyes before he went in, "Yes. Yes, that'll be all right."

He went in. He seemed, instantly, to disappear.

The door, let free on its spring-loaded hinges a foot from where Lim stood with the metal detector on the ground beside him, closed with terrible finality, suddenly, without warning, with a bang.

On the car radio, Hurley said urgently, "He's there! He must be there! He hasn't rung back and I can't get in touch with him!" Hurley said, "It's the old gasworks on Godown Street and Tung Kun Street in North Point—"

"What the hell's he doing there?" In the back, reading the street map, Auden ordered Spencer, "Left! Turn left into Singapore Road, down Singapore Lane, then right into Temple Street and then—" Feiffer, grabbing hard on to the microphone as Spencer swung the car through the cross junction from Shanghai Street and accelerated down Singapore Road, demanded, "Who the hell are you?"

"I'm with the archives and history section!"

"The end of the street—the end of Temple's blocked off—" Spencer, changing down and making the engine roar, turning right back down to run parallel with Shanghai Street, shouted back to Auden behind him, "It's all blocked off! There are pylons in the middle of the road!"

He saw Feiffer turn to look at him or back out through the rear window. He tried not to look as if his legs still hurt. Auden, looking stoic, shouted, "He knocked down a wall at the station, boss!" He looked away down to his map. There were the marks of pylons everywhere. Auden, finding a clear street, shouted above the engine, "When you get to Shanghai, try to bear right and then come up again into Godown Street!"

"What the hell do you mean he knocked down a wall?"

The radio was breaking up into static. Feiffer, pressing hard on the "Send" button to try to clear the fast-breaking transmission, shouted to Hurley, "Who the hell are you? Why the hell is O'Yee there?"

"I can't get into Godown Street from there!" Ahead of him, Spencer could see only more pylons blocking the road. They were everywhere. The whole area was closed off. It was some sort of new development. Spencer, trying to be helpful, trying to catch Feiffer's eye as he turned again into a nameless side street and found himself back where he started, going again for Singapore Road, said to be part of the conversation, "Someone knocked down a wall in the basement too!" He could get nowhere. He was going in circles. Spencer, a moment before the transmission broke up into static and then cleared again, said in protest, "Phil, for God's sake, *read the map!*"

She became stone.

In the factory, in the darkness, in the silence and the faint smell of ammonia and oil and decay, she heard a sound and became stone.

She ceased to breathe or make any sound at all.

She listened. In the cocoon, unmoving, stone, she listened for a whisper, a rasp, a motion.

". . . Jakob . . ." Outside the cocoon there was no sound. She listened for a sound.

In her hand the machete was glittering against the redness, beginning to come alive. She was stone. There was no perspiration. Her hand, feeling the life surging through the wooden handle of the weapon like a tide, a current, was stone and did not move.

". . . Jakob . . ." He had looked up from the words he was writing and seen that it was her. For an instant the pale eyes had looked up at her and an expression had begun on his face. For an instant . . .

She felt the surge in the machete turn into life. She felt it begin to grow.

". . . Jakob . . ." She smiled in the photograph.

She had smiled when she had killed him.

She heard him rasp.

She heard him whisper. She heard him. She heard him move across the stone floor of the factory in the darkness. She heard his shoes grate on something hard. She heard him stop. She heard him draw a breath.

". . . Jakob . . ."

He heard it. It was a whisper, a rasp. He heard it.

". . . twenty-eight . . ."

O'Yee said softly, "Oh my God—!"

He listened, unmoving in the darkness.

". . . twen-ty-*eight!*"

It was a whisper, a rasp. It was barely there.

She listened. She heard him move.

He heard it. Something moved, someone. O'Yee, his mouth dry and like sandpaper, said in a rasp, "Hullo? Are you there?"

He listened.

She heard him.

He was against some sort of wooden packing crate or machine. In the darkness he could only feel it with his outstretched hand. O'Yee, inching his way along whatever it was, in total, pitch black darkness, smelling the smell of oil and dust and ammonia, said in a whisper, a rasp, "I'm here . . . I'm over here . . ."

On the phone to St. Paul de Chartres hospital, Detective Chief Inspector Osgood said in a gasp, "Oh, my God!"

She was gone. She had been gone a week.

On the phone, shouting, Detective Chief Inspector Osgood, the phone electric in his hand, out of control, shrieked back down the line to the psychiatrist registrar, "I know how bloody old she is! She's fourteen years old! You should have told us as well as goddamned Juvenile!" They shouldn't. They should have done exactly what they had done.

They knew it. They knew it better than he did. Osgood, because he could think of nothing else to say, because, somehow, for some reason everything he had ever thought had all gone for nothing, said, "In the name of all that's goddamned holy, for Christ's sake, both her goddamned parents are bloody *dead*!"

"Left!" On the street map, between Shanghai Street and Godown Street he found an opening where there were no pylons. In the back of the car, Auden, tracing it with his finger, ordered Spencer, "Turn left into there—into Cheong Street—into that lane!" The radio was gone, shrieking static. Auden, being thrown against the loaded shotgun propped up on the floor and wincing as the barrel cracked against his left knee, ordered Spencer, "There! That lane there! It goes straight into Temple Street." The lane looked barely wide enough. He sensed Spencer hesitate.

Auden, rubbing at his knee, trying to avoid Feiffer's eyes in the rearview mirror, yelled as an order as the car did a ninety-degree turn in the middle of the street, "Down there! Don't stop! Straight down there and then right!"

"*Mr. O'Yee!*" He could not get the corrugated iron doors open. He could not get his fingers around the opening to pull. The doors were shut, locked. Lim, starting to pound on them with his fists, looking up and down the facade of the building for another way in, starting to panic, yelled, "O'Yee! Mr. O'Yee! I can't hear anything!" He was shouting in Cantonese.

He stopped.

He listened.

He could hear nothing.

Lim, at the doors, pounding on them with both fists, wrenching, prying, trying to get his fingers around the gap to pull it apart, yelled in Cantonese, "Mr. O'Yee! O'Yee—*I can hear a car coming!*"

There was nothing. He was moving in a giant black room full of nothing. He touched a shape, an object: he felt it cold and hard, like metal, and then another, something else, something wooden and with nails in it. From all the boarded-up windows and doors there was no light at all, no chinks or breaks. He was in the middle of night. He was moving toward the center of it. O'Yee, moving, going down and then up, going nowhere, lost, moving away from the center and then turning back into the center, said in a whisper, "Anyone? Anyone . . . ?" There was the smell of oil and dust and disused, rusting machines and the smell of wood and metal—he smelled the metal's coldness or something someone had put on it or spilled on it to preserve it—he smelled the smell of ammonia drifting away from him. His mouth was no longer dry. He felt it full of saliva. He touched at the butt of his gun and felt only the feel of Bakelite and cold, gray metal. He was in darkness. There was only, far off, far behind the way he had come or the way he was going, a distant pounding sound, like throbbing—too far away, somewhere else.

". . . twenty-eight . . ." He heard it. It was faint, three-syllabled: it was like the voice of a child.

It was the voice of someone pretending to be a child.

". . . twenty . . ."

He listened.

He waited.

". . . twen-ty . . ." It was to the left, moving. It was faint. It was the voice of a child's cartoon, a man or a woman pretending to be a child or, even more than that, something a child imagined sounded like—

O'Yee said suddenly, "Oh my God."

He listened.

He froze.

He knew what it was.

". . . twenty . . . twenty . . . eight."

He knew what it was.

O'Yee said, *"Oh my God!"*

He heard it. He heard it move.

He heard a single word. He heard someone call.

It was in front of him, at eye level on a box or a machine or a crate.

He felt its breath.

"Oh my God. Oh my God. Oh my God—"

He saw something metal glitter. There was no light. He saw it gleam like ice.

He saw, he felt, he sensed—

In the darkness he—

". . . twenty . . . Twen-ty-EIGHT!"

"JAKOB!!"

In the darkness, alone, lost, rooted to the spot, O'Yee shrieked, "NO—!"

O'Yee shrieked, "Lim! Lim! LIM!"

He found a side door with the corrugated iron on it hanging loose and rusty.

Lim, wrenching at it, pulling it, tearing it apart, hearing the car coming down the road at full speed, yelled, "I hear you! I hear you!" The iron was pulling away, bending, exposing the door behind it. The door was only plywood with no lock on it, a service entrance. He got the iron free and pulled at it. It was stuck. On the other side there was a nail put into the doorjamb to hold it. It would not come free.

He banged on it with his fists and then his gun butt.

Lim, banging on it with his gun butt, smashing it, breaking it, splintering it, worked at the wood around the nail to get it free. He heard it coming. He heard the nail start to give. The door was opening. In the factory or the gasworks or whatever it was, there in the darkness, the sound—the banging—was echoing, coming back to him amplified, over and over, banging, banging, banging—

They were banging on the doors. In the hospital every morning, they were going up and down the long white corridors banging on all the doors, shouting and calling and making sounds in the kitchen.

All the dreams were gone. In the banging, all the dreams and silence fled and the banging went on and on and on and, everywhere, everywhere in her head, there was the banging as they came down the corridor toward her room shouting and bringing the light and the glare and the day with them, banging and banging and banging—

"Oh Jesus . . ." He was going backward. He touched something. Something near him was moving. In the darkness, something took wing and flew. He felt the wind. He was caught up, falling over. He felt something behind him fall away with a clatter. Bamboo. It was lengths of thin bamboo. His foot was on it as he moved. He felt himself lose balance. He was going backward—going forward in the darkness, the bamboo and the smell and the wooden crates and the metal all caught up. He was still. He was not moving at all. Something was coming toward him. It was a shadow, an impression. He had thought he was going away, but it was something coming toward him.

He heard a pounding, a thumping, a banging like a drum, a pulse. In the darkness it was everywhere, amplified, getting closer, getting louder. He heard someone call his name. He heard—

"MR. O'YEE!" It went. The door and part of the jamb splintered and it went and it was open, spilling light into the place. It was alive, full of birds, the floors covered with dead rats and the remains of other birds. There were holes bitten into the walls, broken bamboo cages. There were holes bitten into the walls where the old gas pipes were.

Twenty-eight!" It was a bird, some sort of parrot. It was in the air, mad, circling and flapping. There were dead rats everywhere, killed, gutted, gnawed down to the bone. They had killed everything that moved in the place and then one another and then they had bitten through into the old pipes and killed everything that was in there or came from there or got into there to try to escape. Lim, frozen at the door, yelled, "Yat's! It's the thing from Yat's! It's—" Lim, his gun out and pointing, yelled, hearing the car coming up fast behind him, "Mr. O'Yee! O'Yee— *where the hell are you?*"

* * *

He saw her only for an instant. Whatever she was, she was not human. The birds with their claws and their beaks had torn her face to pieces.

"MR. O'YEE!"

He saw her only for an instant. The birds with their claws and their beaks had torn her face to pieces. The machete in her hand was running red with blood. She was tiny, a child wearing a man's white coveralls with the word QUARANTINE in red on them. She was a child in adult's clothing. She was looking away toward the door. She was—

"O'YEE!"

He saw her. He saw her see Lim. He saw the giant gun in her other hand. O'Yee shrieked, *"Lim!"* He saw him see her. He saw him start to run back out the door. He saw her face, the machete, her hands running blood. "Twenty-eight!" He saw the parrot wheel overhead and something dark and powerful and quick cover it and then it was gone. He saw—
In the doorway, as he ran, he saw Lim start to turn, to think better of something, to do his duty. It was happening in microseconds, too fast to take in.
"Mr. O'Yee!" He was coming back, spinning at the door to turn around, to come back in, to say—
O'Yee, moving, reaching out, yelled, *"Lim!"* He saw her move. He saw her bring her hand up with the gun in it. He saw her aim.
He thought for an instant Lim was about to say something—
He saw her, in a single shattering explosion that lit her up and turned everything to light, shoot Lim dead where he stood at the half-open, spring-loaded, suddenly closing doorway.

17

There were only the flesheaters left. Everything else had been killed and eaten. It had not been enough—the flesheaters, the birds of prey, themselves were dying. At the wrecks of their bamboo cages, against the walls and boarded-up windows they were colliding, dashing themselves to pieces, falling bloody and flapping and screeching to the floor and into the machines. At the open door O'Yee saw Auden and Spencer going for the piles of wooden crates in the center of the place, Auden with his shotgun out. O'Yee, on his knees, had both his hands pressed down hard against Lim's chest wound to stop it bleeding. The blood gushed out over his hands and drowned them. Lim was on his back with his eyes half open: the blood was saturating him, drowning him, covering him over. He heard someone shout. It was Auden. He was on top of one of the crates, going over it, jumping down the other side, looking for the boarded-up windows. He saw Feiffer only feet from him with his revolver out. Feiffer shouted, "Phil, take out the windows! Get light in here!" There was a crash as Auden found a window and knocked out the glass with the butt of his shotgun, then a second, a louder thump as the boards on the other side of it went out and fell into the street in splinters.

Spencer shouted, "Phil! Another! Here!" He had no idea what was happening. He had no idea where they had all come from.

O'Yee, his hands swimming in blood, his eyes staring, shrieked, *"Harry!"*

"It's all right." He was beside him. Feiffer, trying to pull O'Yee up, said, "It's all right. We're here. It's all right."

"What the hell's happening?" She was running. She was somewhere up on the metal catwalk that led to what looked like a storeroom or a half floor above the machines, running. There were birds everywhere. There was a crash as Auden got another window out and there were shapes and shadows everywhere. O'Yee shrieked, "It's a kid! It's just a kid! I thought—" The blood was welling out in gouts—he could not stop it. O'Yee, pressing, pushing at the wound, shrieked, "I thought she'd been attacked! I thought it was a plastic gun! I thought it was a plastic gun and she—" O'Yee, pressing, pushing, trying to stem the blood that would not be stemmed, shrieked, "We came to help!" He fought against Feiffer's grip as he tried to lift him up and away from the open door. O'Yee, pushing him off with his hand covered in blood, yelled, "Twenty-eight! Twenty-eight! Someone, over and over kept calling—" He heard crashes and the sound of breaking glass as Auden found another window. "It was a bird! It wasn't a person—it was a goddamned bird!"

He couldn't move him. He was too heavy. Feiffer, seeing O'Yee's eyes go, said quickly as Spencer, with the light spreading across the factory, saw the metal stairs to the floor above and started to mount them, "It was a parrot. It was an Australian Port Lincoln parrot. That's their call."

"Are you crazy?"

Feiffer said, "Christopher, Lim's dead."

"Are you crazy?" It wasn't someone else—someone he didn't know—it was Feiffer. O'Yee, shaking his head, said, "What are you talking about? You're Harry Feiffer—I've known you for fifteen years—what the hell do you mean it's an Australian Port Lincoln parrot? You don't know that! I've known you for years and you don't know anything about things like—" O'Yee, his hand sinking into the wound as something deep inside Lim seemed to give way and sag, shrieked, "Harry, what's happening?" He saw Lim's face. He was dead. O'Yee, beginning to shake all over, ordered Feiffer, "He's not dead! Don't say he's dead because he isn't dead!"

From somewhere up high Spencer called, "Up here! I think she's gone up here!" There were thumpings, bangings as he tried to break through a window with only the butt of his revolver. "Rats! Dead rats and—bones and a—" Spencer yelled as something on the other side of the glass gave way and sent a shaft of light down, "Everything's dead!" She was running. She was on a metal catwalk somewhere. He heard her running. Spencer, above the sound of another window downstairs going with the butt of Auden's shotgun, yelled, "She's up here!" He heard a click, he sensed a movement, something stop. Spencer yelled, "I see her! I—" Spencer yelled, "Cover! Take cover!" There was a flash that lit up the catwalk as the blast from the .455 Webley sent a bullet an inch from his head into the glass of another window. Spencer yelled, "She's up on the first floor running toward you!"

"Move!" At the open doorway, Feiffer, wrenching, pulling O'Yee to his feet, shoved him out of the light. Feiffer, holding him back, stopping him going down to Lim, yelled in O'Yee's face, "He's dead! You can see he's dead! *He's dead!*" There were more shots, sharper, as Spencer fired back high into the roof.

Spencer yelled, "She's gone! I can hear her, but she's gone!" He saw Auden in a shaft of light going for the far corner of the warehouse where there was the shadow of a flight of metal stairs. For an instant Spencer saw her. Spencer, firing another shot into the air, yelled, "She's a kid! She's wearing coveralls two sizes too big for her! They're dragging around her ankles!" Spencer, getting no reply from Auden, hearing him clatter onto the stairs cocking the shotgun, ordered him, "She's a kid! Phil, she's a kid! *Don't kill her!*"

They were coming, banging on all the doors as they came. They were coming along the ward, laughing and banging and ending all the dreams and the night, and they were coming, coming. She was on the fire escape of the hospital. She had got out. She had worked all night at the lock on her window until her hands bled and she had finally got it open. On the fire escape all the smell of the antiseptic and the disinfectant and the medicines in little plastic cups they brought around on trays was gone and she was out in the open, clean air.

She had nowhere to go. Out there, high up, she could see all the lights of the city at night, but she had nowhere to go.

She heard them coming. She heard them banging and banging and banging and she ran, going nowhere, with nowhere to go. She ran.

She ran down, going fast, not stopping.

The cocoon swallowed her.

All the lights turned red and the cocoon swallowed her and the cocoon knew what to do.

She heard them banging. She was on the fire escape again, running.

She escaped. She was in the cocoon.

She ran.

She was on the top of the fire escape again and they were banging, banging, coming for her. She— She—

"JAKOB!"

"Jesus Christ!" On the stairs, lit up by the flash from the gun, the bullet missing him by inches and tearing out a chunk of railing, Auden, falling, yelled, "Bill!" The shotgun was going from his hand. He reached for it and caught it by the barrel and, turning it in midair, held it. Auden, recovering, getting his balance, his hand burning with grazes and cuts from the sharp edge of the ventilating rib, yelled, "What the hell's she got?" He was blind from the flash. He could see only sparks and colored lights. He had caught the gun by feel. Auden, hearing something fast and big go over his head in a series of rasping cries, yelled, "Bill, I can't see!"

He was shooting. She was running along the catwalk with the machete and the big gun like some sort of tiny child dressed in her father's clothing and, aiming carefully, shooting above and behind her to herd her away from Auden, Feiffer was to one side of the open doorway with O'Yee with his arm outstretched shooting round after round, placing the shots, punching holes in the roof. He saw her shadow running. He saw her start to turn and, reloading, he fired round after round up at her—yards away—and turned her back and sent her running again. She was covered in blood. Above her, there were shadows, shapes as the last of the birds crashed into walls in panic or took flight and somersaulted, all their strength gone, and fell down over the catwalk and died on the hard stone floor. She was armed. She had the big Webley from Quarantine and the machete. Lim was dead. All he had to do was order, "Kill her!" and— He saw her reach the end of the catwalk and turn into shadows. He heard her start to come down another metal stairs in the darkness. All he had to was— Feiffer yelled, "Bill, I can't see her! Keep down! Get Auden!"

"I'm all right!" On the stairs, Auden shouted, "I can see! I'm all right! It was the flash!" He was going back down the stairs with the shotgun at port. Auden, clattering down the metal risers, yelled, "I can see her! She's on the other stairs going down!"

Auden, getting a quick bead on her as she ran and following her along the aiming rib of the shotgun like a clay pigeon falling down from its parabola, yelled to Feiffer, "Boss?"

It was O'Yee. At the doorway, before he could give an order, O'Yee shrieked, "Don't shoot!" He was by Lim's body with his fists clenched like a child. O'Yee shrieked, "It's a little kid! For Christ's sake don't kill her!"

"*Boss?*" She was going into the shadows. Auden, his finger on the trigger, not wanting to squeeze, starting to squeeze automatically, setting himself up for the order, demanded, "Boss! Harry? Yes or no?"

"No!" She was gone. She was gone into the shadows. Running toward them, his own gun still out, reloading as he went, Feiffer tried to count the shots. She had a six-shot Webley. She had fired one—two . . . She had fired one, maybe two rounds at Lim. Outside, as the car got to the factory he had heard one. Three shots. She had fired three. She had three left. Feiffer, running, crunching over bones and dead rats and birds, ordered Auden, "Go to Spencer!" He saw Spencer smash open another boarded window and send a shaft of light straight down. Feiffer yelled, "Get all the windows out! Get some goddamned light in here!" He thought he lost her. He had seen her only as a shadow. Getting to the bottom of the stairs, shoving broken bamboo cages and packing cases out of the way, there—in that instant—he saw her.

Feiffer said in a gasp, "*Oh my God!*"

There were dead birds and rats everywhere. There were holes in the walls where the birds had bitten through to the old gas pipes and killed everything that came out of there. O'Yee, every muscle in his body shaking as the light seemed to come down in suddenly lit dusty shafts one by one, said to no one, to someone, to Lim, "I thought it was something from a—" His hands were covered in blood. The blood was drying, caking. O'Yee, walking through the shafts of light, said over and over, "I came to help. I told you to wait outside. I did! I told you to wait outside!" There was some sort of dead bird on the floor in front of him, something with broken wings and talons and a twisted beak—some sort of hawk or sea eagle or kite, torn apart like something dead on the road, gutted and devoured by carrion. O'Yee, walking, going nowhere, said shaking his head, "*I came to help!*" He was dead. Lim was dead. O'Yee, shaking his head, trying to make it mean something, shrieked at the top of his voice, "*He's dead!*"

* * *

She was like something from hell. She had no face. Her face had been torn apart by the birds. Only the eyes were there. In the shafts of light the eyes were shining. She was tiny. In the outsized bloody coveralls, she was so small that the machete in her left hand dragged along the ground. She was a tiny child dressed up playing at soldiers with a wooden sword. He saw the gun in her hand. Her hand was a claw, with the blood, dark and unrecognizable. He almost— He almost went forward to take the gun from her because it was too heavy. Feiffer, lowering his own gun, taking a single step toward her, saw her. She was an *amok*. He had heard about them: he had heard stories from people who had served in Malaya. He had heard them say that there was no choice, that when it began, when the eyes glazed and everything locked and all there was was the killing, that the only thing to do was to shoot for the head and—

All he had to do was raise his gun and kill her.

All he had to do was—

He saw, in the shafts of light, the red haze about her the old Malaya hands had spoken of. He saw the gun, the machete. He saw her eyes. The eyes held him. She had no face. He saw only, as she seemed to turn and look at him, her long black hair pinned back.

Feiffer said, "Oh my God . . ."

He saw the pin that held back her girl's hair.

She was fourteen years old.

He saw the pin she put in her hair to hold it back, to look pretty. He saw—

All he had to do—

She was not his. In the cocoon, he still lived. In the cocoon, he was still there with her. It was still that day. It was still the day they had all gone to Yat's. It was the day he had told her things about the birds and the animals and held her hand. It was still the day her mother had carried a camera around her neck and watched as he told her things about all the birds and animals and how they lived.

It was the day she had waited while her mother had said something to him.

"I wish—" She was sitting in the Wishing Chair with the lovely old dog asleep beside her. She was the only one waiting for the Wishing Chair. She was the only one there for the dog to come up to and fall asleep by and dream his dreams of bones and pats.

"Take my picture—"

She had waited there, waited there, waited there.

She saw his face change as her mother told him something and then walk away.

"Take my picture—"

She saw him look at her and she saw his face change.

She smiled at him and pointed to the dog, but it was no good because her mother had said something to him and he didn't like dogs or birds anymore.

He came to her and looked hard at her face.

"Take my picture . . ."

The look on his face made her cry.

Mother: Mata Idris, New China Apartments, North Point. She had read it on her record at the hospital when nobody was looking. *Father: Unknown.*

"Take my picture—"

The look on his face made her cry.

"Take my picture . . ."

He had never said another word to her from that day, to either of them.

"Take my picture!"

She died and left a blank sheet of paper. In the hospital, at night, listening at the door, she heard people laughing about it. One of them had a friend in the police. It was the night Sister. She had cut the article out of the newspaper and given it to her.

"Take my—"

> He thought he saw an Elephant
> That practiced on a fife:
> He looked again, and found it was
> A letter from his wife.
> "At length I realize," he said,
> "The bitterness of life."

She saw him standing there in the light. She saw him looking at her. She saw the gun in his hand, by his side.

"Take my picture—"

"Take my picture!"

She was writing on the back of it.

The girl, her face torn apart, her hair held up by a pin, trying to cry, said in a child's voice that stilled him, that drained all the feeling from his face, *"I don't know what it means!"*

* * *

"HARRY!" He was behind her with the shotgun. Auden, the barrel of the weapon an inch from the back of her head, pointing down to execute something, said, "Harry!"

"Leave her!"

"Wai—" It was the name of the dog at Yat's.

Feiffer, trembling, said as he saw him come out of the shadows to one side of her with his gun drawn, "Christopher—"

"Wai—"

He saw her start to turn, to look around.

Feiffer said softly, "Christopher . . ." He saw Spencer appear from nowhere and take the Webley gently from her hand. He saw him break it open. It was empty. He saw Spencer lean forward, lean down to her and take the machete.

"Christopher . . ." He saw O'Yee weeping.

"Wai . . ." She was fourteen years old with her hair held back by a pin. She had been hurt. She touched at her face. "Wai . . ." She was telling secrets to the dog.

Feiffer said quietly, "Christopher, take her."

"Wai . . ."

O'Yee said softly, "He's dead."

"Take her." He saw Auden's gun come down.

He was weeping. He looked sad.

Auden said softly, "I'm glad. I'm glad I didn't have to—" He looked at Spencer and, seeing his face, looked away and down to the floor.

Mata Idris said, "I'm lost, Wai, I can't find my way home."

There was a silence.

He had children of his own. They were now all grown up. O'Yee said softly, "It's all right."

He had come to help.

"Wai—" Mata Idris, wiping at her face and touching at her hair to be pretty for her father the day he had taken her to Yat's to tell her all about animals and birds—the day she had got pretty to have her photograph taken—said, smiling, "Wai, I was the only one here. I got to pat you all by myself." He took her hand. He squeezed it.

She said so softly he almost didn't hear it as he smiled, she thought wonderfully, at her, "Wai, today is my eleventh birthday. I'm going out with my mother and father to have my photo taken in the Wishing Chair—"

18

At night after Quarantine had caught and killed all the dying birds on the floor of the factory, it came out.

It was a *Podargus strigoides*: a tawny frogmouth. It was scruffy, ragged. In the darkness, flying fast, it went after the boy on the boat.

It would not make it. The boy was too far out to sea. It mattered not at all.

It was the thing that flew above the harbor: it was life, optimism, promise.

It was a denial of death. It was hope.

Out there, too high to see, untiring, it flew.

It soared.

MORE MYSTERIOUS PLEASURES

HAROLD ADAMS
MURDER
Carl Wilcox debuts in a story of triple murder which exposes the underbelly of corruption in the town of Corden, shattering the respectability of its most dignified citizens.   #501 $3.50

THE NAKED LIAR
When a sexy young widow is framed for the murder of her husband, Carl Wilcox comes through to help her fight off cops and big-city goons.
                                                                #420 $3.95

THE FOURTH WIDOW
Ex-con/private eye Carl Wilcox is back, investigating the death of a "popular" widow in the Depression-era town of Corden, S.D.
                                                                #502 $3.50

EARL DERR BIGGERS
THE HOUSE WITHOUT A KEY
Charlie Chan debuts in the Honolulu investigation of an expatriate Bostonian's murder.   #421 $3.95

THE CHINESE PARROT
Charlie Chan works to find the key to murders seemingly without victims—but which have left a multitude of clues.   #503 $3.95

BEHIND THAT CURTAIN
Two murders sixteen years apart, one in London, one in San Francisco, each share a major clue in a pair of velvet Chinese slippers. Chan seeks the connection.   #504 $3.95

THE BLACK CAMEL
When movie goddess Sheila Fane is murdered in her Hawaiian pavilion, Chan discovers an interrelated crime in a murky Hollywood mystery from the past.   #505 $3.95

CHARLIE CHAN CARRIES ON
An elusive transcontinental killer dogs the heels of the Lofton Round the World Cruise. When the touring party reaches Honolulu, the murderer finally meets his match.   #506 $3.95

JAMES M. CAIN
THE ENCHANTED ISLE
A beautiful runaway is involved in a deadly bank robbery in this posthumously published novel. #415 $3.95

CLOUD NINE
Two brothers—one good, one evil—battle over a million-dollar land deal and a luscious 16-year-old in this posthumously published novel. #507 $3.95

ROBERT CAMPBELL
IN LA-LA LAND WE TRUST
Child porn, snuff films, and drunken TV stars in fast cars—that's what makes the L.A. world go 'round. Whistler, a luckless P.I., finds that it's not good to know too much about the porn trade in the City of Angels. #508 $3.95

GEORGE C. CHESBRO
VEIL
Clairvoyant artist Veil Kendry volunteers to be tested at the Institute for Human Studies and finds that his life is in deadly peril; is he threatened by the Institute, the Army, or the CIA? #509 $3.95

WILLIAM L. DeANDREA
THE LUNATIC FRINGE
Police Commissioner Teddy Roosevelt and Officer Dennis Muldoon comb 1896 New York for a missing exotic dancer who holds the key to the murder of a prominent political cartoonist. #306 $3.95

SNARK
Espionage agent Bellman must locate the missing director of British Intelligence—and elude a master terrorist who has sworn to kill him. #510 $3.50

KILLED IN THE ACT
Brash, witty Matt Cobb, TV network troubleshooter, must contend with bizarre crimes connected with a TV spectacular—one of which is a murder committed before 40 million witnesses. #511 $3.50

KILLED WITH A PASSION
In seeking to clear an old college friend of murder, Matt Cobb must deal with the Mad Karate Killer and the Organic Hit Man, among other eccentric criminals. #512 $3.50

KILLED ON THE ICE
When a famous psychiatrist is stabbed in a Manhattan skating rink, Matt Cobb finds it necessary to protect a beautiful Olympic skater who appears to be the next victim. #513 $3.50

JAMES ELLROY
SUICIDE HILL
Brilliant L.A. Police sergeant Lloyd Hopkins teams up with the FBI to solve a series of inside bank robberies—but is he working with or against them?   #514 $3.95

PAUL ENGLEMAN
CATCH A FALLEN ANGEL
Private eye Mark Renzler becomes involved in publishing mayhem and murder when two slick mens' magazines battle for control of the lucrative market.   #515 $3.50

LOREN D. ESTLEMAN
ROSES ARE DEAD
Someone's put a contract out on freelance hit man Peter Macklin. Is he as good as the killers on his trail?   #516 $3.95

ANY MAN'S DEATH
Hit man Peter Macklin is engaged to keep a famous television evangelist *alive*—quite a switch from his normal line.   #517 $3.95

DICK FRANCIS
THE SPORT OF QUEENS
The autobiography of the celebrated race jockey/crime novelist.
                                                                      #410 $3.95

JOHN GARDNER
THE GARDEN OF WEAPONS
Big Herbie Kruger returns to East Berlin to uncover a double agent. He confronts his own past and life's only certainty—death.
                                                                      #103 $4.50

BRIAN GARFIELD
DEATH WISH
Paul Benjamin is a modern-day New York vigilante, stalking the rapist-killers who victimized his wife and daughter. The basis for the Charles Bronson movie.   #301 $3.95

DEATH SENTENCE
A riveting sequel to *Death Wish*. The action moves to Chicago as Paul Benjamin continues his heroic (or is it psychotic?) mission to make city streets safe.   #302 $3.95

TRIPWIRE
A crime novel set in the American West of the late 1800s. Boag, a black outlaw, seeks revenge on the white cohorts who left him for dead. "One of the most compelling characters in recent fiction."—Robert Ludlum.   #303 $3.95

FEAR IN A HANDFUL OF DUST
Four psychiatrists, three men and a woman, struggle across the blazing Arizona desert—pursued by a fanatic killer they themselves have judged insane. "Unique and disturbing."—Alfred Coppel.   #304 $3.95

JOE GORES
A TIME OF PREDATORS
When Paula Halstead kills herself after witnessing a horrid crime, her husband vows to avenge her death. Winner of the Edgar Allan Poe Award. #215 $3.95

COME MORNING
Two million in diamonds are at stake, and the ex-con who knows their whereabouts may have trouble staying alive if he turns them up at the wrong moment. #518 $3.95

NAT HENTOFF
BLUES FOR CHARLIE DARWIN
Gritty, colorful Greenwich Village sets the scene for Noah Green and Sam McKibbon, two street-wise New York cops who are as at home in jazz clubs as they are at a homicide scene. #208 $3.95

THE MAN FROM INTERNAL AFFAIRS
Detective Noah Green wants to know who's stuffing corpses into East Village garbage cans . . . and who's lying about him to the Internal Affairs Division. #409 $3.95

PATRICIA HIGHSMITH
THE BLUNDERER
An unhappy husband attempts to kill his wife by applying the murderous methods of another man. When things go wrong, he pays a visit to the more successful killer—a dreadful error. #305 $3.95

DOUG HORNIG
THE DARK SIDE
Insurance detective Loren Swift is called to a rural commune to investigate a carbon-monoxide murder. Are the commune inhabitants as gentle as they seem? #519 $3.95

P.D. JAMES/T.A. CRITCHLEY
THE MAUL AND THE PEAR TREE
The noted mystery novelist teams up with a police historian to create a fascinating factual account of the 1811 Ratcliffe Highway murders. #520 $3.95

STUART KAMINSKY'S "TOBY PETERS" SERIES
NEVER CROSS A VAMPIRE
When Bela Lugosi receives a dead bat in the mail, Toby tries to catch the prankster. But Toby's time is at a premium because he's also trying to clear William Faulkner of a murder charge! #107 $3.95

HIGH MIDNIGHT
When Gary Cooper and Ernest Hemingway come to Toby for protection, he tries to save them from vicious blackmailers.   #106 $3.95

HE DONE HER WRONG
Someone has stolen Mae West's autobiography, and when she asks Toby to come up and see her sometime, he doesn't know how deadly a visit it could be.   #105 $3.95

BULLET FOR A STAR
Warner Brothers hires Toby Peters to clear the name of Errol Flynn, a blackmail victim with a penchant for young girls. The first novel in the acclaimed Hollywood-based private eye series.   #308 $3.95

THE FALA FACTOR
Toby comes to the rescue of lady-in-distress Eleanor Roosevelt, and must match wits with a right-wing fanatic who is scheming to overthrow the U.S. Government.   #309 $3.95

JOSEPH KOENIG
FLOATER
Florida Everglades sheriff Buck White matches wits with a Miami murder-and-larceny team who just may have hidden his ex-wife's corpse in a remote bayou.   #521 $3.50

ELMORE LEONARD
THE HUNTED
Long out of print, this 1974 novel by the author of *Glitz* details the attempts of a man to escape killers from his past.   #401 $3.95

MR. MAJESTYK
Sometimes bad guys can push a good man too far, and when that good guy is a Special Forces veteran, everyone had better duck.
#402 $3.95

THE BIG BOUNCE
Suspense and black comedy are cleverly combined in this tale of a dangerous drifter's affair with a beautiful woman out for kicks.
#403 $3.95

ELSA LEWIN
I, ANNA
A recently divorced woman commits murder to avenge her degradation at the hands of a sleazy lothario.   #522 $3.50

THOMAS MAXWELL
KISS ME ONCE
An epic *roman noir* which explores the romantic but seamy underworld of New York during the WWII years. When the good guys are off fighting in Europe, the bad guys run amok in America.
#523 $3.95

ED McBAIN
ANOTHER PART OF THE CITY
The master of the police procedural moves from the fictional 87th precinct to the gritty reality of Manhattan. "McBain's best in several years."—*San Francisco Chronicle*.   #524 $3.95

SNOW WHITE AND ROSE RED
A beautiful heiress confined to a sanitarium engages Matthew Hope to free her—and her $650,000.   #414 $3.95

CINDERELLA
A dead detective and a hot young hooker lead Matthew Hope into a multi-layered plot among Miami cocaine dealers. "A gem of sting and countersting."—*Time*.   #525 $3.95

PETER O'DONNELL
MODESTY BLAISE
Modesty and Willie Garvin must protect a shipment of diamonds from a gentleman about to murder his lover and an *un*civilized sheik.   #216 $3.95

SABRE TOOTH
Modesty faces Willie's apparent betrayal and a modern-day Genghis Khan who wants her for his mercenary army.   #217 $3.95

A TASTE FOR DEATH
Modesty and Willie are pitted against a giant enemy in the Sahara, where their only hope of escape is a blind girl whose time is running out.   #218 $3.95

I, LUCIFER
Some people carry a nickname too far . . . like the maniac calling himself Lucifer. He's targeted 120 souls, and Modesty and Willie find they have a personal stake in stopping him.   #219 $3.95

THE IMPOSSIBLE VIRGIN
Modesty fights for her soul when she and Willie attempt to rescue an albino girl from the evil Brunel, who lusts after the secret power of an idol called the Impossible Virgin.   #220 $3.95

DEAD MAN'S HANDLE
Modesty Blaise must deal with a brainwashed—and deadly—Willie Garvin as well as with a host of outré religion-crazed villains.
                    #526 $3.95

ELIZABETH PETERS
CROCODILE ON THE SANDBANK
Amelia Peabody's trip to Egypt brings her face to face with an ancient mystery. With the help of Radcliffe Emerson, she uncovers a tomb and the solution to a deadly threat.   #209 $3.95

THE CURSE OF THE PHAROAHS
Amelia and Radcliffe Emerson head for Egypt to excavate a cursed tomb but must confront the burial ground's evil history before it claims them both.   #210 $3.95

THE SEVENTH SINNER
Murder in an ancient subterranean Roman temple sparks Jacqueline Kirby's first recorded case.   #411 $3.95

THE MURDERS OF RICHARD III
Death by archaic means haunts the costumed weekend get-together of a group of eccentric Ricardians.   #412 $3.95

ANTHONY PRICE
THE LABYRINTH MAKERS
Dr. David Audley does his job too well in his first documented case, embarrassing British Intelligence, the CIA, and the KGB in one swoop.
                                                        #404 $3.95

THE ALAMUT AMBUSH
Alamut, in Northern Persia, is considered by many to be the original home of terrorism. Audley moves to the Mideast to put the cap on an explosive threat.   #405 $3.95

COLONEL BUTLER'S WOLF
The Soviets are recruiting spies from among Oxford's best and brightest; it's up to Dr. Audley to identify the Russian wolf in don's clothing.
                                                        #527 $3.95

OCTOBER MEN
Dr. Audley's "holiday" in Rome stirs up old Intelligence feuds and echoes of partisan warfare during World War II—and leads him into new danger.   #529 $3.95

OTHER PATHS TO GLORY
What can a World War I battlefield in France have in common with a deadly secret of the present? A modern assault on Bouillet Wood leads to the answers.   #530 $3.95

SION CROSSING
What does the chairman of a new NATO-like committee have to do with the American Civil War? Audley travels to Georgia in this espionage thriller.   #406 $3.95

HERE BE MONSTERS
The assassination of an American veteran forces Dr. David Audley into a confrontation with undercover KGB agents.   #528 $3.95

BILL PRONZINI AND JOHN LUTZ
THE EYE
A lunatic watches over the residents of West 98th Street with a powerful telescope. When his "children" displease him, he is swift to mete out deadly punishment.   #408 $3.95

PATRICK RUELL
RED CHRISTMAS
Murderers and political terrorists come down the chimney during an old-fashioned Dickensian Christmas at a British country inn.

#531 $3.50

DEATH TAKES THE LOW ROAD
William Hazlitt, a universtiy administrator who moonlights as a Soviet mole, is on the run from both Russian and British agents who want him to assassinate an African general.   #532 $3.50

DELL SHANNON
CASE PENDING
In the first novel in the best-selling series, Lt. Luis Mendoza must solve a series of horrifying Los Angeles mutilation murders.   #211 $3.95

THE ACE OF SPADES
When the police find an overdosed junkie, they're ready to write off the case—until the autopsy reveals that this junkie *wasn't* a junkie.   #212 $3.95

EXTRA KILL
In "The Temple of Mystic Truth," Mendoza discovers idol worship, pornography, murder, and the clue to the death of a Los Angeles patrolman.   #213 $3.95

KNAVE OF HEARTS
Mendoza must clear the name of the L.A.P.D. when it's discovered that an innocent man has been executed and the real killer is still on the loose.   #214 $3.95

DEATH OF A BUSYBODY
When the West Coast's most industrious gossip and meddler turns up dead in a freight yard, Mendoza must work without clues to find the killer of a woman who had offended nearly everyone in Los Angeles.   #315 $3.95

DOUBLE BLUFF
Mendoza goes against the evidence to dissect what looks like an air-tight case against suspected wife-killer Francis Ingram—a man the lieutenant insists is too nice to be a murderer.   #316 $3.95

MARK OF MURDER
Mendoza investigates the near-fatal attack on an old friend as well as trying to track down an insane serial killer.   #417 $3.95

ROOT OF ALL EVIL
The murder of a "nice" girl leads Mendoza to team up with the FBI in the search for her not-so-nice boyfriend—a Soviet agent.   #418 $3.95

JULIE SMITH

TRUE-LIFE ADVENTURE
Paul McDonald earned a meager living ghosting reports for a San Francisco private eye until the gumshoe turned up dead . . . now the killers are after him.   #407 $3.95

TOURIST TRAP
A lunatic is out to destroy San Francisco's tourism industry; can feisty lawyer/sleuth Rebecca Schwartz stop him while clearing an innocent man of a murder charge?   #533 $3.95

ROSS H. SPENCER

THE MISSING BISHOP
Chicago P.I. Buzz Deckard has a missing person to find. Unfortunately his client has disappeared as well, and no one else seems to be who or what they claim.   #416 $3.50

MONASTERY NIGHTMARE
Chicago P.I. Luke Lassiter tries his hand at writing novels, and encounters murder in an abandoned monastery.   #534 $3.50

REX STOUT

UNDER THE ANDES
A long-lost 1914 fantasy novel from the creator of the immortal Nero Wolfe series. "The most exciting yarn we have read since *Tarzan of the Apes.*"—*All-Story Magazine*.   #419 $3.50

ROSS THOMAS

CAST A YELLOW SHADOW
McCorkle's wife is kidnapped by agents of the South African government. The ransom—his cohort Padillo must assassinate their prime minister.   #535 $3.95

THE SINGAPORE WINK
Ex-Hollywood stunt man Ed Cauthorne is offered $25,000 to search for colleague Angelo Sacchetti—a man he thought he'd killed in Singapore two years earlier.   #536 $3.95

THE FOOLS IN TOWN ARE ON OUR SIDE
Lucifer Dye, just resigned from a top secret U.S. Intelligence post, accepts a princely fee to undertake the corruption of an entire American city.   #537 $3.95

JIM THOMPSON

THE KILL-OFF
Luanne Devore was loathed by everyone in her small New England town. Her plots and designs threatened to destroy them—unless they destroyed her first.   #538 $3.95

DONALD E. WESTLAKE
THE HOT ROCK
The unlucky master thief John Dortmunder debuts in this spectacular caper novel. How many times do you have to steal an emerald to make sure it *stays* stolen? #539 $3.95

BANK SHOT
Dortmunder and company return. A bank is temporarily housed in a trailer, so why not just hook it up and make off with the whole shebang? Too bad nothing is ever that simple. #540 $3.95

THE BUSY BODY
Aloysius Engel is a gangster, the Big Man's right hand. So when he's ordered to dig a suit loaded with drugs out of a fresh grave, how come the corpse it's wrapped around won't lie still? #541 $3.95

THE SPY IN THE OINTMENT
Pacifist agitator J. Eugene Raxford is mistakenly listed as a terrorist by the FBI, which leads to his enforced recruitment to a group bent on world domination. Will very good Good triumph over absolutely villainous Evil? #542 $3.95

GOD SAVE THE MARK
Fred Fitch is the sucker's sucker—con men line up to bilk him. But when he inherits $300,000 from a murdered uncle, he finds it necessary to dodge killers as well as hustlers. #543 $3.95

TERI WHITE
TIGHTROPE
This second novel featuring L.A. cops Blue Maguire and Spaceman Kowalski takes them into the nooks and crannies of the city's Little Saigon. #544 $3.95

COLLIN WILCOX
VICTIMS
Lt. Frank Hastings investigates the murder of a police colleague in the home of a powerful—and nasty—San Francisco attorney. #413 $3.95

NIGHT GAMES
Lt. Frank Hastings of the San Francisco Police returns to investigate the at-home death of an unfaithful husband—whose affairs have led to his murder. #545 $3.95